A DETECTIVE TOBY MYSTERY

Other Books by Mary M. Cushnie-Mansour

Novels

Night's Vampire Series
Night's Gift
Night's Children
Night's Return
Night's Temptress
Night's Betrayals

Children's Titles

A Story of Day & Night (novel)

The Day Bo Found His Bark/Le jour où Bo trouva sa voix
Charlie Seal Meets a Fairy Seal/Charlie le phoque rencontre une fée
Charlie and the Elves/Charlie et les lutins
Jesse's Secret/Le Secret de Jesse
Teensy Weensy Spider/L'araignée Riquiqui
The Temper Tantrum/La crise de colère
Alexandra's Christmas Surprise/La surprise de Noël d'Alexandra
Curtis The Crock/Curtis le crocodile
Freddy Frog's Frolic/La gambade de Freddy la grenouille

Short Stories

From the Heart
Mysteries From the Keys

Poetry

picking up the pieces
Life's Roller Coaster
Devastations of Mankind
Shattered
Memories

Biographies

A 20th Century Portia

Are You Listening to Me?

Mary M. Cushnie-Mansour

CAVERN
OF DREAMS
PUBLISHING

Are You Listening to Me?

Copyright © 2017 by Mary M. Cushnie-Mansour

Publisher's Note: This is a work of fiction. Names, characters, places, and incidents are a product of the author's imagination. Locales and public names are sometimes used for atmospheric purposes. Any resemblance to actual people, living or dead, or to businesses, companies, events, institutions, or locales are entirely coincidental.

Ordering Information:
Books may be ordered directly from Cavern of Dreams Publishing or through booksellers.
A list of Cavern of Dreams publications is available on the 49th Shelf:
http://49thshelf.com/Lists/Members/2015-26/Cavern-of-Dreams-Publishing

Cavern of Dreams Publishing
Brantford, ON , Canada
1-519-753-4649
info@cavernofdreams.com
www.cavernofdreams.com
Discounts are available for volume orders.

Library and Archives Canada Cataloguing in Publication

Cushnie-Mansour, Mary M., 1953-, author
       Are you listening to me? / Mary M. Cushnie Mansour ; illustrations by Jennifer Bettio.

Issued in print and electronic formats.
ISBN 978-1-927899-38-0 (paperback).--ISBN 978-1-927899-40-3 (PDF)

       I. Title.

PS8605.U83A74 2017   C813'.6   C2016-901346-4
                                                 C2016-901347-2

Acknowledgements

I would like to thank my friend, Brenda, for inspiring me to participate in NaNoWriMo (National Novel Writing Month) back in 2009. Being challenged to write 50,000 words in 30 days sounded epic to me, at first, until I broke it down into daily increments. "Are You Listening to Me?" was my first NaNo attempt, and I completed the 50,000 words in 11 days as the story started to take on a life of its own. I continued on, so enwrapped in the story had I become, and finished the novel's first draft with just over 95,000 words in 19 days! I must also thank a couple of other friends, Ella and Myra, for reading the story and enjoying it so much that they encouraged me to publish it, and they suggested I write a Toby Detective series.

Inspiration comes from many sources, and the initial inspiration for this story came from an old orange tabby cat sitting on a windowsill in a house in Hamilton, Ontario. As my mom and I walked past the house, there he was, just staring at us. I turned to my mom and said: "I wonder what the old fellow has witnessed looking out his window?" From there, I wrote the first story about Toby—The Witness—which was a three-part short story for the Brantford Expositor.

My love and understanding of cats, something I believe I inherited from my mom, and her mother before her, is echoed loud and clear in Toby's voice. Thanks Mom … and grandma Small.

Again, as always, I would like to thank my editor, Bethany Jamieson, for her edit on the final manuscript, and Cavern of Dreams Publishing for publishing yet another of my books.

Thanks go to Jennifer Bettio for the cover art. She managed to capture exactly how I wanted the three main characters in the book to look. Adding the finishing touches to my cover, as always, is Terry Davis from Ball Media. Collaborating with Terry to finalize the details is always a creative pleasure. And, never to be forgotten, Randy Nickman from Brant Service Press, for the fine printing job.

As always, last, but never least, thanks to my husband and family for their continued faith in my dream.

PREFACE:

It's been a while since my last big case, so I will jog your memory about who I am. My name is Toby, and I live with Jack Nelson, a retired cop. I used to be quite stout, but since venturing into police work, I have put myself on a rigorous routine of fitness and healthy eating. That doesn't always work out for me because, as my nature dictates, I am inclined to be a tad lazy sometimes—most of the time, actually. And I never miss a meal or a snack if I am passing through the kitchen. My hair is red; I once heard someone say redheads were God's chosen people, so I assume that goes for cats too.

Now do you remember? Yes, I am a cat—Detective Toby. I solved a crime about six months ago when Jack's friend went loony and kidnapped his own kids. I saw through him right from the beginning; Jack didn't. If it hadn't been for me, goodness knows what would have happened to those kids. I was a hero, and everyone was grateful to me. The police department awarded me with a framed certificate, which certified I was a 'Class-A Detective.' I was told I was welcome any time down at the police station, which I take full advantage of every time Jack visits the captain, Bryce Wagner.

There have been a lot of changes in the past six months. Jack renovated the back door. I now have my own special cat door so I can come and go from the house as I please. Jack figured if another crime needed investigating, I wouldn't have to wait for someone to open the door to get out and about detectiving if I had my own. There have also been some significant changes on the street. The old gym that used to be owned by Mardy Hampton was sold, and the new owners tore down the old building and are constructing a new one. I heard Jack say they were hoping to have it up and running by early spring. Jack has been talking about getting out of the neighbourhood for a time because he can't sleep well with all the banging going on. Personally, I can sleep through most anything, but the 24-hour noise is starting to get to me, too.

At first, I thought Jack was going to move us completely out of the neighbourhood, but was relieved when I saw him just packing for a camping trip in his old campervan. I knew he wouldn't leave me behind since I accompanied him most places now. I won't bore you with the details of our month-long excursion through Northern Ontario because it isn't relevant to the story that is going to unfold in the pages to follow.

Enough introductions. You know who I am now and you will be hearing more from me as the story of what happened during the summer of 2009 on the street where I live unfolds.

Friday, May 1, 2009

Camden Gale had decided it was time to move on. He knew his sister would not be happy about the decision, but he had accomplished everything he'd needed to here. He was also aware Doctor Hatfield wouldn't be happy, and he dreaded the lecture he was about to receive. Camden pushed open her office door. The secretary scowled at him. He was late, as usual—something her boss continuously chose to overlook. It was an inconvenience to the other patients because Doctor Hatfield always took the full amount of time with Camden—sometimes even longer.

The secretary was going to relish the day he would no longer need the doctor's help. Of all Doctor Lucy Hatfield's patients, this one gave her the creeps.

"Would you like me to book you in for next week, Camden?" she asked.

"That won't be necessary. I won't be returning."

The secretary couldn't help the smile that slipped across her lips. "Oh, Doctor Hatfield never informed me…"

"She doesn't know yet." Camden noticed the smile. He had never liked her. She was pretentious. Maybe she should have been one of his Chosen, but at the time he was considering his options, he had figured she would be too close to home. Besides, she never went to the gym, which would have made it tough. Camden smiled back at her. The secretary looked away from the underlying evil in his smile.

Doctor Hatfield opened her door and beckoned Camden in. "Hello Camden, let's get started. Would you like a drink?"

The secretary winced at the possibility of having to serve him something, but to her surprise, he declined. Camden sat in a chair in front of the doctor's desk—not his usual place. Doctor Hatfield looked surprised.

"Wouldn't you be more comfortable on the couch, Camden?"

"Not today, doctor. I won't be here long."

"You have someplace else to be?"

"You might say that."

"Mind sharing?"

"Not your business." Camden's voice had a sharp edge to it.

Doctor Hatfield tapped her pencil on the paper pad. She took her glasses off and studied the young man in front of her. He wasn't what she would call handsome, but he wasn't difficult to look at either. His crow-black hair curled tightly to his head, and his penetrating blue eyes were set deep in their sockets. Camden's nose was sharp, but not overly large. His lips spread thinly above a rounded chin. His skin had a permanent tan to it. Camden was of a medium build, and Doctor Hatfield noticed the rippling muscles in his arms: he clearly benefited from the gym where he was employed.

Camden had been assigned to her about six months before—a troubled young man with a history of mental illness, according to his records from former therapists. Doctor Hatfield had made progress; she thought she was breaking through Camden's tough exterior. She had discovered the little boy under the crust and was beginning to draw him out, helping him deal with his many past issues, she believed. But looking at Camden now, she saw the return of the hostility she had dealt with during the first couple months.

"Okay, Camden, this is your choice. I don't have to know where you are going." Doctor Hatfield smiled.

Camden liked her smile. It was genuine. She was genuine. Not like some of the other doctors he'd seen—he had seen right through them. But Lucy—that is how he referred to her in his thoughts—she had been serious about trying to help him, so he allowed her into places he had never allowed anyone before. It had felt good, at first. But then the old urges had started to return, especially after he had begun working at the gym. He started being more cautious with her, careful about what he shared. Careful because he didn't want to make a slip and end up back in the hospital again, or worse.

"This'll be my last visit," Camden stated.

Doctor Hatfield raised her eyebrows. "Oh, why is that, Camden? We are making such substantial progress; do you think it is wise to stop now?"

"Actually, I'm moving. I've been offered a job at a new gym in Brantford, Ontario. I need a change. So does my sister."

"How does Emma feel about the move?" Doctor Hatfield had met Emma a couple times. She was Camden's twin sister—a solemn young woman who barely spoke. Emma had a much softer look than her twin. She was the opposite colouring, her skin being the shade of cream, with poker-straight, strawberry-blonde hair kept in a long braid, which brushed against the small of her back. Her eyes were blue, like Camden's, but they were a vibrant blue made even more outstanding by the black circle around the iris. Her tiny, button-nose had a light sprinkling of freckles, and her lips were full, but not pouty. Emma's body looked frail beside her brother's lean muscles, and she was about five inches shorter than Camden.

Emma had a passion for plants and that was one thing Camden made sure his sister had lots of. He had built her a little greenhouse at the back of their rented house, and it was full of exotic foliage. Lucy couldn't see Emma wanting to leave her home.

Camden smiled. "She's excited."

"Is she really?"

Camden picked up the doubt in Doctor Hatfield's voice. What kind of game was she playing? And why now? It was beginning to appear she was just like all the others, just taken longer for her spots to show. "Yes, she's excited—very excited," Camden confirmed. "In fact," he continued, "it was her idea to move. She doesn't like this place. Vancouver is becoming too dangerous. Just the other day she was telling me there's too much crime, she wanted to move. She reads the news all the time; my sister is terrified of living here. I wouldn't make this move if it weren't for her." Camden thought that would satisfy the doctor. Placing the blame on Emma should take the heat off him.

"I see. I hadn't realized Emma was so unhappy here. You never mentioned it in any of our sessions."

"I didn't see the relevance of declaring my sister's desires when it was me you were supposed to be helping. And, help me you have," Camden's voice was smooth, almost sweet. "I feel good about myself. I feel ready for what life has to offer me, and I thank you for that."

Doctor Hatfield stood and came around her desk. She stopped in front of Camden, sat on the edge of the desk, and studied the young man. Yes, he had come a long way, but, in her professional opinion, not far enough. Especially over the past month. She had noticed several dark, delusional moments that had flickered through during their sessions; however, Camden had been quick to cover them up. "If you like, I can look up the name of a good therapist in Brantford for you," she suggested.

"Won't be necessary." Camden saw the worry in Doctor Hatfield's eyes. "Tell you what, if I feel myself falling, I have your number. I'll call you … I can still talk to you if I don't live here, can't I?"

"Of course." Doctor Hatfield returned to her chair.

Camden stood. "Well, Doctor—Lucy," he dared to call her, thinking, what the heck, it was probably the last time he would ever see her. He extended his hand. "I guess this is it. Thanks again for your time and for all you've done for me. You're better than most." He smiled again.

Doctor Hatfield took his offered hand and shook it. His fingers were cold. She looked into his eyes and saw the iciness there and wondered if she shouldn't try harder to follow through on exactly where he was going and if he was really going to be doing what he said he was. The story of getting a job at a new gym fell in with the kinds of jobs he had held in the past, and with his current one. But lately Camden had voiced lots of dissatisfaction with working there. He had complained that most of the clientele were phoney at the best of times and that he felt they didn't appreciate him for all he did for them. He'd even gone so far as to blame some of them for a couple of the reprimands he had received. It was in the moments he was sharing such information that Doctor Hatfield saw his darkness the most.

"Good luck, Camden. Keep in touch ... I mean that."

Camden smiled—stiff and deliberate. "Sure, doctor, I'll make a point to do that." He turned and walked out of the office.

He didn't bother to acknowledge the secretary. If only he had a bit longer in Vancouver, he would show her. But things were closing in on him—heating up—he needed to move on. All there was left to do was go home and tell Emma. At least this time he had everything in place ahead of time. He had a job and had rented a house just down the street from where he would be working. He had seen pictures of the house. It would be perfect for Emma and her plants, with its three-season room attached to the kitchen.

Doctor Hatfield asked her secretary to hold off before sending in the next patient. He wasn't due for another half hour. She returned to her desk, pulled out Camden's full file, and opened it to the beginning notes— notes that were not hers—information she had managed to gather about him from other places where he had lived.

February 2006: notes on a new patient, Camden Gale ... patient very agitated when admitted to hospital ... admitted himself. He was under the delusion someone was out to get him—actually, several people. Camden works at a local gym doing odd jobs: cleaning, front desk, and serving drinks to the clients when other employees are on their breaks. Upon first sight, he appears to be quite normal and during most of our sessions, he is. Odd living situation, though—lives with his sister. Asked about meeting with her but he refused to allow such a visit, mentioning his sister had been through enough. I never managed to find out what that was. Camden was only my patient for a couple of months, he just stopped coming. I found out later he had moved to Calgary when a colleague of mine contacted me, asking for some advice. He was dealing with a troubled young man who had been admitted to the hospital. When I asked the name, and found out it was Camden Gale, I shared what I could. I forwarded him any notes and information I had on Camden, which wasn't a lot. We both agreed, on the surface, Camden possibly suffered from paranoia brought on by illusions of mistreatment, and misconceptions people were out to get him all the time...

Doctor Hatfield read through the rest of the notes, sorry she hadn't done so as thoroughly before. It might have saved some time, but she always liked to start fresh with her clients and not have a tainted view of them from other doctors. She made a note to give Doctor Morgan a call and moved on to the next set of records in the file.

April 2007: today I met the new fellow, whom a colleague told me about. He had not been able to take him on, saying he was already weighed down with cases. After a few sessions with Camden Gale, I had the feeling there was more to the good doctor's decision than work overload. On the surface, Camden appears quite normal. However, when certain buttons are pushed, such as discussing issues to do with family and work, he becomes agitated and irritable—paranoid that everyone is out to get him. I finally managed to find out he felt he had been neglected by his parents while growing up. In fact, upon deeper research, I discovered he and his sister, Emma, whom he lives with, were in foster care for several years. After our fifth session, I concluded that Camden Gale is paranoid delusional...

Lucy read on. She went to the next file dated January 2008, eleven months before he had come to her in November of 2008. Her phone rang. It was her secretary announcing her next client was getting impatient. Lucy glanced at her watch. "Tell him five minutes, please." Lucy continued reading the last file, which was from a Winnipeg doctor. The same theme ran through his notes. Lucy wondered how many other doctors might have treated Camden, whose files did not make it into the shared medical records. She closed the folder and buzzed the secretary to send in her next client.

~

The house was quiet when Camden arrived home from the doctor's office. Emma was either having an afternoon nap or was in the greenhouse. He dreaded having to tell her about the move. She had not been happy about the other moves, not understanding why they had to leave places where she was perfectly content. Camden thought Emma was the luckier of the two of them; all she had to worry about was her plants. He looked after everything else. But that is the way it should be—she had been through so much—especially after the rape she'd endured at their last foster home. Once they escaped there, Camden had made it his mission to protect his sister. No one would ever hurt her again!

"Emma, you here?" Camden called out.

Silence.

Camden called out again. "Emma."

This time he was rewarded with his sister coming through the back door, followed by their dog, Duke, a Doberman/Sheppard cross. He had often wondered if he and Emma were even related, let alone twins. She was as pale in colouring as he was dark. There were times Camden thought her skin was transparent. But unlike most of the women who came to the gym—women who were not happy with their skin colour or their hair colour and spent lots of money on tanning beds and hair dye—Emma's skin was unblemished. She was also pure and innocent of heart.

"What's up, Cam?" Emma was the only one allowed to call him Cam.

"Sit down, Emma." Camden directed her to a chair at the kitchen table. "I have something to discuss with you. Camden noticed her shoulders droop, as though she knew what he was about to say. Her question confirmed this.

"We aren't moving again, are we, Cam?" Emma was getting good at picking up on the usual signs before a move. She had felt her brother's restlessness in her bones.

"I'm afraid so, Emma. I have a job in Ontario, in a small city called Brantford. Everything is arranged. I didn't want to say anything until I had things in place. I even have a house rented for us. I saw pictures of it online. It has a three-season room on the back for your plants."

Emma interrupted her brother. "Ontario! That's far away from Vancouver, Cam. How will we get my plants there without killing them?"

Camden scowled, but only fleetingly. "We'll rent a U-Haul for our furniture, and with what little we have, there'll be plenty of room for your plants. The weather is warm enough that they won't be damaged."

"When do we leave?"

"I have to be in Brantford on May 19^{th,} just a couple days before the gym's grand opening. So we don't have much time. I'd like to leave within a couple days."

"Don't you have to give proper notice to your boss?" Emma queried.

"Already did," Camden lied. If all went well, his last victim wouldn't die until he and Emma were well on their way to Ontario.

Emma sighed. She was tired of moving. She was tired of being dragged around the country. But, she loved Camden. He was all she had, despite the dark moods she noticed he sometimes had.

Saturday, May 16, 2009

Camden and Emma pulled into the driveway of their new home. Duke was anxious to get out and stretch his legs and mark his territory in the backyard. The real-estate lady Camden had dealt with drove up behind them. When she saw the dog, she didn't look too pleased.

"You never mentioned you had a dog, Mr. Gale."

"Didn't I?" Camden feigned an apologetic look. "Sorry. I guess in my hurry to find a place, I forgot to mention it. He really is no bother, though, as big as he is. I assure you the neighbours will hardly know he's here." Camden pointed to his sister, who was now in the backyard with Duke. "It's her dog, really. Barely ever leaves her side. She doesn't work outside the home. I feel so much better she has Duke with her, especially since I will be doing different shifts at the gym where I'll be working." He pointed down the street to the new facility.

"Oh, you have a job there?"

"Yes, that's why we came to Brantford. My sister wasn't feeling safe in Vancouver with all the crime. Too many gangs. It was her idea to move. I didn't really want to. I had a decent job as a manager at a gym in West Vancouver. Oh well, that's life, I guess." Camden laughed. "What we won't do for family sometimes, eh?"

"I hear you." The real-estate lady smiled. "Well, I have a house showing. Here are your keys and my card if you should need anything. The children of the old lady who used to live here are out of the country. They left me in charge of the property. Hope you like it."

"I'm sure we will. Thank you very much." Camden took the keys and card, turned, and walked to the house.

He wrinkled his nose when he stepped inside. It smelled old. But of course it would, it had been owned by an elderly person. Her children had left quite a bit of the furniture, which was a good thing for him and Emma since they hadn't been able to fit all their stuff into the U-Haul. He walked into the kitchen and noticed the fridge and stove were small and an older style. He opened the fridge door. It was not self-defrosting. He would put that on a list to get for Emma. She was so fragile; he didn't want her to have to do any more work than necessary. Scraping ice from a freezer was not his idea of necessary.

Camden noticed the sliding door leading out into the three-season room. He stooped over and removed the piece of wood in the trail that was being used as extra security, and then slid the door open. The room had been neglected for quite some time. A set of wicker furniture sat in one corner. Camden noticed a couple electrical outlets, which was good because some of Emma's plants needed extra heat, especially when there might be the threat of a late spring frost. Yellowed vinyl blinds hung on some of the windows. He would have to remove them to let as much light in as possible. Emma would love this room, and he would be able to assure her, once again, this was a good move for them. He felt everything was going to work out perfectly here. Maybe this is what they needed to do—him and Emma—move away from the west where the ghosts lived. Surely they wouldn't follow him here.

Duke was standing at the back door of the three-season room. He growled softly. Camden opened the door and the dog bounded in. Emma followed, her face glowing.

"Did you see the flowerbeds, Cam? I don't think whoever lived here before was looking after them, not lately anyway, but at one time they seem to have been well-tended." She smiled. "I'll have fun revitalizing them."

Camden smiled. He hadn't seen Emma so excited for a long time. "So you're not mad at me anymore for making you move?"

Emma reached out and hugged her twin. "No, Cam. You know I could never stay mad at you for long. You are just too good to me."

Camden stroked his sister's long hair and breathed in her musky smell. She always smelled good—not like him. He had to make sure he showered twice a day so as not to offend people around him. Why did that bastard have to do that to her—take her innocence—heap another destruction upon their already damaged life? He hugged Emma close and then gently pushed her away.

"We have to get our stuff in before dark, especially your plants. This is the perfect place back here for them, don't you think?" Camden smiled at Emma.

She clapped her hands gleefully. "Yes, it's perfect. How could I have ever doubted you?"

Camden and Emma spent the next hour unloading the van. Noticing how exhausted Emma was, Camden told her to stay in the back room and arrange her plants where she wanted them; he would look after bringing the rest of their stuff in. They could take their time organizing it later. She nodded and headed for the back room, Duke close on her heels.

Finally, Camden shut the door on the U-Haul. Everything was in the house. He checked his watch. If he hurried, he had just enough time to take the van to the local dealer, saving him another day's rental. He opened his computer case and pulled out a map he had run off before leaving Vancouver. It was a good thing he thought of this stuff.

"Emma, I'm going to take the U-Haul to the dealer. Would you like me to pick up some supper on the way back?" Camden called out to his sister.

She looked up from the plant she was tending and smiled. "That would be wonderful, Cam. That way you won't have to worry about your supper."

Camden nodded and smiled. There she was, always thinking of him. "What do you fancy?" he asked.

"Chicken, I think. What do you say, Duke? Shall we have chicken tonight?"

Duke barked.

"Chicken it is then," Camden chuckled.

The directions took him quickly to his destination. Brantford wasn't as big as he had anticipated. He arrived about ten minutes before closing time. From there, he called a cab and headed to Swiss Chalet on Lynden Road and picked up a take-out order for his and Emma's supper. He would worry about getting groceries tomorrow. He was tired and was getting one of his headaches so asked the cabbie to stop at a drugstore so he could pick up some medication and a newspaper. He wanted to buy a used van to get around in; cabs were expensive. When he got home, Emma was waiting for him in the kitchen.

Emma headed to bed early after supper. Camden wanted to check his emails. He had a mobile internet that he could hook into anywhere he went. He perused down his inbox. Nothing of any importance. He switched to his sent file and clicked on his *special* email, the one he had used a number of times in the past. He studied it and contemplated deleting it off his computer, hoping not to need it here in Brantford. But what if he did? What if things didn't change? Camden decided to keep it for now. He shut off his computer and headed to bed.

Camden and Emma spent the next two days unpacking and cleaning their new home. Camden kept a close eye on his sister and was soon satisfied she was content. Most of her plants had survived the trip. Duke appeared to be enjoying his new backyard, as well.

Emma insisted on accompanying Camden when he went for groceries, something she hadn't done for a long time. That pleased him. Maybe this move was going to turn things around for them. Maybe he wouldn't get those spells and do the things he did. Then again, it wasn't his fault—others made him do it—it was their fault.

By Monday afternoon Emma had had enough. She looked exhausted. Camden asked her if she would like to go for a walk and explore the area. He had been talking to the corner store owners, and they had told him about a beautiful park where they could go and walk around for free. Emma said she would rather stay home and have a nap; he could go, she would be okay.

"I want to get started on fixing the flowerbeds tomorrow," she said.

"I could help you when I get home from work," Camden suggested.

"It's okay, Cam. I won't overtax myself. You'll be tired after your first day at the new job. I want to do this myself. My head's been spinning with ideas ever since we arrived."

Camden reached over and hugged his sister. "Okay. Just promise me you'll pace yourself. I'm going to go and check that park out." He smiled. "Sure you don't want to come?"

Emma returned his smile, shook her head no, and headed up the stairs to her room. From her window, she watched her brother leave. She worried about him sometimes. She wondered why they always had to move. He would seem so happy when they first settled in a place, and then as time went, he would grow bitter. Emma had learned to recognize the signs. She knew when he was getting restless and was going to tell her they were moving. This time had been the worst yet. Emma turned and headed to her bed. Duke was lying by the doorway. As she closed her eyes, Emma said a prayer, asking God to make this the last move—at least for a long time, anyway.

Tuesday, May 19, 2009

Jack had driven all night to get home. It had been great to get away from all the confusion, but he was looking forward to crawling into his queen-size bed and stretching his limbs to their fullest. He could tell Toby was happy to be heading home, as well.

"What do you say, old boy, shall we send out for a fish dinner for lunch?"

Toby looked up at Jack, meowed and licked his chops. Jack reached across the seat and scratched Toby behind the ears. "I'll take that as a yes."

As they pulled onto their street, the first thing they both noticed was that the gym was completed. There was a sign out front announcing the grand opening. "Times are changing, old boy," Jack pointed out.

Toby raced to the van window as he and Jack passed by Miss Mildred's house. *"What's that van doing in her driveway?"* he wondered. *"I'll check it out later while Jack is unpacking our stuff. There are benefits to being a cat—all the luxury without having to do any of the work."*

Jack stopped in front of his house and then backed the van into the driveway. He got out and waited for Toby to jump down. He thought it was strange how Toby had taken to the outdoors after all the years of being an inside cat. Toby headed down the street to Miss Mildred's.

"Don't you be gone long now, Toby. I don't want you to miss your fish lunch," Jack called after the disappearing tail.

Toby paid no attention. He was on a mission. He slunk up to the old wire fence that meandered around Miss Mildred's yard. *"What the heck is that? Miss Mildred doesn't have a dog!"* Toby saw Duke lying in the middle of the yard. Then he noticed the girl kneeling by the flowerbed. *"Maybe someone has come over to help her fix things up."*

The girl was humming. It was a melodic sound, yet mournful. Toby observed how pretty she was, and frail. Her long strawberry-blonde hair swept the grass. Toby moved closer to the fence for a better look. Duke's ears pricked forward. Toby stopped. The last thing he wanted was that great hulk of a dog charging at him when nothing but a flimsy wire fence separated them. Duke growled.

"What's the matter, Duke?" Emma looked up.

Duke stood and trotted over to Emma. He lay down protectively at her side, still growling. Emma patted his head. "Have you had enough of the outdoors, Duke?" She checked her watch. "Oh, it's lunch time already. I wonder where Camden is. Oh, I remember, he went to look at the gym, but that was an hour ago." She stood. "Well, he should be back for lunch; shall we go in and make him some?"

Toby kept very still as the girl and the dog moved across the yard to the back door. He noticed all the plants in Miss Mildred's three-season room; they hadn't been there before. *"Something really strange is going on here,"* Toby thought as he turned around and headed for home. *"No sense missing out on a good fish lunch, though."*

When Toby arrived home, Jack hadn't even started lunch. Toby could tell because he could smell fish a mile away on a rainy day. Jack was sitting on the front step talking to a strange young man. Toby climbed the steps, sat down and glared at Jack, who paid him no attention. Toby meowed.

"Hey there, old man," Jack finally noticed Toby.

"I wish you would quit 'old manning' me! I have a name, Jack. You wouldn't like it if I kept calling you old man, would you?" Toby stared at the young visitor.

"Toby, this is our new neighbour, Camden. He and his sister have moved into Miss Mildred's old place. Unfortunately, while we were gone, she passed away. Camden, this is my cat, Toby," Jack introduced.

Toby circled around on the porch, eyeing Camden. Camden was eye-balling Toby. *"Something wrong with this fellow. Don't like what I see behind those eyes!"* Toby prided himself on reading people.

"Does the cat really understand when you speak to him? It isn't like he's going to remember my name or anything." Camden's statement caused Jack to raise his eyebrows, but then he laughed.

"Oh, Toby understands more than you might think. He's a very smart cat. Actually solved a crime about six months ago and was awarded an honorary detective certificate," Jack explained.

Camden stared at Toby. "You don't say. Well, my sister and I will sleep much better knowing how protected our new neighbourhood is." He laughed and then checked his watch. "Wow, I didn't realize it was lunchtime. Emma will be worried." He stood and extended a hand to Jack. "It was nice meeting you, always good to know your neighbours."

"Likewise," Jack said as he shook Camden's hand. "Come around anytime. Bring your sister."

"Will do. Emma doesn't go out much, though." Camden stooped over to pet Toby.

Toby arched his back and hissed. *"Don't you be touchin' me!"* Toby raced to the door and meowed.

"Looks like your cat doesn't like me," Camden pointed out to Jack.

"You bet my paws, I don't!"

"Oh, Toby just gets a little cantankerous sometimes," Jack chuckled. "You'll get used to him."

"No, he won't!" Toby hissed again.

Camden shrugged his shoulders and left.

Once inside the house, Jack looked at Toby. "What's the matter with you, old boy? Not everyone is out to commit a crime. That isn't any way to welcome someone new into the neighbourhood. He and his twin sister have just moved here from B.C.; he has a job at the gym. Told me his sister isn't well, so she doesn't work. Their parents died when they were eighteen, and he's just always been there for her. Quite a young man who would sacrifice his life to be there for his sister when she needs him."

"Still don't like him … can't fool an old cat like me!" Toby walked over to the refrigerator and sat down.

"Okay, okay ... I get the message," Jack snickered as he picked up the phone and dialled the local fish and chip shop. "Lunch will be here in half an hour," he said as he headed for the living room and his favourite chair.

Toby followed and jumped up on the back of the couch. He stared out the window. Things were changing too fast in the neighbourhood, and he didn't like it one bit. He watched the workers over at the gym as they put the finishing touches on the front flowerbeds. He thought of the girl in the yard ... the big, black dog ... the young man who had just left. Yes, things were changing in the neighbourhood and Toby was not a happy cat!

~

Emma had lunch on the table when Camden walked in. He gave her a hug. "Sorry, I'm late. I stopped by our neighbour's house and had a nice chat. He seems like a nice fellow. His cat's a bit weird, though. Didn't like me much."

Emma giggled. "Well, Cam, you never were much of a cat person, you've always liked dogs. Let's eat before the lunch is cold."

"I have an orientation at the gym this afternoon," Camden mentioned. "Just for a couple of hours. Manager wants to go over some details with the employees."

"Good. Maybe you'll meet some nice people, maybe even a sweet girl," Emma grinned. "You can't spend your entire life looking after me, you know."

Camden looked up from his dish. "And why can't I do that, Emma? Are you unhappy?"

"Of course I'm not unhappy, Cam. It's just that it isn't normal to live with your sister for the rest of your life. Besides, maybe I want some nieces and nephews." Emma reached over and touched Camden's hand. He pulled it away.

"What's wrong, Cam? I'm sorry if I offended you," tears began to brim in Emma's eyes.

"I don't ever want to get married, Emma; you know that. You shouldn't want to either after what we've been through! Look at our parents, the exemplary pair they were!"

"But that was them, Cam; we aren't them."

"I thought you wouldn't want to have anything to do with men after what happened to you!"

"I've been reading some books on healing after traumatic events. I know I'll never forget what happened to me, but I know now I can heal and move on with life. I think it would be lovely to have a husband and children. We don't have to be like our parents, Cam. We can learn from their errors. Actually, I thought, once we get settled, I'd like to get some counselling."

Camden's fist came down on the edge of the table. "Out of the question, Emma. There's no way I'd agree to let you relive that! No way! Subject closed! We're doing just fine; why stir the pot?" Camden pushed his plate away. "There now, see what you've done—spoiled my lunch." He shoved his chair back from the table and stood. "I'm going for a walk to cool off before I have to be at the gym. I can't show up all upset." Camden slammed the front door on his way out.

The tears that had threatened earlier released. Emma pushed her plate aside. Duke came and laid his head on her lap. She stroked his neck. "It's okay, Duke, Cam's just nervous about his new job. He'll calm down, he always does." Emma went into the living room and lay down on the couch. The disagreement had worn her fragile state down. Duke stretched out on the floor beside her.

~

Camden was in a frantic state of mind. The last thing he needed was Emma going to some shrink and talking about all the happenings in their past, and about how many times they had moved, and about him—especially about him. Camden knew he lost it on her sometimes and he also knew she wondered about what was really going on with him. He saw the way she looked at him when he was in one of his moods.

He walked a few blocks until he felt settled, and then turned around and headed to the gym. It would be good to show up early. He pushed the front door open and entered. Everything smelled new. There was no one in sight, so Camden sat on one of the couches in the front lobby. The front door opened and a young girl entered. She walked over to Camden and held out her hand.

"Hi, I'm Paige Young. I've been hired on as the main receptionist." Paige's voice was pleasant. "And you are?"

Camden stood. "Camden Gale. I guess I've been hired on to do odd jobs and fill in wherever needed."

"Pleased to meet you, Camden Gale." Paige smiled. "Are you from around here?"

"No." Camden offered nothing further.

"Well, that's a bonus. I've lived in Brantford all my life. Probably will live here the rest of it, too." She laughed. "So where do you come from, Camden Gale?"

Camden didn't like to tell strangers too much about himself, but she did look kind—not like some of the others he had met at the gyms he'd worked at. "British Columbia," he finally answered.

"No shit! I've always wanted to go there. Are the mountains as beautiful in real life as they are in pictures?" Paige's eyes were bright with enthusiasm.

"There are no words to actually describe their majesty," Camden answered, sure that was what Paige wanted to hear. "You should take a trip out there someday and see for yourself."

The front door opened again and two young men walked in. They introduced themselves as Vincent Reid and Nolan Innis. They had been hired on as personal trainers. Just before two o'clock another girl showed up, introducing herself as Sophia Vasser, a personal trainer.

The group stood around looking at each other. "I wonder where Miss Hanley is," Sophia said.

"Right here." An older woman came around the corner. "Sorry, I was checking out the women's change

21

room. For anyone who doesn't know me, I am Isabella Hanley, the manager." She smiled. "Follow me, everyone."

Isabella directed the small group to a room just off the reception area. "This is where we will have our staff meetings," she informed. "This is also where you will have your lunches and breaks." She pointed to the lockers on the end wall. "You will each be assigned a locker for your personal effects; you will be responsible for your own lock. The owner of the gym will not be responsible if your belongings are stolen." She looked at her watch. "Mr. Rawlings will be here around two-thirty. I am to show you around until then."

Camden stuck close to Paige as they walked around the Gym. Isabella explained to everyone what their responsibilities were and said they would each be given a procedure's manual to look over before the grand opening on Thursday. Isabella had spoken directly to everyone except Camden. Finally, she turned to him.

"I'm sorry; I have not had the pleasure of meeting you in person. I understand you applied for a position here from out of province. Mr. Rawlings said you have worked in the gym environment before and he's hired you for general duty and fill-ins. I will give you a list of your tasks before you leave. You and Paige will also be responsible for selling the protein drinks and bars at the front desk. I would like you two to come in for a couple of hours tomorrow so I can show you where everything is there. Is ten o'clock okay with both of you?"

Paige and Camden nodded in agreement.

A friendly, deep voice boomed through the building. "Isabella, you back there?"

"Over by the treadmills, Mr. Rawlings."

A tall, heavyset man walked around the corner. He had a friendly face. Camden remembered him being pleasant on the phone when they had talked about the job. He had also been very sympathetic to Camden's situation, especially when Camden told him of Emma's health issues and that she had been recommended to see a specialist in Brantford.

"How is everyone today?" he asked. "Ready for a busy few days I hope. I have advertised a pretty tantalizing opening price for membership and am expecting a line-up at the door." Mr. Rawlings paused and looked at the group of young people. He walked up to Camden. "You must be Camden. How was your trip? How is your sister?"

"Trip was good, sir. My sister is settling in fine. She sees the specialist next week," Camden returned.

"Good, good. Where are you living?"

"We actually found a house to rent right on this street."

"Excellent." Mr. Rawlings turned to the others. "Well now, for the next few minutes, I want you all to humour me. You humour me because I own the business," he chuckled. "Actually, you humour me because I want the best gym in town. I know what I am talking about and if you follow what I am about to say, and what you read in your booklets, which Miss Hanley is going to give you, you will all continue working here for a very long time—if you want to." He laughed again.

For the next half hour, Mr. Rawlings went over in great detail what he expected of his employees. In return, he would treat them well. He wanted everyone to be like a big happy family. Camden winced at those words: in his mind, there was no such thing as a happy family.

When the orientation was over, everyone left except for Camden and Isabella. "Come to my office, Camden," Isabella directed. "I have that duty sheet for you."

Camden followed her, and she handed him a piece of paper. "I'm sure you have done most of these things before if you've worked at gyms. If you have any questions, please don't hesitate to ask me. As we get busier, Mr. Rawlings will probably hire someone to help you out, but he is not the kind of man who over-hires and then lets people go. We might have to work a little harder at the beginning until we know exactly where we stand. I hope that's okay with you."

"Yes, ma'am; I don't have a problem with working hard, or working long hours."

"Mr. Rawlings asked how your sister is—is she ill?"

Camden was caught off-guard. He wanted to make sure he didn't say anything different to different people, especially those he worked with.

"It's okay—you don't have to tell me. I didn't mean to pry. Just know, if you ever need to talk about anything, my door is open. We like to make sure our employees are happy." Isabella laid her hand on Camden's arm.

Camden pulled his arm away. "Thank you."

Isabella was shocked by his reaction. "Well, I guess we are done here; I'll see you in the morning at ten."

"For sure."

As Camden left, Isabella couldn't help thinking there was something very strange about him. She made a mental note to ask Mr. Rawlings exactly what he knew about Camden Gale.

Wednesday, May 20, 2009

Camden was waiting at the front door of the gym when Isabella arrived at 9:45. She smiled. "Good to see an employee who likes to be on time."

"I don't believe in giving any employer an excuse to fire me," Camden replied. "If I do my job and show up every day, and on time, what reason would they have to let me go?"

That hadn't been the answer Isabella would have expected from a new employee, but she also had the feeling Camden was far from your ordinary employee. She hoped he was as good as he dictated he was. Time would tell. She opened the door, and they stepped inside. Camden followed her to the front desk and watched as she pulled some papers from under the counter. She then went around to where the drinks were served, retrieved a booklet and set it on the countertop.

"Ever mix drinks at the gym where you worked?" she asked.

Camden smiled. Isabella wondered why her question would elicit such a strange smile. "Of course," Camden replied. "Actually, that was my main job at the last gym I worked."

"I see. Then all this should be familiar to you. Most gyms serve the same kinds of drinks because the clients usually want something quick, filling, and healthy." Isabella glanced at her watch. "I hope Paige is not going to be one of those people who come in at the last minute."

No sooner were the words out of her mouth when Paige came flying through the front door. "I'm so sorry, Miss Hanley. I missed my bus and had to call a cab, and it took forever to get to my house and…"

Isabella interrupted: "Well, you are here now. Try to make sure you are in good time from tomorrow on."

Camden threw Isabella a dark look. Fortunately, she didn't see it. He was upset for Paige. She had explained it

25

wasn't her fault. Things happen. Why didn't some people understand that? Why was Miss Hanley so curt with Paige? Who the hell did she think she was anyway? She would get hers one day. Camden felt a throbbing in his head. He drew in a deep breath in an attempt to alleviate the pain.

The next hour was spent going over the registration form and how to mix the drinks. There was a cash register at the front desk and a separate one for the drinks and body building powders. If they were on the same shift, they would always count the cash floats together. They would be held responsible for any shortages.

"What about overages?" Camden asked.

"If it was intended for a tip, then you take that immediately and put it in a tip jar. If it wasn't, then it stays in the till and is recorded as a sale."

"But the shortages come out of our pockets?" Camden's words sounded clipped.

"Yes, that's right." Isabella moved on to the next subject.

Camden wasn't paying attention anymore. His head continued aching. He was thinking how unfair the system was. He thought he and Paige shouldn't have to pay shortages if they couldn't keep overages. Who were these people anyway? He started to shake. Beads of sweat broke out on his forehead. He felt a hand on his arm and was about to pull away when he realized it was Paige's.

"You okay, Camden?" there was genuine concern in her voice.

"I think I need to go to the washroom for a minute. Be right back."

Camden stopped at the sink and splashed water on his face. He gazed at his reflection in the mirror. There were dark circles around his eyes. He always got those when his headaches started. He began to pace. He needed to settle down; it was too early to get this upset. What excuse would he give Emma if he said they had to move again so soon? And he wouldn't have time to do what had to be done before leaving. He really didn't want to, he was getting tired. He wanted to stop—truly he did, but others just wouldn't let him. They needed to be taught a lesson. Camden breathed in deep, splashed some more water on his face, dried it, and then rejoined Isabella and Paige.

"Sorry," he mumbled. "Don't know what came over me."

"Are you okay now?" Isabella questioned with genuine concern.

"Yeah, I'll be fine. Must've just been a bit of travel-lag catching up with me. It's been a long couple of weeks."

Isabella looked at her watch. "Well, I guess we have finished here anyway. I'll see both of you tomorrow morning at nine o'clock sharp."

Camden and Paige walked out together. He was feeling queasy. He wanted to ask Paige if she would like a ride home, but he was too nervous. She smiled at him and waved as she headed to the bus stop. "See you tomorrow, Cam."

She didn't see him wince. Only Emma could call him Cam.

~

Toby was laying on the back of the couch by the front window when Camden passed by on his way to the gym. Toby's ears flattened and his tail swished angrily. Jack was sitting in his easy-chair, drinking his morning coffee and flipping through the newspaper. He looked up when he heard Toby's tail tapping the couch.

"What's the problem, old boy? What's got you so upset this early in the morning?" He stood, walked over to Toby and glanced out the window just in time to catch a glimpse of Camden. "Is that what you're upset at? It's just our new neighbour."

"*Just my point,*" Toby's ears went even flatter. He looked at Jack, shook his head, and jumped down from the couch. "*I'm outta here … see you later.*" Toby pushed through his cat door.

Jack returned to his chair. "Crazy cat," he mumbled as he picked up the newspaper and commenced reading.

Toby headed down to Miss Mildred's house. He still considered it hers. He wanted to do some investigating while Camden was out of the way. Hopefully the big dog was locked up somewhere. Toby wasn't afraid of the girl; it might be nice to get to know her. He approached the backyard cautiously, eyes wide open, searching for the dog. After skirting the perimeter, Toby was relieved the yard appeared empty. He noticed a movement in the back porch—the girl working amongst her plants. He found an opening in the fence, just big enough for him to squeeze under.

"Boy, that was a tight fit; I'll have to do something about that. Maybe I'll tell Jack he should have me on the light diet stuff ... come to think of it, he already does ... oh well, maybe I should just skip my bedtime snack ... yeah ... that should do it." Toby was trying to rationalize the extra pounds he was carrying around.

Once through the fence, Toby took another guarded look around to make certain the dog was not in the yard. He walked up to the back door and meowed. The girl didn't hear him the first time, so he meowed louder. This time she looked up. As she did, Toby heard that dreaded sound: *woof!* He turned just in time to see the dog come racing around the corner of the house. The girl moved quickly to the door and opened it.

"Hurry, kitty, come in for a minute. Duke does not take kindly to cats, especially those in his territory." Emma's voice was pleasant to Toby's ears as he slipped through the opening just in time to miss being eaten by Duke. He rubbed around Emma's legs to show his appreciation.

Emma knelt and scratched behind Toby's ears. "Where did you come from, fellow? My, you are a handsome boy!"

"Bet your bottom dollar I'm a handsome boy, and smart, too!" Toby purred.

"So, why have you come to visit me?"

Toby jumped up onto a nearby stool. *"Just welcoming you to the neighbourhood, sweetheart."*

"Do you have a name ... yes, you must ... you're wearing a collar. Let me see, what does it say? Toby. Well, isn't that a lovely name for a big, strong kitty like you."

Toby liked the girl more and more.

"Well, my name is Emma, and I live here with my brother, Camden. I call him Cam, but no one else can. We just moved here from Vancouver." Emma sighed. "We're always moving. I hope Cam will settle somewhere one day and be happy." She paused. "I'd get you a treat, but all I have are dog treats. If you come over and visit once in a while, I'll make sure to have some kitty ones on hand. Would you like that, Toby?"

"You bet I would! How to handle the dog, though ... a cat my age could have a heart attack if a dog that big got too close. I could've been a goner this morning!" Toby stood on the stool, circled, and arched his back.

"These are all my plants; do you like them, Toby? Cam lets me keep them, no matter where we live. He's so good to me. I wish he'd get out though and have some fun of his own." Emma had a wistful look in her eyes. "You know, Toby, I think it's time we both moved on. Things happen in life. I've been reading some books—Cam doesn't read much—these books say we can heal from traumatic events if we want to ... that's the answer, Toby— if we want to. I want to be healed, but I'm not sure if Cam does. Oh, here I go, rambling on to a cat; you must think I'm pathetic."

"Not really ... I think you're in danger ... I think your brother is crazy!" Toby meowed and arched up for a backrub.

"Well, Toby, Cam'll be home soon. He had to go to the gym this morning for some training. Big grand opening tomorrow. I'll go and let Duke in my front door. Better yet, here," Emma scooped Toby up in her arms, "I'll let you out the front door."

Toby could feel Emma's heart beating. He felt comfortable in her arms and hoped he wasn't too heavy for her. "Come anytime, Toby. Just meow at the front door if you want. Duke is usually in the backyard, and if he is in the house when you come over, I'll let him out. I'd have gotten a cat when Duke was young so they could have grown up together, but Cam doesn't like cats. It will be fun to have you around." Emma set Toby down on the front step. "See you again, Toby."

Toby meowed and headed for home. Emma went to the back door and let an anxious Duke into the house. "It's okay, Duke. It was just a kitty. He isn't going to take your place." Duke growled. Emma patted him on his head. "We better get lunch ready; Cam will be home any time now."

~

Toby pushed through the cat door and headed straight for his dish. Jack had forgotten to fill it. He meowed loudly and was rewarded with Jack coming through the kitchen door.

"What's up, old man?" Jack set his coffee cup on the table. "Oh, sorry, forgot to fill the dish this morning. Where you been, anyway? You've been gone for quite some time. Find yourself a girlfriend somewhere?" Jack laughed.

"*Sort of.*" Toby meowed louder and stared at his dish.

Jack chuckled. "Some things'll never change, will they, buddy?" he said as he poured the kibble.

Toby dug in. "*I've had quite the morning, especially the part where I was almost eaten by a big dog. Thank God, Emma was there. I'll do anything to make sure she is safe.*" Toby purred as he gobbled down his lunch.

~

"I had a visitor today," Emma mentioned as she and Camden sat down for lunch.

Camden's face tightened. He didn't like visitors, especially if he wasn't home. Emma was too trusting.

Emma noticed the look on her brother's face. "Oh no, Cam … it wasn't a person; it was a big, orange cat. He just showed up in the yard. Duke almost got him. Good thing I was in the back room. I let him in, and we had quite the chat. His name tag had Toby on it; I think he lives somewhere close by."

Camden relaxed slightly. "Big orange cat, eh? Was he old?"

"He looked very mature."

"Probably the cat that lives a couple of doors down. Met him the other day. He didn't like me. Don't you be getting friendly with him; he spat at me."

"Oh Cam, he's just a harmless kitty. He probably won't even bother coming over again. I think he must have visited the old lady who used to own this place."

"Well, don't be letting him in the house. I don't want Duke getting upset, and I'd hate for something awful to happen to our neighbour's cat. I like Jack … seems like a real decent fellow." Camden smiled.

Emma wasn't sure if she liked his smile.

Thursday, May 21, 2009

I t was Grand Opening day at the new gym. People lined up outside the door long before opening time. Toby was staring out at them, annoyed his morning sleep had been cut short. Even Jack was irritated because a few impatient horns had blasted into the morning silence.

"I don't think this neighbourhood is ever going to be the same again," Jack commented as he poured his coffee. He went to the front door and retrieved his newspaper. People were lined up on the sidewalk in front of his house.

"Mr. Rawlings must be offering something exclusive to the first so many customers—maybe a half price membership."

Toby jumped down from the back of the couch and ran to his dish. It had been a long night. Jack had been on the ball; the dish was full. Toby wondered if it would be safe to go and visit Emma this morning. *"Probably not with all those people out there, but maybe I should check on her. Her brother will be at work, and she seemed sort of timid. What if one of these people tries to break into her house? She'll be terrified! I better get down there. At least if something happens I can run back here and get Jack."* Toby went into the living room, meowed at Jack, and then ran to his cat door.

Jack laughed. "Go on, old boy. If you dare go out in that madhouse, I can only wish you luck."

Toby was gone before the last words were out of Jack's mouth. He raced through the backyards to get to Emma's house, and saw her in the three-season room watering her plants. From the front porch railing, he meowed as loud as possible. Finally, she looked up and smiled. Emma held her finger up, indicating one minute and Toby watched her let Duke out into the yard before coming to let him in.

~

Camden was up and out of the house early the morning of the Grand Opening. It was going to be a long and stressful day, and he wanted to take a relaxing walk before going to work. The employees had been instructed to come in the back door this morning; Isabella would be there to let them in. Camden had discovered a little park down the street and spent a half an hour there just sitting on a swing, swinging and thinking. Swinging and hoping things would be better here. But he wasn't sure that was the way it was going to be. Isabella had already shown an icy side when she had been so unsympathetic about Paige being late. Camden watched the bus stop, hoping to see Paige.

Perhaps Emma was right: maybe he did need someone else in his life. Paige seemed kind. But, people—Isabella—walked all over her. He would help her—make it okay for her—just like he did for Emma. The bus pulled up and stopped, but Paige didn't get out. He got a lump in his throat. Maybe she was going to be late again and then she would get fired. Camden sighed and headed to the gym. As he was going around the corner to the back door, a car pulled into employee parking.

"Hey there, Camden," Paige got out of the passenger side of the car. "You ready for this big opening? Did you see all those people?" Vincent Reid got out of the driver's side.

Camden curled his hands into fists. He breathed deeply. He could have picked Paige up if she had asked. Paige came up to him. "Vincent lives a few blocks from me and has offered to give me a ride when we are on the same shift; isn't that nice of him?"

"Very," was all Camden could manage as he headed for the back door. The day was not starting well.

"What's wrong with him?" Camden heard Vincent ask Paige.

"I don't know. He gets a bit weird sometimes," Paige answered. However, Camden didn't hear her last words. "Seems like a nice guy, though." Had he heard them, maybe his day would not have gotten even worse.

"Pull yourself together," Camden mumbled. "You need this job. Emma needs you."

"Good morning, Camden," Isabella greeted him. "Just head to my office; we are going to have a short meeting before we open the doors. I think you three are the last here so we can get started now."

At nine o'clock the doors opened and the people poured in. They took a number and, as Jack had thought, the first fifty were given their membership at half price. Camden was too busy to think any more about his perceived morning problem. Most of the early birds were young adults in their twenties and thirties. One young mother asked if there was a day-care room.

"Not yet," Camden replied. "But I believe the owner is looking into putting one in."

"When?"

"Not sure of the time-frame."

"Well, I guess I can get my friend to babysit for me until then. Where's the form to sign up?"

After people had registered, Isabella took them in groups to show them around. Vincent, Nolan, and Sophia were ready to help people with the equipment and get them signed up for a fitness program. By one o'clock the line-up was finished and only the odd straggler was coming in, mostly for information.

Paige plopped down in a chair. "Boy, wasn't that something, Camden? I wonder how many of these people will stick it out for more than a month." Paige pointed to someone at the drink counter. "Do you mind serving them, Cam? I really have to go to the washroom."

Camden winced, then nodded and went to help the customer. "What can I get for you, miss?"

The young woman barely looked at Camden. "I'll have a banana/strawberry smoothie please."

As Camden mixed her drink, she looked away. He placed the beverage in front of her. "That will be $3.50," he said. She threw $4.00 on the counter, picked up her drink, and told him to keep the change.

"Snob," Camden muttered under his breath as he put the money in the till and took out his tip. He made a mental note to find out her name. She appeared to be the type that would just walk over people whenever she felt like it. He didn't like those kinds of individuals. There had been too many of those type of people in his life. She had that look, too. However, he usually fixed them. Camden noticed Paige returning. "My turn, Paige," he said, and headed to the washroom without waiting for her acknowledgement.

Camden stood in front of the mirror. The black circles were appearing again, and his head was starting to ache. He splashed water on his face; his nausea increased. He ran into one of the stalls and threw up. "Please, God, not so soon; give me time." Camden pounded his fist on the side of the stall.

"You okay in there?" a voice asked.

Camden didn't answer.

"You okay in there?" the same voice repeated.

Camden opened the stall door. "I'll be fine; just a little queasy."

The voice belonged to Nolan. "Been a crazy morning, hasn't it? I thought it would never end." He paused. "Hey, how say we go out for a drink after work … you're new in town, aren't you? I could show you some of the best watering holes." He laughed.

"Thanks, but no thanks," Camden responded. "I have to get home."

"Maybe another time then, eh?" Nolan patted Camden on the back.

Camden winced. He hated people touching him. "Maybe."

Camden managed to make it through the rest of the afternoon without further upset. The gym closed at four o'clock, and by five all the employees were headed for home. Camden didn't bother to say goodbye to anyone. He just needed to get out of there, go home, and have a good night's sleep. Tomorrow would be a better day. Tomorrow he would start fresh. Nicer people would come to the gym tomorrow. He had to remember to look for the woman who had ignored him while he served her drink. He wanted to find out her name.

~

Toby was curled up on his usual perch on the back of the couch by the window facing the street. His eyes opened just in time to see Camden walk by. *"Darkness reeks on that young man,"* Toby thought. *"My poor Emma, what she must put up with."* Toby had spent an enjoyable morning with Emma, watching her tend her plants. They had gone out in the garden, and he had followed her around out there too. She was magic, the way she handled the shrubberies. Toby had heard Duke barking periodically from the house. *"Ha! She prefers me, you big sack of bones. Of course, who wouldn't prefer someone like me?"* If one looked closely, they would have seen Toby smiling. *"Yes, it was a good morning."*

~

Camden ate his supper in silence. Emma was worried as she looked at him and noticed the dark circles around his eyes. It was starting too soon. It had never come on this quickly before. What was wrong with her brother? She wished she could reach him, but every time she tried to open the subject of what was bothering him, he would get angry and shut her down.

"Everything go okay today?" Emma finally ventured.

Camden looked up. He didn't want to bother his sister with his issues. "Everything went fine. I'm just tired. Need an early night." He stood and headed for the stairs. "Thanks for supper, Emma. It was delicious."

Once Camden was in his room, he went straight to his computer and turned it on. He checked his emails—nothing but junk. He went to his sent file and clicked on the *special* file. He stared at it.

"Dear ... You are receiving this email because you have been very, very naughty. Do you know what happens

to very naughty people? Think about it! When was the last time you ridiculed someone ... ignored someone just because ... blamed someone wrongfully? When was the last time you were nice to someone ... really nice? When was the last time you helped someone ... really helped? You are so pathetically naughty that I can't stand it! Only you can turn this around and do something about it. I have given you the warning; now, it is up to you to seek reconciliation. If you don't, maybe retribution will come your way ... if you have any friends who are just like you, pass this on to them so they can get help too. For every friend you try to save, the retribution on yourself will be lessened. You know the drill: six to ten, maybe you won't die ... one to five, you will ... signed: 666."

Camden exited out of his emails and crawled into bed. "Please don't force me to use it ... please don't force me to use it," he garbled into his pillow. The last sound he heard before sleep overtook him was Emma's soft footsteps passing by his room on her way to bed.

Wednesday, May 27, 2009

The morning sky opened with a sprinkling of rain that promised to increase as the day went on. Toby sat on the back of the couch staring out at the dreariness. He knew he wouldn't be venturing down to see Emma today. He noticed Camden running down the sidewalk, headed for work. Camden had stopped by a couple of times over the past week to talk to Jack. Toby wasn't happy about the visits because he always came at an inappropriate time—when he and Jack were having *their time*—TV time.

Camden, in Toby's opinion, complained too much. Jack just listened patiently. Jack had a lot of patience. Camden complained mostly about the clients and how they were such snobs and how many of them pushed him around and took him for granted. Most had no manners either. Camden went on and on. He never mentioned any names, and sometimes Toby wondered if what Camden was saying was true or if it was all in his head. *"Most likely in his head. Personally, I think he's a nutcase, and I wish Jack wouldn't be so cozy with him."*

Toby stood up and arched; stretching in the mornings was good. He could hear Jack making coffee in the kitchen, so sauntered over to his dish, meowed, and then walked over and rubbed around Jack's legs.

"Just give me a minute, old boy." Jack finished pouring the water in the coffee-maker and then pulled Toby's box of kibbles from the cupboard and filled his dish. Toby finished his breakfast and returned to his perch on the back of the couch. Jack had poured a coffee and was reading his newspaper in his favourite chair.

"How would you like it if we moved, Toby?"

"Must be something severe if Jack is calling me Toby." Toby opened his eyes and looked at Jack.

"It just isn't the same around here with that gym next door. People coming and going all day long, and, from what

38

I hear, eventually the gym is going to be open 24-hours a day. Just a matter of time. The other day when I came home, someone was parked halfway in my driveway. I had to go over to the gym. Good thing Camden was working because he went right back into the workout areas and found out who it was. I think he's right about some of those people. The guy didn't even apologize. Camden was furious, but I told him it was okay—no biggy."

"Oh, Jack, it is a biggy for Camden—be careful."

"Anyway, as I was saying, I'm thinking of putting the house up for sale and maybe get us a little place on the edge of the city." Jack paused and took a sip of coffee. He shook his newspaper page and continued to read. "Just a thought, old man—just a thought."

~

Camden was meticulously watching a couple of people. The first one was the woman who had thrown him the money on the first day at the gym. He had tried several times to be friendly with her, but she wanted nothing to do with him. Once, she had even spoken quite sharply and asked him if he had a problem. Camden had looked up her file. Her name was Brianna Gates; she was a school teacher. He copied down her email address.

The other person Camden was watching was a fellow named Tyler Acton. He was a machinist and thought he was really something. Camden had been checking the guys' washroom for supplies one day, and Tyler had bumped into him and knocked the supplies out of his arms. The bastard hadn't even bothered to apologize or help to pick them up. Camden had gotten into trouble from Isabella for taking so long in the washroom because Paige was really busy at the front desk and he was needed at the drink counter. Camden copied down Tyler's email address.

So it was, on that particular rainy day, May 27th, when things really began to fall apart for Camden again. There were others, too—others he was watching, but he hadn't made any final decisions on them yet. On May 27th,

Brianna had brushed by him without even a smile. In fact, she had appeared to be sneering at him. Tyler had been leaving at the same time Camden was headed for home and hadn't even thanked him for holding the door open.

Toby was sitting by the window when he saw Camden running past. He observed the look on Camden's face and hoped Emma would be okay. She had never said anything about her brother being mean to her, but Toby had the feeling he could be.

When he arrived home, Camden was still enraged. Luckily, Emma was resting on the couch. He assumed she'd had a stressful day, too. Rainy weather affected her like that. Duke was lying on the floor beside her and he looked up when Camden came into the living room, then put his head down and went back to sleep. Camden headed straight for the back porch—straight to the *special* plant that he took such care to make sure went with them no matter where they lived. He picked some of the seeds and then headed to his room. Camden opened the closet door and reached up for a box on the top shelf. Inside was a mini coffee grinder, which he took over and set on his desk. He pulled a zip-lock bag out of the top drawer of his desk and then put the seeds into the grinder and turned it on. The seeds ground quickly. He poured the powder into the baggie, sealed it, and tucked it under his pillow. He put the grinder back in its box and returned it to the shelf in his closet.

Camden breathed deeply as he sat down at his computer and went to his email account. He had given Paige his email, but she hadn't sent him anything yet. He'd noted she had not given him hers. Camden had two email accounts: one that could be traced easily, one that couldn't. It was the account that couldn't be traced easily that he opened on May 27th. He scrolled to his *special* email, the one he had sent several times over the past few years. He smiled as he read it, picturing the faces of Brianna and Tyler when they read their mail later. He copy/pasted the document into a new email and then typed in Brianna's email address. When hers was sent, he opened another blank document and pasted the letter again, this time typing in Tyler's address. He pushed send and sat back in his chair for a moment. Camden smiled as he closed his computer and headed downstairs. His step was light, as though the weight of the day had evaporated.

Emma was in the kitchen starting supper. Duke was lying in front of the sliding doors to the three-season room. Emma looked up as Camden entered. "Sorry, Cam, I had a headache and decided to lay down for a bit. I overslept. You know how rainy weather affects me."

"No problem, Emma. Maybe I can help you. What are you cooking?"

"I was going to make spaghetti. You look like you've had a good day."

"Pretty good. What can I do?"

Emma put her hands on her hips. "Well, I guess you could chop the onion for me." She passed him an onion, a knife, and a chopping block.

Camden laughed. "Ah, is that what I get for offering to help—the onions!"

Emma joined in the laughter. She was happy to see her brother relaxed. Maybe things were going to work out here after all.

~

Brianna had gone for groceries after her workout at the gym. She didn't need much, but it would save her from going on Thursday or Friday night when the stores were crowded. On the way home, Brianna went through the Swiss Chalet drive-thru and picked up a quarter-chicken dinner with a side Caesar salad. She figured the meal would go nicely with a glass of rosé wine. It had been a long day. She hated rainy days because the students had to stay in for recess. Those were the days when she most questioned her teaching vocation. But, on the whole, Brianna enjoyed the kids. Next year she would apply to teach grade five; grade two was beginning to bore her.

Sylvester, Brianna's cat, greeted her at the door. "What do you want, kitty? Miss me?" Sylvester rubbed his head on one of the grocery bags and meowed. He was a big, black and white male that her brother, Neil, had needed to find a home for a couple of years ago. She'd said she would take him temporarily, but the cat had grown on Brianna, and he was good company on the lonely nights, especially since Greg had left.

Brianna put her groceries away and then warmed the chicken dinner in the microwave. She poured her wine while waiting. When the dinger went, she placed everything on a tray and headed for the living room and turned on the television. Sylvester joined her on the couch. When her meal was finished, she flipped through a few channels, but finding nothing of any real interest, Brianna shut the television off and went over to her computer. Sylvester followed, jumping up on the desk and stretching out in front of the monitor.

"I'm going to have to get a monitor riser if you get any bigger, Sylvester," Brianna giggled. Sylvester rolled over for a belly rub.

Brianna clicked on her email and went to the in-box––five new emails. Three were junk mail; one was from her brother, and there was one that said 'JUST FOR YOU' in the subject line. She didn't recognize the sender but didn't delete it. She clicked on her brother's and read through it quickly. Short and sweet—as always. He was backpacking around Europe for the summer and stopped at internet cafés every once in a while to update the family. She would call her sister tomorrow to give her the news. Her sister had three kids and no computer. Neil was doing well. He was in France now and would be heading to Italy in a couple of weeks. The hostels were not always the best, but they were a roof over one's head, which was especially important if it was raining. Neil had put a smiley face beside that comment. Brianna pushed print to run a copy, and then she opened the last one.

"What the..." Brianna sat in shock as she read her screen. *"Dear Brianna: You are receiving this email*

42

because you have been very, very naughty. Do you know what happens to very naughty people? Think about it! When was the last time you ridiculed someone ... ignored someone just because ... blamed someone wrongfully? When was the last time you were nice to someone ... really nice? When was the last time you helped someone ... really helped? You are so pathetically naughty that I can't stand it! Only you can turn this around and do something about it. I have given you the warning; now, it is up to you to seek reconciliation. If you don't, maybe retribution will come your way... if you have any friends who are just like you, pass this on to them so they can get help too. For every friend you try to save, the retribution on yourself will be lessened. You know the drill: six to ten, maybe you won't die ... one to five, you will ... signed: 666."

Brianna's finger was shaking as she hit the delete key. "What a sicko!" she exclaimed. She looked at her watch. "Better get to bed, I have preschool yard duty in the morning." She got into her pyjamas, brushed her teeth, and crawled under the covers. Sylvester curled up at her feet. Brianna was having a difficult time falling asleep, still thinking about the email, so she flicked on the television for the eleven o'clock news and pushed the sleep button for sixty minutes.

"If anything can make me forget that nasty email, world disasters, wars, and murders should!" Brianna burrowed down into her comforter. Sylvester looked up for a second, then settled again. An hour later the television shut off. Brianna was breathing softly, sound asleep.

~

Camden checked his computer before heading off to bed. He had set that email account up to show automatically when an email was received. He grinned when he saw one of them had been opened. Camden hoped Brianna had a good night's sleep.

Thursday, May 28, 2009

Tyler Acton had been annoyed leaving the gym Wednesday night. He'd actually been annoyed before he had even gone to the gym, and had thought he could improve his mood by pumping some iron. Pumping iron had felt good, and he was starting to feel some release, but then he had accidentally bumped into one of the gym workers in the washroom. He would have stayed to help him clean up the mess, but he was on a tight schedule and needed to finish his workout. The guy had looked really upset and Tyler had thought if looks could kill, he would be dead. Tyler remembered looking at his name tag, but couldn't remember the guy's name now.

Then on the way out the front door, the guy had held the door open for him, but he was in such a hurry he hadn't said thanks until the guy was way down the sidewalk. He'd thank him today if he saw him. Tyler had gone straight to work from the gym. He was on the night shift this week at his uncle's machine shop. There wasn't much work around, and he was thankful to have a job, but he had been late a few times and his uncle had warned that he couldn't keep giving Tyler special privileges.

When Tyler got home from work, he decided to check his email before heading off to bed for a few hours. He tapped his fingers impatiently as the computer loaded up. It was old and slow, like he felt sometimes. He would be thirty on his next birthday and didn't have anything to show for it. He lived in a dingy little apartment; hadn't had a steady job in six years; didn't have a girlfriend now, and hadn't had one since Veronica had left six months ago and she had only been around for seven months. He didn't have anything in his bank account either because he had felt it was more important to have fun than to save for a rainy day.

When the rainy days hit and he lost his job at the factory where he'd been doing assembly work for four years, he had no trade to fall back on. After a month, he had gone to his uncle and asked for a job—told his uncle he would do anything, even sweep the floor. Tyler remembered his uncle stroking his chin and looking at him with the condescending look he gave just before the big speech was released. And Tyler had listened. What choice did he have? He needed to pay the rent, and he needed to eat. He couldn't keep sponging off his mum, who was on a limited income. He had sucked it up and taken the night-shift job from six p.m. to four a.m., cleaning the machines and sweeping up the shop and offices.

When Tyler had read about the new gym opening and saw the price for membership, he had decided to get himself in shape again. That was the reason he had been late to work a couple of times because he had taken some extra time on a piece of equipment. "Three strikes and you're out, Tyler," his uncle had said. He had almost been late last night, just making it to the shop as the buzzer went off.

Finally, the computer was booted up. Tyler clicked on his email. He deleted the usual pesky junk mails and then clicked on the one that said: JUST FOR YOU. "What the hell is this?" he shouted. *"Dear Tyler: You are receiving this email because you have been very, very naughty. Do you know what happens to very naughty people? Think about it! When was the last time you ridiculed someone ... ignored someone just because ... blamed someone wrongfully? When was the last time you were nice to someone ... really nice? When was the last time you helped someone ... really helped? You are so pathetically naughty that I can't stand it! Only you can turn this around and do something about it. I have given you the warning; now, it is up to you to seek reconciliation. If you don't, maybe retribution will come your way ... if you have any friends who are just like you, pass this on to them so they can get help too. For every friend you try to save, the retribution on yourself will be lessened. You know the drill: six to ten, maybe you won't die ... one to five, you will ... signed: 666."*

"Sick bugger! Who'd send this to someone!" Tyler grumbled angrily as he pushed the delete button. "I mean, I've had chain letter emails telling me if I didn't forward it on something bad would happen, but they were silly things, like my hair falling out or..." Tyler mumbled as he shut the computer off.

He went into the kitchen, poured himself a glass of milk, and looked in the cupboard for something quick to snack on before hitting the pillow. All he found was a box of crackers, and they were a bit stale. He would have to set his alarm earlier than normal so he could grab a few groceries before hitting the gym before work. Tyler headed to his bedroom, pulled the blinds, and crawled under the covers. The nasty email was already forgotten.

~

The first thing Camden did when he woke in the morning was turn his computer on to check if Tyler had opened his email. He smiled when he saw the notice. Good.

Camden wasn't all bad. He might give them both a second chance. Nevertheless, his final decision would depend on how they behaved the next time he saw them. He turned off his computer, retrieved the baggie from under his pillow, and headed downstairs for breakfast. He could smell the bacon cooking. He was humming as he entered the kitchen.

Emma looked up and smiled. "Do you mind grabbing the eggs from the fridge? The bacon is almost done."

Camden retrieved the eggs. "Where's Duke?"

"He wanted out. I think he's agitated about Toby coming over so much."

"Toby comes over a lot? Thought I asked you not to get too close to that cat. He doesn't like me, Emma."

"Don't be silly, Cam. Toby is just an old cat, and he's always out of here before you get home." She paused. "Almost as though he doesn't want to meet up with you," she giggled.

Going to the back door, Camden whistled for Duke, who came running immediately. "Good boy, Duke," Camden patted the dog as he came through the door. "We don't like big orange cats, do we?" Duke let out a muffled growl.

Camden's happy mood had been spoiled with the mention of the cat. He plunked himself in a chair and waited for Emma to serve the breakfast. He studied her back, wondering what was getting into her lately. She seemed to be changing, and Camden wasn't sure if he liked the change. She had mentioned she was doing some reading and wanted to see a counsellor; how did he know for sure she wasn't sneaking out to see someone while he was at work? It was a good thing they lived so close to the gym; he would start popping in to check on her during breaks and lunch hour. Camden made a mental note to call the house more often during the day.

Emma noticed her brother's mood change, as well.

~

"Think I'll invite Camden and his sister over for supper tomorrow night," Jack mentioned during his and Toby's usual morning ritual. "I'd like to meet his sister, and it will be our way of welcoming them to the neighbourhood."

"You already welcome him enough; you don't need to have him sitting at our table with his dark looks daggering at me!" Toby sat up and glared at Jack. *"But, it'd be good to have you meet Emma. That way I could get to see the interaction between the two of them and confirm what I'm thinking: that guy isn't as wonderful as he portrays he is to his sister!"* Toby jumped down and headed for the kitchen, his tail held high.

"Where you going, old man? I thought you'd like that since I see you always going down to their house in the daytime. I think it's time I met the sister."

"Don't need to explain yourself, Jack. I'll just hide if the guy gets too creepy. I have my corners where I can spy from." Toby let out a meow and headed for his cat door.

Once outside, he headed for the front of the house and sat down on the edge of the sidewalk. If his timing was correct, Camden should be coming along any time now, headed for work. Toby noticed the front door of Emma's house open. Camden stepped out and he didn't look happy. Toby planted himself right in the middle of the sidewalk, laid down, and stretched across the full width. He kept his eyes focused in the direction where Camden would be approaching.

Camden stopped about a foot from Toby. "Get out of the way, cat," Camden ordered. "This sidewalk's for people, not overweight, lazy cats!"

Toby rolled over but made no move to get up. *"Go around me, buddy."* He rolled back so he could face Camden. Toby noticed Camden's foot start to move toward him. *"Dare you!"*

Just then the front door of Jack's house opened, and Jack stepped out onto the porch. "Hey there, Camden, glad I caught you. I was wondering if you and your sister would like to come over for supper tomorrow night."

Camden's foot rested back down on the walkway. He threw Toby a nasty look and muttered, "Next time, cat." Then he turned to Jack. "That would be nice. What time?"

"Around six, good?"

"I have to work until six; could you make it six-thirty?"

"Sure. Anything in particular you guys don't like?"

"Nah, we pretty well eat anything."

"See you tomorrow night then."

"Looking forward to it. I gotta get to work now, though." Camden threw another nasty look at Toby and then stepped around him.

"Didn't see that did you, Jack? He was going to kick me—kick your best friend!" Toby sat up and moved off the sidewalk after Camden had passed. He decided to go back to the house and have another rest; he was shaken.

"Not going down the street this morning, Toby?" Jack asked.

Toby threw Jack a disdainful look and jumped up on the back of the couch. *"What do you care? You just invited*

48

that guy over to our house ... the guy who would have kicked me if you hadn't opened the door to ask him over for supper. I could be lying out there on the sidewalk bleeding to death..." Toby closed his eyes.

"Well, you have a good nap there, old man. I'm headed out to have coffee with the captain; been a while since Bryce and I got together, and he called me last night."

"I won't wait up for you," Toby didn't even bother to take note of Jack's exit.

~

Brianna had not slept well. The email kept repeating over and over in her mind. But, one thing she did not do, unless she was at death's door, was call in sick to work. Of course, of all days, she had to be there early today. Brianna crawled out of bed, staggered to the bathroom and turned on the shower. She let the water pour over her until her eyes began to open and her mind cleared.

She had deleted the email, but it would still be in her deleted mail file; she hadn't emptied her recycle box yet. She wondered if she should show it to someone, and then thought better of it. Probably just some punk trying to scare people. But, it was addressed directly to her. Brianna ran through a mental list of her friends, trying to figure out which one of them might pull something like this. Not one she could think of. By the time she got dressed and ate breakfast, Brianna had run out of time. She flew out the door and put the email out of her mind.

It was an extra busy day at work and to top it off, Brianna's principal called an emergency staff meeting. When it was over, all she wanted to do was go home and crash; she decided to forfeit the gym. "One night won't kill me," she mumbled as she got into her car and headed for home.

~

Tyler slept through the alarm. He either had to delay getting groceries or forego his gym workout. As he was splashing water on his face, his stomach gave him the answer. He pulled on a pair of jogging pants, slipped into a T-shirt, and headed out the door to the grocery store. He went through Harvey's drive-thru on the way home and picked up a burger combo. As he returned to the apartment, there was just enough time to put his groceries away and make lunch before he had to head out the door to work. The gym would have to wait until tomorrow night—that way he could spend longer because he didn't work Friday nights.

Any thoughts of the weird email had totally slipped his mind.

~

Camden was watching the clock from three o'clock on, the usual time when Tyler showed up for his workout. Brianna should be arriving shortly after four. By five he assumed neither one was going to show. He was hoping he hadn't upset them so much that they wouldn't be back for a few days. That would disrupt his schedule. What if they didn't return at all? Camden started to hyperventilate just thinking about that possibility.

"Camden … you okay?" Paige's voice cut into his thoughts. "There are a couple of customers waiting for drinks. Should I get them?"

"No … no, I'm fine." Camden turned to the customers. "Sorry about that; I guess my mind was wandering. Getting close to my shift's end. What can I get for you, miss?" he asked the lady first, not being sure which customer had been there first.

"I was here first," the male customer inferred.

"Sorry, I didn't realize. I…"

"You should pay more attention to your job, Camden." The young man poked Camden's name tag. "This isn't the first time you've screwed up, and the gym has only been open for a week."

Camden's face turned a dark red. His head began pounding. The young woman looked displeased. "It's okay," she said, a hint of sarcasm in her voice, "if the big man wants his drink first, by all means, serve him first."

"No!" Camden almost shouted. "He's being rude. He can wait. What would you like, miss?"

Paige noticed what was going on and she came around the corner. "Need some help here? How say I serve this guy and you assist the lady, Camden." She paused. "Oh my God, Owen Bains! It's you causing this ruckus. What has gotten into you?"

Owen laughed. "Paige, could you get me a banana/pineapple smoothie please—I know it will be extra sweet, too, if you make it." He paused. "I guess you better make it because, after the way I've treated Camden, he would probably put some poison in my drink, or something!" He laughed again.

"Oh, Owen, you are too funny." Paige giggled.

Camden's face drained of colour. He made a mental note to look up Owen's information. The guy was a real jerk. Isabella had heard the commotion from her office and she was coming across the floor, heading for the drink counter. "*Oh God,*" Camden thought, "*now I'm going to be disciplined for being rude to a customer, and it wasn't my fault. I don't even know why he was such a jerk to me.*"

"Everything okay here?" Isabella asked.

"Everything is fine," the young woman answered her. "This nice young man was just getting ready to mix me a strawberry smoothie, weren't you, Camden?"

Camden hesitated a second before replying: "That I was; what size did you want?"

"Large."

Isabella looked puzzled but decided not to make anything more of it. Obviously whatever had been going on had been dealt with. She would pull Paige in later, when Camden wasn't around, and ask her what had happened. Isabella had noticed Camden's shortness with some of the clients, and she intended to speak to Mr. Rawlings about him. She didn't care if he had been hired all the way from

British Columbia. Sometimes her boss was too trusting and gave the wrong people a job. He had done the same thing at a former gym he had owned, and it had almost backfired on him. One of the clients was ready to sue the gym, but Isabella talked them out of it. It would be unfortunate if Camden lost his job, but that wasn't her problem. The bottom line profit of the gym was her problem and cynical employees affected that bottom line.

Paige and Camden served the clients their drinks, and then Paige returned to the front desk to buzz through a new arrival. Camden hoped it might be Brianna or Tyler. No such luck. He sighed. It was getting late anyway; his shift would be over before they would finish their workouts. He began to clean the counter and tidy the shelves. Camden didn't like to leave a mess.

"It's kind of quiet now, Camden; could you please cover here for me for a sec?" Paige asked. "I have to go to the washroom."

"Sure, no problem." Camden thought it would be the perfect opportunity for him to look up Owen's email.

Paige didn't take as long as Camden expected. He was just writing down the last few letters on a piece of paper when she returned. He quickly clicked off the computer screen. "What are you doing, Camden?" Paige asked.

"Nothing."

"What did you write on that piece of paper you just shoved in your pocket?" she pushed.

"Nothing. What's it to you anyway?"

"Were you looking up my phone number, Camden?" Paige grinned mischievously. "Come on, admit it ... yes ... you were, weren't you ... you were looking up my phone number!"

"No, Paige. I was not. I told you it was nothing." Camden's voice sounded edgy.

"You are one weird dude, Camden Gale," Paige laughed. "Oh well."

Camden returned to the drink counter and mixed a drink for another lady. She was nice and left him a one dollar tip. He looked at the clock. Five to six. "I'm going to take off now, Paige," he called over to her.

"No problem, it's not so busy."

Camden retrieved his belongings from his locker and headed home. He was pondering whether to send the email to Owen tonight. No, better not—he had to deal with the other two first. Maybe he would send them another one. Yes, that was what he needed to do. As he passed by Jack and Toby's house, he glanced at the picture window.

"Lazy old cat," he muttered when he noticed Toby on the back of the couch. Camden raised his middle finger in the direction of the window. Then he paused at the spot where Toby had lain across the sidewalk earlier that day and made a kicking motion. "Stupid cat. You'll be sorry you ever tried to cross me. One day you'll come trotting over to my house, and I'll be there, and Duke will be extra agitated. If there's one thing Duke is not fond of, it's cats!"

Camden figured Toby was sleeping and was just a dumb animal. He didn't realize the old cat saw everything. Toby noticed the tension in Camden's face and once again worried for Emma. He should have gone to visit her today. Oh well, he would see her tomorrow night. The only problem was that he would have to suffer through Camden's company, as well.

Emma had supper ready and was watching television when Camden stormed in the house. "Cam, what's wrong?" she jumped up from the couch.

"Some jerk almost got me in trouble today. I may still be in trouble. I don't think Isabella thinks much of me and I get the feeling she's always watching me. It doesn't seem to matter what I do, it's never good enough!"

"I'm sorry to hear you had a rough day, Cam." Emma went up to her brother and gave him a hug.

He pushed her away. "Not now, Emma. I need to go to my room for a bit. You go ahead and eat. I'll be down for something later."

Duke growled when Camden pushed Emma. "It's okay, boy; Cam didn't mean anything by it." Duke walked over to Emma and stood protectively by her side. Camden stomped up the stairs to his room.

Once inside his room, Camden took the baggie out of his pocket and placed it under his pillow again. He turned on his computer, sat down and waited for it to fire up. Camden put his hands on his temples and began to rub, hoping to alleviate the escalating pain. Finally, he could get into his email. He checked the regular account; still no message from Paige. Then he moved into his other account and brought up his special message.

"Yep … I think those two need another warning." He started with Brianna, making a few changes first. Send. Camden sat back and smiled. Then he sent a copy to Tyler. Camden hummed a little tune. He felt much better now. He shut the computer off and went downstairs for supper.

"Sorry, Emma." He planted a kiss on her forehead. "I shouldn't take my work frustrations out on you." He lifted the lid of the pot on the stove. "What do we have here?"

"Chicken and dumplings—your favourite."

"Oh, by the way, I accepted an invitation to supper at Jack's place tomorrow night. I didn't think you would mind since you are so attached to Jack's cat."

"That will be lovely." Emma was pleased. It wasn't often Cam liked someone enough to socialize with them. Maybe this Jack fellow would be good for her brother. Maybe they would stay here longer if Cam made a good friend. Then she could make friends, too.

~

Brianna arrived home at six o'clock. She rummaged in her freezer for a leftover she could throw in the microwave. Finally, she was rewarded with a container of stew. It looked a bit frosty, but she really didn't feel like cooking a meal from scratch.

The principal had been concerned with the amount of violence on the playground. Brianna thought he was overreacting. Kids would be kids. They would wrestle, especially the boys. But there was no tolerance for violence of any kind across the school board, and Mr. Cunningham followed that policy to the letter. The result had been a big meeting, and there would now be three teachers on outside duty instead of the usual two.

While her supper was heating up, Brianna turned her computer on. She had forgotten to send a reply to her brother last night. She noticed another strange email: this one said: 'ARE YOU LISTENING TO ME' in the subject line. *"Dear Brianna: you are still being very, very naughty. I told you what happens to very naughty people. Did you think about it? Did you ridicule someone today ... ignore someone just because ... blame someone wrongfully? Were you nice to someone ... really nice? Did you help someone today, just because ... really help? I doubt you even gave my message a second thought. Oh, believe it, you are so pathetically naughty that I can't stand it! You might still be able to turn this around and do something about it. I am being generous giving you another warning, but it is still up to you to seek reconciliation. If you don't, retribution will come your way ... and don't forget all those selfish, naughty friends of yours who are just like you. Pass this on to them so they can get help too ... for every friend you try to save, the retribution on yourself might be lessened. You know the drill—six to ten, maybe you won't die ... one to five, you will ... signed: 666."*

Brianna hit the delete button again, but not before putting a block sender on the letter. "There, that should fix you, you sick prick!"

~

Tyler got home from work in the wee hours of Friday morning. His uncle had talked to him about possibly signing on as an apprentice. He had said it would be good to get a trade, something he could take with him anywhere in the world. Tyler knew his uncle felt a sense of responsibility for him since Tyler's dad had died when he was ten years old.

He had told his uncle he would think hard about it and then thanked him for the opportunity.

It had been a long day, and Tyler was too tired to check his email. He gulped down a glass of milk and headed off to bed. "Nothing that can't wait until tomorrow," he reasoned.

~

Before Camden went to bed, he checked to see if either of the emails he had sent had been opened. Just Brianna's. Oh well, Tyler would open his eventually. It was only a matter of time before those two got their just desserts. Camden crawled under his covers, curled into the fetal position, put his thumb in his mouth, and fell asleep.

Friday, May 29, 2009

Tyler got up at two o'clock in the afternoon. He wasn't hurrying to get out of the apartment, not having to punch a clock tonight. After showering, Tyler packed his gym bag and made some eggs and toast. He flipped through the sports' channels on the television while eating.

Just before Tyler was going to leave, he remembered he had to call his mum. He hadn't talked to her for a couple of days. She answered on the third ring.

"Hello." Her voice sounded sad.

"Hey there, Mum, how are you? Sorry, I haven't been in touch—been really busy."

"Tyler!" His mum's voice picked up. "I was going to give you a call today if I didn't hear from you. Everything okay? Do you need anything?"

"Oh, maybe just one of your delicious home-cooked meals on Sunday," Tyler laughed.

"That can be arranged." She giggled softly. "How's work?"

"Good. Uncle George offered me an apprenticeship."

"Oh, Tyler, that would be wonderful. Having a trade is a good thing."

"That's what he said."

"Are you going to do it?"

"I told him I'd think about it."

"Well, you should, you know. You aren't getting any younger. You need to settle down. I wouldn't mind being a grandmother before I die."

"You aren't going to die anytime soon, Mum."

"One never knows when their time will be up," Tyler's mum interrupted.

"I have to find a girl that will put up with me first," he chuckled.

"What happened to the last girl, Veronica?"

"She couldn't put up with me." Tyler chuckled again. "Anyway, gotta go. I was just on my way out to the gym."

"Maybe you'll meet a lovely girl there," his mum suggested.

"Maybe."

"Think about what your Uncle George offered you."

"I will. See you on Sunday. Bye."

"Bye, Tyler."

Tyler hung up the phone, double-checked to make sure he had turned off his stove and then headed out the door. He didn't bother to check his email. It could wait until tonight. On his way to the gym, he stopped for gas and made a phone call to a buddy to get together with after his workout. He smiled. Life was getting better. Tyler tapped his fingers on the steering wheel and hummed along with the song on the radio.

When he entered the gym, he smiled at Paige, who was at the reception desk. "And how are you today, beautiful Paige?"

Paige grinned widely. "Just fine, Tyler—missed you yesterday."

"Had to get groceries—man has to eat, you know. Have to keep this gorgeous body of mine in good shape for the girls," Tyler flirted.

Camden was pouring a drink for someone when he heard Paige say Tyler's name. He breathed in deep. Good, one of them was here. He looked at the clock: four o'clock. He patted his pocket to ensure the baggie was still there. Camden smiled at the client at the drink counter. "That will be two-fifty," he said.

The girl put three dollars on the counter, "Keep the change," she said as she walked away. She was one of the nice girls.

~

Brianna managed to get out of the school by four o'clock. It had been a good day with the kids. On the way to the gym, she called her sister. "Hey, Caitlin, what are you up to later?" Brianna could hear the kids in the background. "Is Mitch home tonight?"

Caitlin sounded tired. "Mitch is never home on a Friday night, Brianna. You know that."

"I thought maybe he would sacrifice one Friday night so your sister could take you out for a movie or something fun."

"Dream on, sis. You can come over here if you like. I could make us supper, and we could do a movie here after the kids go to bed. They'd love to see their Aunt Brianna, you know—it's been a couple of weeks." There was a slightly accusatory tone in Caitlin's voice.

"I know, sis. I've been really busy with school, and I started working out at this new gym."

"Finally over Greg, eh?"

"Why do you say that?"

"You're working out again," Caitlin laughed.

"I need to work out if I'm going to fit into my summer clothes. The winter has added a few pounds to my hips."

"You've nothing to worry about, skinny sister of mine."

"Oh, by the way," Brianna changed the subject; "I had an email from Neil. He's doing fine; I ran a copy for you and will drop it off after my workout."

"Great. Are you going to have supper with the kids and me, and stay for a bit?"

"Sure, I can do that, I guess—unless I pick up some hot young stud at the gym!" Brianna smiled into the phone. "Well, sis, I'm pulling into the parking lot now; I'll see you later."

"See you … have a good workout."

Brianna was humming a tune as she walked into the gym. "Hey there, Brianna," Paige greeted her. "Nice to see you."

Camden's ears perked up for the second time in a half an hour. He snuck a quick look around the corner.

"Paige, could you watch the drink counter for a few minutes; I have to go and check the garbage cans. You know how fast they fill up with paper when we're busy. Good, though. Some gyms I've worked at were not as strict about wiping down the equipment after each use."

"Sure, Camden."

Camden followed Brianna to the entrance of the women's change room. She felt his presence and turned. "Are you following me?" Her voice sounded harsh.

He blushed. "Oh, no ... no ... I ... I ... I was j ... just on my way t ... to empty the garbage p ... pails." Camden stuttered.

Camden didn't hear Brianna mumble sorry. Brianna was upset with herself for being rude. He was just a guy doing his job. Somehow, as she crossed the gym floor she remembered the email, and it had made her a bit jumpy, especially when Camden had been following so close. She changed into her shorts and t-shirt and then went out to find an empty treadmill. They were all being used.

Tyler, who was just finishing up on his treadmill, saw Brianna waiting. "Here you go, beautiful lady. I'm done here." He stepped off, sprayed the handles and face of the mill, bowed low, and waved his arm with a flourish. "All yours."

"Thank you," Brianna grinned.

"Do you have a number?" Tyler boldly asked.

"I do."

"May I have it?"

Brianna laughed. "I don't usually give my number to strangers."

Tyler feigned a hurt look. "We aren't strangers; I just gave you my treadmill." He stuck his hand out. "Name's Tyler."

"Brianna." She shook his hand.

"Maybe have a smoothie after our workout?" Tyler wasn't going to give up.

"Depends."

"On what?"

"Whether we finish at the same time."

"I'll wait for you at the drink counter—how does that sound? We can talk and get to know one another, and then you can give me your number." Tyler was persistent, and he had no idea why other than the fact that Brianna was kind of cute, and the echo of his mother's voice telling him she wanted grandchildren was still ringing in his head. Plus, he felt great: life was beginning to look up for him.

"We'll see … maybe." Brianna pouted saucily, put her earphones on, and turned the treadmill on slow speed to start.

Camden was emptying the garbage can closest to the treadmills. He lingered long enough to hear the conversation. *Good,* he thought; *I can kill two birds with one stone.* As he passed by Brianna's treadmill, he nodded and smiled. She didn't acknowledge him. *What a creep that guy is,* Camden continued thinking. *Hitting on her … and her … she looked like she was enjoying every minute of it. The world will be better off without them!* Camden headed for the back door to take the garbage out to the bin, and then returned to the drink counter. There was no way he was going to miss this opportunity.

At five-thirty, Tyler sidled up to the drink counter. Camden noticed Brianna heading over. She stopped and put her hand on Tyler's arm. "I just have to get changed. Do you mind ordering my smoothie … strawberry … medium? I won't be but a few minutes."

Tyler smiled. "I'll even pay for it."

"That won't be necessary." Brianna hurried off to the change room.

Tyler turned to Camden. "Could I have two smoothies: one medium strawberry and one large banana."

Camden nodded. "*Creep,*" he thought; "*didn't even say please. No manners.*" His blood began to race as he mixed the drinks. He leant over and pulled the two cups from under the counter. It took him a few extra seconds to drop the poison powder in each one.

"What are you doin' down there?" Tyler was looking over the edge.

Camden stood up quickly. "Sorry, I just dropped something."

"Not in my cup, I hope." Tyler laughed.

"Oh no." Camden smiled and opened the fridge to get out a pre-packed package of strawberries. He dumped them into Brianna's cup and then poured the liquid in and set it on the mixer. While it was mixing, he peeled a banana and repeated the process for Tyler's drink. When the orders were finished, he put the lids on and handed them to Tyler. "That will be five-fifty, please."

Tyler pulled out his wallet and threw six dollars on the counter. "Keep the change," he said and then turned to watch for Brianna. As soon as he noticed her, he picked up the drinks and walked toward her, pointing to the couches in the front lounge. "Want to sit over there while we drink our smoothies?" he asked.

"Good idea," she replied.

Camden glanced over at them every once in a while to make sure they were still drinking. They were laughing. Tyler was touching her thigh, and she was touching his arm. *Sickening—intimate so soon, and they hardly know each other.*

Finally, Tyler and Brianna stood. Tyler picked up the empty cups and threw them in the garbage. They shook hands, and both headed out the door. Camden didn't see whether they had exchanged numbers or not. It was almost six o'clock; time for him to leave.

"I'm just going to empty the lobby garbage before I go; looks like it's getting full," he informed Paige.

"No problem, Camden. See you on Monday."

"Yep." Camden took the garbage out to the back bin. He made sure it was well-covered with other papers. No sense taking any chances. He replaced the garbage can in the lobby, fetched his things, and headed home to get Emma. They would be just in time to be at Jack's for six-thirty.

~

Toby looked up lazily from his perch on the back of the couch when the doorbell rang. Jack came out of the kitchen, apron on, ladle in hand. The house smelled delicious; Toby hoped Jack would fix him a dish of whatever he was cooking, as well. Jack opened the door.

"Welcome guys, come on in and make yourselves at home. I'll just be a few more minutes." Jack turned to Emma. "You must be Emma. Camden has told me a lot about you."

Emma blushed. "All tall tales, I'm sure," she said, her voice barely a whisper. "Cam has a habit of exaggerating where I am concerned."

"I'll bet he exaggerates a lot where everything is concerned." Toby stood and stretched. He didn't want to be in the same space as Camden, so he'd wait to see where Emma sat before he settled again.

"Hello, Toby," Emma knelt and scratched Toby behind the ears before he had a chance to escape. She sat down on the couch and patted beside her for Toby to jump up.

Toby looked at Camden, who was standing awkwardly in the middle of the room. He was glaring at Toby, and if Toby guessed correctly, the glare was one filled with hate. *"I haven't done anything to you yet, bub."* Toby glared back and then jumped up beside Emma. He stretched his body out so there wouldn't be enough room for Camden on the couch.

Jack laughed. "Toby, you couch hog ... or is it Emma you are trying to hog?" He pointed to an easy-chair. "You may as well sit there, Camden. We wouldn't want to disturb the king of the household." Jack didn't notice Camden's pursed lips as he sat down. Toby did, though.

Before long Jack was calling everyone into the kitchen. "Supper is served." He showed Camden and Emma where to sit and then took a seat. Toby was a bit put out because there was no dish of food waiting for him yet. "I'll get you yours, old boy, after the guests are served."

Jack had outdone himself. He had cooked a leg of lamb seasoned with rosemary and mint, garlic and pepper. A dish of mushrooms and onions, one with Parisian potatoes sprinkled with mozzarella cheese and chives; and a plate of glazed baby carrots was passed around. Toby had no interest in the vegetables but couldn't wait to dig into the lamb. The final dish was a garden salad. Toby would pass on that, as well.

"Do either one of you say grace?" Jack asked.

"I do," Emma said in a hushed voice.

Toby noticed the shocked look on Camden's face. *"He doesn't know his own sister says grace. Is she afraid to tell him?"* Toby walked over and sat down beside Emma. He looked up at her adoringly.

"I think you have a friend there, Emma," Jack mentioned, pointing to Toby. "Would you do us the honours of saying the blessing then?" he added.

Emma bowed her head. "Thank you, Lord, for the food we are about to receive and thank you for the fellowship we are about to have with Jack and Toby. Amen."

Once the plates were filled, and Jack had cut up some lamb and put it in a dish for Toby, Jack ventured a conversation. "So, Emma, Camden says you move around quite a bit due to your health."

Toby noticed the shocked look flit across Emma's face.

"Have you had the appointment yet with the specialist here?" Jack continued.

Emma looked helplessly at Camden.

"No, Emma hasn't seen him yet," Camden intervened. "I think the appointment is in a couple of weeks, isn't it, Em?" Toby noticed how Camden was looking at his sister—also, how he emphasised the words 'isn't it, Em?'

Toby glanced at Jack. He was oblivious to what was really going on here. "So what's wrong with you?" Jack continued innocently. "Camden never really told me."

Emma looked at her brother. "Why don't you tell him, Camden; you know how I hate to talk about it."

"Oh, no ... no ... please, I didn't mean to pry," Jack was quick to say. "Some things are best kept private." He paused and then changed the subject. "So how was your first week at the gym, Camden?"

"Not that great at the beginning, but as the week went on things improved."

"Probably just had to get into the swing of things, eh?"

"Yeah, that's probably it. Takes a while to adjust to a new place. Hopefully this will be the last one for a while. I think Emma really likes it here; so do I. It would be nice to put down roots."

After supper, Emma and Camden offered to help Jack clean the dishes. "Oh no," he waved them off. "Let's just go in and sit down. I'm retired and have lots of time to clean up. Maybe Toby will help me tomorrow—how about it, old man?" Jack chuckled.

Toby headed to the living room and jumped up on the couch where he and Emma had been sitting before supper. When she came into the room, he looked at her and meowed.

"Okay," she said and came and sat beside him. Toby cuddled up as close to her as possible without infringing directly on her lap. "I guess you will have to sit in the chair again, Cam," Emma giggled.

The rest of the evening went by slowly for Toby—and Camden. Everyone listened as Jack told stories about his days on the force. The only time Toby perked up was when Jack began the story about how Toby had solved the mystery earlier that year. About nine o'clock, Camden stood and said he thought they had better get home. Emma jumped up immediately; Toby felt a cold spot on his back.

"I've been asked to work for a bit tomorrow. Boss has hired another guy to help out up front since they are expanding the gym hours," Camden explained. "I have to go in at noon and show him the ropes."

"Well, that will take some pressure off you, won't it?" Jack said as he stood. "It has been a pleasant evening; I hope you folks enjoyed yourselves." He began to walk them to the door. "It was a real pleasure meeting you, Emma." Jack extended his hand to her.

"Likewise," she answered. "And I loved your stories. You've had a very exciting life. Bye, Toby. Come on over to the house anytime. I missed you today."

"Wish I could tell you about your brother and what he tried to do to me … wish I could warn you that I think he's up to something." Toby jumped down from the couch and went over to the door. He rubbed between Emma's legs and meowed.

Camden curled his arm into Emma's. "Let's go, sis. I'm sure Jack wants to go to bed, and even surer the old cat's had enough for one day." He laughed. Jack and Emma looked at him, puzzled. Emma shrugged her shoulders and walked out with her brother. Jack just shook his head and closed the door.

"Strange young man, sometimes," was all he said before locking the door and shutting off the lights. "I'm bushed, old man. We'll clean up in the morning. My bed's calling me."

"You'll clean up in the morning!" Toby returned to his perch by the window and watched Camden and Emma as they walked home. It was too bad Toby couldn't hear what they were talking about because it looked like it was a pretty intense conversation.

Emma was visibly upset and Camden figured he knew why. It was confirmed with her first question. "Why did you tell Jack we moved here because I was ill and needed to see a doctor?"

"It was easier that way."

"I don't understand; how was it easier, Cam? Our moves are never because of me; it is always you who wants to relocate. So I'm asking you again, why would you tell it otherwise?"

Camden's face turned hard. He didn't like to be challenged about his decisions. Whatever he did was to protect Emma, but now she was questioning his motives. He took his hand from her arm and started to walk away. "I just did. It's no big deal, Emma, and it doesn't matter to anyone else why we moved here. It seemed like the easiest explanation at the time. Now, leave it there!"

Emma stopped and looked at her brother. She was beginning to wonder how much she really knew about her twin.

Toby closed his eyes after Emma and Camden disappeared into their house. He was not happy about the scene he had just witnessed, and he was even more worried for Emma now.

~

Brianna drove straight from the gym to her sister's house. Caitlin had already fed the kids, but she had waited to eat.

"The kids are watching television," she said as Brianna came through the door. Maybe we can have supper undisturbed for a change, although, I'd guess you don't have much to disturb your meals. Oh, God, I better shut my mouth before the other foot goes in it." She paused. "You look smug about something, sister of mine. What's up?"

"I'll tell you while we eat. What's for supper?" Brianna asked even though she knew it would probably be something to do with pasta. Caitlin was so stressed with the three little ones—all a year apart—all boys. Brianna studied her sister for a minute, her eyes travelling to her belly. She hoped that little bump was just still left over from the last baby.

"Macaroni casserole," Caitlin replied.

"Sounds good."

The sisters sat down and served themselves. After a few minutes of silence, Caitlin asked, "So ... what's up?"

"Not much." Brianna smirked. Then, "I met a guy at the gym this afternoon. He seems nice. Bit cocky, though. We had a smoothie together after our workouts."

"Did you give him your number?

"No!" Brianna was shocked by her sister's question. "I'll be having a few more talks with him before handing out my number!"

"You are getting old, Brianna," Caitlin laughed. "You don't want to be old enough to be a grandmother before you have your own kids!" She paused. "So, what does he do?"

"He works in his uncle's machine shop. Told me his uncle offered him an apprenticeship."

"So what's he do there now?"

"He cleans up at night and runs machines."

"How old?"

"Didn't ask, but he looks around my age." Brianna put down her fork after popping the final pieces of pasta into her mouth. "Why don't we spend some time with the kids before they go to bed? I can help you clean up later."

"Why don't you visit with them and I'll clean up—I see them every day—every hour of the day and sometimes through the night. They'll love spending time with Aunt Brianna."

"Are you sure?"

"I'm certain."

Brianna spent the next forty-five minutes with the boys. It wasn't what she would have considered quality time—watching television—but it was time.

"Time to get ready for bed, boys," Caitlin announced.

The usual bedtime complaining resounded through the room, but Caitlin remained firm. She had heard all the excuses and none of them worked with her anymore. Within half an hour the boys were all tucked into bed, and the two sisters were slouched on the couch. Caitlin flipped through the television channels. "This looks like it might be an entertaining movie," she mentioned.

But Brianna had started to feel unwell. Her stomach was queasy, and she was sweating. "You know, sis, it's been a long week; I think I'll call it a night. I'm not feeling well. Think we could do a movie another time?"

"Are you sure? I was looking forward to spending time with you tonight."

Brianna stood shakily. Her legs felt like jelly. "I was too, but I really don't feel well. I think the sooner I get home and crawl into bed, the better. I'm really sorry."

"Okay, if you must go, you must." Caitlin followed her sister to the door. "Give me a call when you get some free time," she suggested before closing the door.

"Will do," Brianna answered as she raced to her car. When she was inside the car, her stomach started churning, and she felt as though she were going to vomit. It couldn't have been the casserole her sister had served, Caitlin and the boys weren't sick. Maybe she had picked up a bug from one of the kids at school.

By the time Brianna got into her house, she barely made it to the bathroom before throwing up. She felt her stomach churn again and staggered to the toilet: diarrhea poured out of her. When she stood, she noticed blood in the toilet bowl. "What the hell?" She stumbled to the sink and splashed water on her face. She felt as though her heart was pumping at three times the typical rate. She staggered out of the bathroom and into her bedroom. If she could just make it under the covers and fall off to sleep before the next wave of nausea, maybe she could sleep through this.

~

Tyler left the gym and headed to the pool hall. He had arranged to meet his friend there and have a couple games of pool before heading home. The beer went down real smooth, and he thought he better order some wings before he got intoxicated.

"You look pretty smug there, Tyler," his friend Jason mentioned. "Got a hot date when you're finished with me tonight?"

"No, not really." He paused for effect. "But I did meet someone really hot at the gym this evening."

"Get her phone number?"

"Nah, not yet; she wouldn't give it to me."

"Loser."

"Am not! She says she usually waits to get to know someone before handing out her number."

Tyler and Jason dug into the wings when they arrived at the table. Tyler washed his wings down with his last swig of beer. His stomach felt queasy. Maybe the wings had been too greasy, or maybe the beer hadn't mixed well with the smoothie he'd had at the gym.

"What's wrong with you, man, you're sweating?" Jason asked.

Tyler wiped his forehead. He shoved his chair back and excused himself to the washroom. By the time he got there, his stomach was lurching, and he leant over the toilet and threw up all the wings and beer he had just consumed. When he returned to the pool hall, his face was as white as a ghost and he was shaking.

"Holy shit, man! You look like death warmed over." Jason looked worried.

"Yeah … don't know what came over me. Think I'll call it a night and get home before I get any worse."

"You okay to drive, man? I could give you a lift."

"No, I'll be fine." Tyler grabbed his keys off the table and headed out the door.

As he walked through his apartment door, another wave of nausea struck him; he headed straight to the bathroom and threw up again. He splashed water on his face and went and sat down at his computer. He was still sweating. He turned his computer on and waited for it to boot up. Before he could check his email, he had to hit the bathroom again—this time with diarrhea. As he went to flush, he noticed the blood.

Feeling slightly better, he returned to his computer and clicked on the email icon. He was shocked to see what came up on one of the subject lines ... ARE YOU LISTENING TO ME, *"Dear Tyler: you are still being very, very naughty. I told you what happens to very naughty people. Did you think about it? Did you ridicule someone today … ignore someone just because … blame someone wrongfully? Were you nice to someone … really nice? Did you help someone today, just because … really help? I doubt you even gave my message a second thought. Oh, believe it, you are so pathetically naughty that I can't stand it! You might still be able to turn this around and do something about it. I am being generous giving you another warning, but it is still up to you to seek reconciliation. If you*

70

don't, retribution will come your way … and don't forget all those selfish, naughty friends of yours who are just like you. Pass this on to them so they can get help too … for every friend you try to save the retribution on yourself might be lessened. You know the drill—six to ten, maybe you won't die … one to five, you will … signed: 666."

"Who the hell would send something like this?" Tyler ran his fingers through his hair. It was obvious that the email was a follow-up to the previous one. He hit the delete button and headed to the bathroom for the third time. Tyler splashed more water on his face and then stumbled into his room and flopped on his bed. If only he could just close his eyes. Sleep finally came to him, but it was fitful and filled with pain. He could hardly wait for the morning when he would be able to call his mum. He thought a couple of times—when he woke slightly—that maybe he should get himself to a walk-in clinic. His heart seemed to be beating too fast, and he couldn't stop sweating. But as he drifted off to sleep again, he reasoned that it would be morning soon.

Saturday, May 30, 2009

Brianna's night hadn't gone any better. She had gotten up several times and thrown up and had diarrhea until there was absolutely nothing left in her stomach. Nevertheless, she wouldn't break down and call anyone because that was the kind of person she was—never wanting to bother anyone. But by seven o'clock in the morning, she felt like death had already taken her. Sylvester hadn't left her side the entire night. She picked up the phone and called her sister.

Caitlin answered on the third ring. "Hey, sis," Brianna's words were barely audible; "I need you to come and take me to the hospital."

"I'll have to call someone to come and sit with the kids; Mitch got called into work. He wasn't any too happy about it either because he sort of tied one on last night. But we need the money…"

"Caitlin," Brianna could barely talk. "Please … get here … soon … please." She dropped the receiver.

When the line went dead, Caitlin realized how severe the situation was. She also knew her sister didn't ask for help unless she was on her last straw. She picked up the phone and dialled her friend Marny to come over and babysit.

Marny's voice was full of sleep. "Hello … this better be good, calling me at seven o'clock in the morning."

"I need you to come and watch the kids for me. Brianna called, and I have to take her to the hospital. She sounded horrible. Last night when she was here, she got sick all of a sudden and rushed home."

"Did she say what was wrong?"

"No, she could barely talk."

"I'll be right there. Give me twenty to get out of bed and throw some clothes on."

"Hurry … please."

~

Tyler crawled out of bed at six o'clock. His stomach growled its displeasure, but the very thought of putting food in his mouth made Tyler want to pitch it up before it even left the dish. He noticed blood in the toilet again, and he was getting more than a little concerned. He felt drained, and he was still sweating. Tyler figured he should go to the hospital but knew he wouldn't be able to drive in his shape. He had no choice but to call his mum; she was the only person he knew that would be up this early in the morning. She answered on the second ring.

"Tyler? You okay?"

"How'd you know it was me, Mum?"

"I have call display now—too many solicitors calling."

"I'm really sick, Mum; can you come over and take me up to the hospital ... don't think I should be driving." Tyler's voice was nothing more than a scratchy whisper.

His mum didn't wait for another word. She dropped the phone, grabbed her purse and keys, and headed for the car. Within ten minutes she was bursting through Tyler's door. Her breath caught in her throat when she saw the shape her son was in. "Let's go!" she ordered. Tyler followed her. He didn't even bother to lock the door. He bumped into the walls of the hallway and almost fell down the one flight of stairs that led to the parking lot.

Tyler had never seen his mother drive so fast in all his life. She came to a screeching stop at the hospital's Emergency doors, ordered him to stay put, and then ran inside. Within a few minutes a nurse, pushing a wheelchair, returned with her. Together they helped Tyler out of the car.

"Hello, Tyler, my name is Karen. How long have you been sick, sir?" the nurse asked.

"Started last night."

Karen pushed him through the Emergency doors and called for someone to help her get Tyler onto a gurney. She turned to his mum. "Come with me, and we'll get the paperwork filled out. I don't think your son is in any shape to answer questions right now. Lisa will take his vitals while we do that."

No sooner had she spoken, Tyler started to vomit. Lisa grabbed a dish and managed to catch most of it. When he was finished, she set the bowl aside and called for someone else to come and help get Tyler changed. By the time Lisa finished taking Tyler's vitals, his mum and Karen had returned. Lisa pulled Karen aside.

"I think we need to get a doctor over here, stat!" she said. "This young man's blood pressure is exceedingly low, probably because he has been throwing up. He also mentioned he had diarrhea and it had blood in it. So does his vomit."

"I'll page Doctor Campbell," Karen said and headed for the nurses' station.

Doctor Campbell was just finishing up an emergency appendectomy, and his nurse told Karen he would be there within the half hour. He had passed a message on to put the young man on an intravenous drip to replenish some of his lost fluids.

Lisa had a hard time finding a vein to put the needle and tube in. Finally, with a little luck, and lots of wiggling around, she managed one on the back of Tyler's hand. As the liquid started seeping into his system, he began to relax and his blood pressure stopped plummeting.

Karen came over with a clipboard. "I need to ask you some questions, Tyler. Answer the best you can, please."

Tyler nodded.

"What did you eat last night?"

"Chicken wings and beer at the pool hall."

"How long after you had eaten the wings did you start to feel ill?"

"Not long."

Tyler's mum intervened: "Do you think he has salmonella poisoning from the wings?"

"Possible. But that doesn't explain most of your son's symptoms," Karen added. "We will have to wait and see what the doctor says."

After another ten minutes, Doctor Campbell arrived. Tyler's mum thought he looked as haggard as Tyler. Must have been a long night for him. She hoped he was on the ball enough to take care of her son. The doctor looked over the information on Tyler's chart. He looked in his eyes, tapped his stomach, checked his breathing—the usual stuff doctors do.

"Looks like he might have a touch of food poisoning based on the fact that the symptoms started after he ate the wings," Doctor Campbell surmised. "Possibly has picked up a flu bug, as well, and that would explain the severity of what is going on. Keep him on the intravenous until it is finished and then send him home." The doctor turned to Tyler's mum. "Make sure he drinks plenty of liquids and gets some rest. This should pass through his system by tomorrow. If he gets worse, bring him back in, but I think he will be okay. He looks like a strong young man."

Tyler's mum wasn't too sure about the diagnosis, but he was the doctor. She nodded her head and then sat down in the chair beside her son and waited for the intravenous to finish. At noon they went back to his apartment. Tyler still looked dreadfully pale.

"Are you sure you don't want to come and stay with me?" his mum asked him.

"I'll be okay. I feel a bit better. I'll call you if I get worse again. Boy, whatever this is, it sure is horrible. I won't be eating chicken wings for a while."

"I'll bring over some chicken soup for you later if you like."

"That'd be nice. Thanks, Mum."

Tyler's mum made sure he got into his apartment and that he had some juice and water beside his bed. He snuggled under the blankets and fell off to sleep. She left, content the worst was hopefully over.

~

Caitlin paced in the kitchen. The clock's ticking was annoying. What was taking Marny so long? Finally, she heard the car pull into the driveway, and Marny came racing into the house and threw her keys to Caitlin. "Take my car. Boys still sleeping?"

"Yes … you know where everything is," Caitlin said as she raced out the door.

It should only have taken Caitlin ten minutes to get to Brianna's place, but she ran into an accident at the bottom of West Street hill. She had come upon it before realising it was an accident, and by then she had passed any street she could have detoured down. She tapped her fingers impatiently on the steering wheel. "Damn!" she cursed.

The police had blocked off three lanes and were directing traffic through on the one open lane. Finally, it was her turn, and once she was through, she put her foot down on the gas and sped up. She didn't care if a police officer followed her; she wouldn't stop for them. They would understand when she arrived at her destination. Lucky for her, they were all too busy with the accident to notice the little blue car that burned rubber through the intersection.

In the meantime Brianna had gotten worse. After she had made the call to her sister, she managed to crawl to the bathroom. Her heart was going a mile a minute. She was sweating rivers of water, causing her clothing to cling to her body as though she had just climbed out of a pool. The pain in her stomach was excruciating. Suddenly her entire body began to shake. The ceramic tiles on the bathroom floor were cold. She felt herself slipping into unconsciousness. The last thing she saw was her cat, Sylvester, pacing back and forth at the bathroom door. The last thing she heard was his meowing mingled with her sister calling her name.

~

About an hour after Tyler's mum left him, he woke up with more throbbing in his stomach. He reached for the water on his night table, but it slipped out of his hand and crashed to the floor as his body was wracked with another pain. Nausea followed, but before he could make it to the bathroom, he began throwing up. Once again, he noticed blood. Tyler started to sweat. He wasn't sure if it was from the illness or from fear. He had never been this sick in his life.

"Why now?" he mumbled. "Just when things are looking up for me." Tyler felt like he was dying and there was nothing he could do about it. He whispered a prayer. His bowels gave way, and he didn't care. His body went into convulsions.

When his mother arrived at four o'clock with a pot of soup, Tyler was on the floor. At first she thought he was just sleeping, but when she realized that wasn't the case she dropped the soup on the floor and it mixed with her son's vomit. She walked slowly to the living room, picked up the phone, and called the hospital.

~

Camden was having a good afternoon. He liked the new fellow Mr. Rawlings had hired and thought they were going to get along fabulously. His name was Graham, and like Camden, Mr. Rawlings had hired him from out of province. Graham caught on quickly, too, for someone who had never worked in a gym.

At four o'clock Camden said goodbye and headed home. He was too happy to bother checking if Toby was sitting in Jack's front window.

When he walked into the house Emma and Duke were in the three-season room, so he headed straight upstairs to his room and turned on his computer. Once it loaded, he pushed the email icon.

Camden leant back in his chair and smiled when he saw Tyler had opened his mail. He also smiled because if all had gone well, Brianna and Tyler should be history by now. Camden had given them just enough of his special powder to ensure their deaths but had not wanted their demises to be too quick. Drawn out and painful, but not enough time for anyone to figure out what was wrong so the illness could be stopped.

When Emma walked into the house, the sound of Camden's laughter sent a chill through her body.

Monday, June 1, 2009

Jack was reading the obituaries in the Monday morning newspaper. He was shocked to see that two young people, not even thirty yet, had passed away. "Can you believe this, Toby?" he exclaimed. "The woman, Brianna Gates, was a schoolteacher. She was only 28. The fellow, Tyler Acton, was in his thirtieth year. It doesn't give a reason for death or anything—just says 'suddenly' for both of them. Strange. Not often this happens. Doesn't appear from the relatives listed they knew each other either."

~

Camden walked to the corner store early Monday morning to get a newspaper. When he got home, he flipped immediately to the obituary page. The first name was Tyler Acton. He scanned down the column until he came to Brianna Gates. Camden leant back in the kitchen chair and smiled. *"Boy that worked fast this time,"* he thought.

"What are you so happy about this morning?" Emma walked into the kitchen, still in her nightgown.

Camden didn't answer her directly. "You look tired, Emma. You could've stayed in bed longer. I don't have to work until one today; they're staggering our shifts now that we are open later."

Duke barked at the back door. Emma walked over to let him out. "It's okay, Cam. I don't want to get into any bad habits again. The book I'm reading says one of the best things one can do to get through depression is to get on a good schedule. So, what would you like for breakfast?"

Camden closed the paper and jumped up from the table. "Why don't you let me make breakfast for you for a change? You can still stay up, but you can be waited on."

"I really don't mind…"

"Emma, let me do this for you just for one morning. If you're up to it, we could take a walk after breakfast. Looks like a beautiful day. Then, I'd like to take you shopping and out for a nice lunch before I go to work."

Emma smiled. "What's the occasion, Cam?" Deep inside she was happy to be able to get out. It would be a real test for her to see how she managed to be out in public. Jack's place, for supper, had been safe because Toby had been there.

"Just because," Camden answered her. "Just because I want to celebrate our move here and because I want to show you how much I appreciate you. Now, what would you like to eat for breakfast?"

"Just some toast and jam will do me fine."

After breakfast Camden and Emma went for a long walk. As they passed by Jack's house, Emma glanced in to see if Toby was on the back of the couch. "Toby must be having breakfast, or maybe he's on his way to see me," Emma stated. "We shouldn't go too far just in case."

"Don't worry about the cat." Camden's voice was tense for the first time that morning. "He's just a dumb old cat with a grumpy attitude. Did I tell you what he did the other morning to me?"

"No, do tell," Emma grinned, expecting that if it had something to do with Toby, it would be funny.

Camden told Emma about the incident on the sidewalk. To his amazement, Emma laughed. "That's hilarious!" she exclaimed and then skipped ahead of her brother. She felt light-hearted but had no idea why. "Catch me, Cam—just like when we were kids!"

The two ran down the sidewalk and then crossed the street into the local park. Emma reached the swings before Camden. "You never were a fast runner, Cam!" she giggled as she started to swing. "Let's see who can get the highest!"

"You know I always beat you in that, Emma!"

An elderly lady, passing by, was happy to hear such joy coming from the park. But someone else sitting in the bushes wasn't. Toby had been headed for Emma's house when he had seen her and Camden start their walk. He had followed them to the park, at a discrete distance. *"I wonder what he's so cheerful about today. I actually haven't seen him happy since he moved here."* Toby was puzzled.

Finally, Emma and Camden left the park and headed for home. Toby followed, again, at a distance. He was disappointed when they got into their van and left. *"Oh well, guess I'll have to catch her later."* Toby turned and headed for home. He found the house empty; it appeared Jack had abandoned him too. He had a little snack and then jumped up to his spot in front of the window. He would wait for Emma to return, and for Camden to go to work.

~

Tyler's mother was beside herself. She called his uncle. "George, there's something terribly wrong here. I had Tyler at the hospital on Saturday, and the doctor passed it off as food poisoning and a touch of the flu. They pumped him with intravenous fluids and sent him home. I saw how ill Tyler was. I've never seen anything like it before."

"What are you saying here, Olivia? Do you think there's more to this than food poisoning?" George's voice had a slight edge to it. He knew how Olivia could sometimes exaggerate. "Maybe you should order an autopsy?"

George was surprised when she said she thought that would be a good idea. "Of course … don't they usually do that anyway if someone dies in their own home?"

"Most times, but not always. If Tyler was at the hospital and the doctor had already made a diagnosis of food poisoning, well then, that's probably what the cause of death will go down as." George was trying to be patient.

"I think I'm going to call our doctor and ask for an autopsy," Olivia revealed her intention. She would not be satisfied until she had a concrete answer as to what had killed her son.

"That means the funeral will have to be postponed. Do you really want to do that?" George asked.

"I want the truth. I don't believe my son had food poisoning, George. I'll get back to you on what the doctor says." She hung up the phone.

George shook his head. After his brother had passed away, Olivia had lived for Tyler. Why, he couldn't figure out. He was a lazy, son-of-a-gun who hadn't amounted to much. George doubted Tyler was even going to take him up on his offer of an apprenticeship. He had only given Tyler a job for Olivia's sake after she had begged him to help. Too much booze and drugs were probably the reasons behind his nephew's untimely death; George knew there had been a lot of that in Tyler's past.

A couple of hours later Olivia called her brother-in-law. "We're going ahead with the funeral, George, but it will just be a memorial service. I'm going to cremate Tyler later." She paused. "After the autopsy."

George sighed. "Whatever you like, Olivia—whatever you like."

~

Caitlin was devastated by her sister's death. She couldn't understand why and she felt if she had gotten to Brianna's house sooner, she would have been able to save her sister. She hadn't been able to reach their brother, Neil, so she had to handle all the funeral arrangements herself. Caitlin had never seen such a mess in Brianna's house. There were trials of vomit everywhere and the toilet had not been flushed. The picture of her sister's twisted body lying on the cold ceramic floor in the bathroom wouldn't leave her mind.

There was no thought of having her sister's body autopsied. She just wanted to get the funeral over with. The tears wouldn't stop, and she had three little boys who needed her. She had three little boys who would probably forget their Aunt Brianna because they were so young. And that was a crying shame.

Tuesday, June 2, 2009

"This is interesting, Toby," Jack said as he read the morning paper. "One of the young people who passed away over the weekend ... his mother contacted the hospital and requested an autopsy on her son. She must have talked to a reporter to get an article in the paper. Looks like there might be some foul play." Jack paused for a minute so he could read more. "Wow!" he exclaimed. "Listen to what she says his symptoms were: severe vomiting, diarrhea, sweating, drop in blood pressure, severe stomach cramps—sounds like it was more than a touch of the flu or food poisoning. The lady goes on to say that she thinks the poor doctor who looked in on her son was almost as haggard looking as her son. She also believes the doctor misdiagnosed her son, reason why she's asking for an autopsy." Jack dropped the paper on his lap.

There was a knock on the door: Jack got up to answer it. "Hey there, Camden, come on in," Jack invited. "Would you like a coffee?"

"No thanks. I was just on my way to work but don't really have to be there for another half an hour, so thought I'd stop in and say hi and tell you again how nice it was for you to invite Emma and me over the other night. It really meant a lot to Emma."

"No problem. Have a seat. I was just reading about the young fellow who died over the weekend. His mother is going to have an autopsy done."

Toby sat up and stretched. He hadn't been overly interested in the article Jack had been reading, but the fact Camden was here made him want to leave the room. However, Toby noticed the look that crossed over Camden's face when Jack mentioned an autopsy. *"Why would that upset him? He didn't know the guy—or did he?"*

"An autopsy, eh?" Camden repeated. "Do they suspect foul play then?"

"I believe the mother thinks the doctor at the hospital misdiagnosed her son's condition. She isn't convinced it was a flu or simple food poisoning."

"Oh, is that what the doctor said it was?" Camden inquired.

"Well, there was some mention in the article about the young man having had some chicken wings the night before, so the doctor blamed his condition on them."

"I see."

Toby was studying Camden thoroughly. *"He appears kind of jittery all of a sudden, as if he murdered the guy or something!"* Toby was pondering the possibility.

Camden glanced at Toby, noticing the glare. "I don't think your cat likes me, Jack," he mentioned, a strange curl to his lips.

"Ah, Toby's okay. He either likes someone, or he totally dislikes them. Nothing in between with him, and no rhyme or reason to his choices," Jack laughed.

Toby was disgusted with the explanation. He jumped off the couch and headed for the kitchen. Since Camden was going to work, he could go over and visit Emma. It had been a few days. Toby heard Jack saying goodbye to Camden just before he slipped out the cat door. "Anytime, son. You have a good day ... talk to you later."

"Holy, mackerel fish! Now Jack's calling that guy 'son!' Jack, you're too trusting. Camden's the kind of kid who'd kill a parent in their sleep!"

Toby's thoughts went wild.

~

Mitch was skimming through the morning paper. He was trying to relax, knowing it would be a long day at the funeral home. His wife was a mess. Her brother, Neil, had called late last night to say he had gotten the message about Brianna but there was no way he could get back in time for the funeral on Wednesday, he was miles from an airport.

Neil had said he wouldn't be able to make it until next week, but he was going as fast as possible. Mitch's eyes caught onto one of the headlines: MOTHER DEMANDS AUTOPSY: SON'S DEATH MYSTERIOUS. He read the article and then called to Caitlin.

"Hey, honey. You should read this."

"Read what?"

"Remember there was another young person who passed away on the weekend?"

"Yeah ... what about it?" Caitlin didn't care about anyone else, she was too buried in her own grief.

"The mother is ordering an autopsy. She talked about all the symptoms her son had; they sound pretty similar to Brianna's."

Mitch's last statement piqued Caitlin's interest, and she came into the kitchen. Mitch was worried as he looked at his wife's red-rimmed eyes. He knew how close she was to her sister. "Didn't you say Brianna had terrible stomach cramps, and, she'd been vomiting and having bad diarrhea?"

"Yes."

"So did this guy. Only his mum had taken him to the hospital. The doctor passed it off as food poisoning, escalated by a touch of the flu, but the mum doesn't think chicken wings could make someone that ill!" Mitch paused. "Did Brianna say anything to you about eating chicken wings that day?"

"No, she'd just come from the gym ... she was in a happy mood until she started getting the stomach cramps. She'd met some guy—wouldn't tell me his name—said there might be a possibility for a second date."

"Do you think maybe we should get an autopsy ordered too, just to check it out?" Mitch posed the question.

"No. I don't want an autopsy. I don't want my sister's body all cut up. I just want to get this over with!" Caitlin turned and left the room, another burst of tears releasing from her heart.

Wednesday, June 3, 2009

Camden was feeling pretty good; things were going well at work. The new guy, Graham, was working with him this week and he was less bossy than Paige. Camden had given up trying to be friends with Paige. She was too flirty with the male customers and with the trainers, Vincent and Nolan. He had seen her leave work a couple of times with both of them. They hadn't even bothered to ask him to come along, not that he would have. He'd noticed them looking his way, laughing.

On Wednesday morning a new lady came in to sign up and Graham, who hadn't done an actual new client registration, asked Camden to help him out. "Good morning, miss," Camden greeted her. "Shall we have a seat over here at the table? My name is Camden. This is Graham; he's new here, so I'll guide him through the process if you don't mind. It won't take much longer than normal."

"Sure." The reply was not said with much sincerity. The woman glanced at her watch. "I only have a limited amount of time though, so I hope it won't take too long."

"It shouldn't," Camden assured. "Your name?"

"Emily Foster."

Camden went down the page and filled in all the boxes as Emily answered the questions. "We need your banking information and where you work so we can fill in this section for automatic withdrawal," Camden pointed to the last section on the page.

Emily told Camden she was a nurse at the Leisure World Nursing Home and she gave him her bank account information. Camden gathered the papers: "There ... that didn't take too long, did it?" he commented cheerfully.

"Long enough," was Emily's curt response.

Camden's head began to pound. She was not a very nice person. In fact, she was quite rude. He handed the papers to Graham. "Put these in the 'to be processed folder', and when I get back from showing Miss Foster around, I'll help you enter her information into the computer. She'll be able to pick up her membership card on her way out."

"I don't need you to show me anything," Emily said. "I had a tour the other day: I don't think you were working. A lovely young lady showed me around."

Camden didn't like her tone of voice. It insinuated he wasn't nice, but he had done his best to be cordial. Some people were ungrateful, unappreciative of those who were particular about how their jobs were done. "I'm sorry, Miss Foster; I didn't realize you already had the tour. Are you going to be doing a workout today?"

"No," her voice was sharp; "there is no time now. I have to get to work. I'll pick up my card tomorrow." She turned, and as she passed Camden, she bumped him. He was waiting for her to say she was sorry. She didn't.

Camden watched her go out the door and then returned to the front reception desk. "You okay, man?" Graham asked. "You look upset."

"It's nothing. Just some people think they are so special! She was rude, but we're taught the customer is always right, so we just smile. Doesn't mean we have to like it, does it?" Camden pulled her file from the folder. "Here, I may as well show you how to process this." He took careful note of Emily's email address. He wouldn't be using it yet, but he had a pretty good notion she might be next if she didn't shape up her attitude.

~

Emily was upset with herself at having been so rude to the young man. She should have just waited until the next day to sign up at the gym because she had known her time was short. She had an employee meeting before work, and she also wanted to stop in and check on Mrs. Silva who was probably not going to see the end of the week. Mrs. Silva had wiggled into a special place in Emily's heart, and it was going to be dreadfully painful to see her go.

When she arrived at work, she noticed Mrs. Silva's daughter's car in the parking lot. Emily prayed she wasn't too late, but realized, as she walked toward her friend's room, she was. She could hear Maria crying. Emily turned and walked the other way. She couldn't handle this now. She should have come earlier so she could say her goodbyes in private.

Friday, June 5, 2009

Emily didn't return to the gym until Friday. She decided to go early in the morning so she would be able to go to the funeral home in the afternoon and evening. Mrs. Silva's funeral was on Saturday. She walked up to the front desk. "I signed up the other day but didn't get my card yet, the name is Emily Foster."

Paige reached under the counter and flipped through the cards until she came to Emily's. "Here you go, miss."

"Thank you. By the way, the young fellow who signed me up the other day ... I believe his name is Camden ... is he in? I was rude to him ... I'm not usually like that. I'd like to apologize."

"Camden isn't in until 12:00 today," Paige informed.

"Oh, I'll be gone by then. Could you pass the message to Camden for me, tell him I'm sorry."

"Sure, no problem."

Emily finished her workout and headed to her car, which she had parked on the street. Camden was walking down the sidewalk, heading for work. She didn't recognize him even though she looked straight at him. But he recognized her. She got into her car and drove away.

"Hi, Paige," Camden greeted as he walked past the front counter on his way to his locker.

"Hey, Camden," she returned.

At three o'clock Paige left for home, forgetting all about Emily's message she was supposed to have passed on to Camden.

~

It was a beautiful afternoon for a stroll. Toby decided to pay Emma a visit. She was in the backyard with Duke, so he meowed and rubbed against the fence.

"Well, hello there, Toby," Emma stood and brushed the dirt off her knees. Duke rushed over to the fence and started barking.

Toby backed away, even though he knew the fence was secure, despite its rickety look. *"Watch it, dog; I'll scratch your eyeballs out!"* He hissed.

"Duke!" Emma shouted. "Bad dog." She grabbed Duke by the collar and put him in the house. "You can come in now, Toby."

Toby crawled under his usual spot and was soon getting a lovely belly rub from his friend.

"You are a funny old cat," Emma began. "I wish Cam would let me have a cat. I love Duke and all, and Duke is actually more my dog than he is my brother's, but he's so big and—well, I'd just prefer a cat."

Toby rolled over and purred. Emma went back to pulling weeds from the flowerbeds. "You know, Toby, I'm a bit worried about my brother again."

Toby picked up on the word 'again.'

"He's been acting strange lately. The other day when I came in from outside, he was upstairs in his room, laughing. It wasn't a typical belly laugh; it sounded evil. At supper I asked him what was so funny, but he wouldn't tell me.

"He's been getting a lot of headaches, too. I don't understand; I thought he liked this town. We usually move when he gets these headaches, not long after they start. He always makes up an excuse that where we're living isn't good for his health. We were in Vancouver for eight months. He saw a doctor while we were there—Doctor Lucy. I met her a couple of times. She was nice and was helping Cam work out some of the stuff that happened to him in our childhood. He always takes everything to heart, and he's always protecting me from issues—at least that's what he tells me."

Emma was in a talkative mood and Toby decided he could learn a lot more by just sitting there and listening. "I don't think the doctor actually helped Cam too much, though, as pleasant as she was. Eventually his headaches returned, and then we were moving again. This is the furthest we've ever moved, though. I'm hoping we won't have to leave this place. I like it here. I like you, and I like Jack."

Toby rubbed his head against Emma's leg. He purred as loud as possible, making sure he got across the point that he really liked Emma, too. She stood and looked at her watch. "Wow, I didn't realize how late it is. I guess I should let Duke back out. Sorry, Toby."

Toby got the message and headed for his opening in the fence. His mind was filled with all the new information. He had definitely been right—there was something strange about Camden. But how was he going to get that point across to Jack?

Saturday, June 6, 2009

t was raining when Emily woke up on Saturday morning. *Dreary day for a gloomy day*, she thought as she slipped into a pair of black slacks and put on a black blouse, then packed her gym bag because she figured a workout might do her good later. Emily had traded a shift with one of the other nurses so she could attend Mrs. Silva's funeral. It was at eleven o'clock.

The funeral was difficult for her because her boyfriend, Chris, was out of town on business for a few days. Emily didn't have him to lean on in her time of need. He was due back later tonight. She was looking forward to his return because she had the feeling he was getting ready to pop a major question to her.

After the internment at the cemetery, Emily opted out of returning to the funeral home for the reception. Instead, she drove to the gym. She noticed Camden was working, however, assuming Paige had passed her apology on, and not really being in the mood to talk to anyone, she walked by without acknowledging him. Her eyes didn't even notice he tried to smile at her.

Later, while she was working on the elliptical machine, Camden was emptying the garbage bin by her. She heard him speak but didn't realize he was talking to her. Emily was thinking of Mrs. Silva. She failed to notice the look on Camden's face when he walked away.

Emily finished her workout, took a shower, and decided to get a smoothie before heading out. The other young fellow was at the counter. Camden was tidying up the front lobby when he heard Emily order a cherry smoothie. He also heard her being sweet to Graham. All she would have had to do today was be nice to him, too—that would have saved her. But no, she hadn't been, and now her fate was sealed.

"That was delicious," Emily said as she finished the last sip of her smoothie. "I think I'll have a large one next time." She smiled. "Good night, Graham, see you tomorrow."

"I'm off tomorrow," Graham said. "I think Camden is on."

Camden didn't hear if Emily replied to that because he had moved on to tidy up around the equipment. It was upsetting him that he was doing more cleaning and less counter work, causing him to wonder what was going on. Maybe he would discuss this with Isabella.

Emily headed for home. She wanted to prepare a late-night snack for Chris. She pulled a package of hors d'oeuvre from the freezer so they could thaw and then sat down and threw a video in. Within minutes she was asleep on the couch, which is where Chris found her when he arrived home at nine o'clock.

"Hey, babe, wake up." Chris leant over and kissed Emily's cheek. "How's my girl been doing without me?"

Emily stirred. "Not so good, Mrs. Silva died. Her funeral was today." She reached her arms up and pulled Chris down on the couch beside her. "I missed you."

"I'm sorry, babe, I couldn't be in touch with you. My boss was strict about not having calls come in or go out."

"That's okay. I don't know why I'm so sentimental over this lady. I've witnessed so many deaths since working in the nursing home. None of them has affected me like hers, though. I might look for another job in the fall––maybe even go back to school for something."

"That sounds fantastic." Chris reached into his pocket. He handed Emily a blue velvet ring box. "Why don't you wait to get a new job until after we're married? That way we can take a beautiful honeymoon without you having to beg for time off."

Emily opened the box. "Oh my God, Chris! Yes! Yes, I will marry you!"

"Of course you will marry me; who else is there in your life that is better looking and more talented than I?" Chris drew her into his arms and held her close. "All your dreams are going to come true, babe. I'll make sure of that.

For now, don't worry about a thing. Just close your eyes and rest. Tomorrow is another day."

It wasn't long until Emily had fallen back to sleep. Chris picked her up carefully, carried her to her bedroom, and tucked her under the covers. Then he headed for his apartment. They had agreed, quite early in their relationship, they wouldn't move in together until they were at least engaged.

~

Just before bedtime that night, Camden sent an email to Emily.

Sunday, June 7, 2009

Emily woke early on Sunday morning. She felt warm and rested. Stretching her arms in the air, she noticed the ring on her left hand. She smiled and hugged herself. Chris was fantastic. She would let him sleep a bit longer before phoning and inviting him over for breakfast. Emily got out of bed and turned her computer on before going to the bathroom. It had been a few days since she had checked her email.

When she returned to her room, she heard a voice say: "You've got mail." She smiled. Chris had hooked that up for her. Emily sat down at her desk and pushed the email icon. She scrolled through the several forwards from friends and then noticed one that said: JUST FOR YOU. She double clicked it. "What the…"

"Dear Emily: you are receiving this email because you have been very, very naughty. Do you know what happens to very naughty people? Think about it! When was the last time you ridiculed someone … ignored someone just because … blamed someone wrongfully? When was the last time you were nice to someone … really nice? When was the last time you helped someone … really helped? You are so pathetically naughty that I can't stand it! Only you can turn this around and do something about it. I have given you the warning, now it is up to you to seek reconciliation. If you don't, maybe retribution will come your way … if you have any friends who are just like you, pass this on to them so they can get help too. For every friend you try to save the retribution on yourself will be lessened … you know the drill … six to ten, maybe you won't die … one to five, you will … signed: 666."

Emily dismissed the email into the recycle box. In her mind, it was best to ignore such things. Besides, she didn't want anything to upset her day with Chris. Today they would set their wedding date: she was happier than she had been for a long time. No sick email was going to take that away from her.

Monday, June 8, 2009

Camden was assured Emily had opened her email. He slipped down to the three-season room early in the morning, before Emma got up, and picked some of the seeds. Camden pulled a bag from his pocket and dropped the seeds in it. There was time to grind them up before he had to use them. He had decided to maybe give Emily one more chance.

He heard Duke's paws approaching. That meant Emma would not be far behind. Just as he was returning to the kitchen, his sister appeared.

"You're up early, Cam."

"Couldn't sleep, so I got up and came down to look at your plants. Em, you sure have a way with them, a real green thumb." He headed upstairs. "I'll be back down in a sec; I forgot something in my room."

"No problem; I'll get breakfast started."

~

Emily headed to the gym after her shift on Monday afternoon. She was still sparkling from her day with Chris. They had set their wedding date for September. They both wanted a small wedding, and since there were not too many relatives on either side, they knew that would be easy to accomplish. She would have her best friend, Candice, as her maid of honour; Chris was going to ask his brother, Derek, to be his best man. That would be it for a wedding party. Candice had insisted on accompanying Emily when she went dress shopping, and they had agreed Saturday would be a good day to start. Emily was deep in thought about her wedding when she walked into the gym.

She swiped her card and kept going, not even looking up to see who was at the front desk. Unfortunately, for her, it was Camden. He began to wish he had some powder with him now so he could get on with what needed to be done. He would make sure to be ready tomorrow if she came in.

On the way out, Emily ordered a large cherry smoothie. Paige was at the drink counter. Camden didn't care; he'd just have to make sure he was there the next time Emily came through. Isabella came out of her office.

"Camden, could you come in here for a few minutes; I need to talk to you about something."

"Uh oh, Camden's in trouble," Paige joked as she was whipping up Emily's smoothie.

Camden frowned. "I don't think that's funny, Paige. I've done nothing to be in trouble for, and you shouldn't say things like that in front of the customers. You don't want them to think I can't do my job."

"Oh for God's sake, lighten up, man!" Paige handed Emily her drink. "You don't have a problem with Camden, do you? Even if he is getting into a little trouble?"

Emily giggled. Camden took her reaction as her making fun of him. He stormed over to Isabella's office. Emily picked up her drink, said goodbye to Paige, and headed out the door.

"Close the door please, Camden, and sit down. Don't look so worried. This is nothing major. It is just that a couple of the customers have complained about you loitering around their machines and it bothers them."

"I don't understand." Camden's head began to ache. "I only go out there when I have to change the garbage cans or clean up around a machine if someone has left their belongings on it. I don't waste time, Isabella. I'm a good employee."

"No one is saying you aren't, Camden. I am just passing on what I have been told, and I am asking you to be a bit more conscientious about what you are doing when working around the clientele. That's all. You may return to work now."

Camden stood and pressed his hands to his temples.

"Are you okay, Camden? Your face is quite red."

"I'll be fine," he mumbled as he walked out of the office.

"Weird boy," he heard Isabella say as he closed the door.

Camden was happy when his shift was over. He couldn't wait to get home and send another letter to Emily. When he got home, there was a note on the kitchen table telling him his supper was in the microwave. Emma had gone to bed early; she'd been working all day in the garden. Camden took his dish and put it in the refrigerator. He wasn't hungry.

He had forgotten to turn his computer off that morning, but Camden knew his sister never snooped around in his room. That was one thing they respected— each other's privacy. Too much of their privacy had been violated when they were children. He moved the cursor and opened his email box. Camden scrolled until he found the one he wanted, then copy and pasted it into a new email, changed the name, and sent it off to Emily. Then he crawled into bed, curled up into the fetal position and tried to go to sleep. But the nightmares returned; it was a restless night.

Tuesday, June 9, 2009

Emily crawled out of bed. It was early—five o'clock––too early for anyone to have to get up, but she was on first shift all week and had to be to work by quarter to six. She actually should have been up a half an hour earlier, but she had pressed the snooze button. The extra thirty minutes hadn't helped, and now she had to rush.

On the way to work Emily grabbed a coffee at the local coffee shop drive-thru. "This should keep me awake for a few hours," she said to the attendant as she paid her.

It was an overly busy day at the nursing home. Several of the patients were in need of extra attention. One of the nurses joked that it must be around full moon time, everyone was so crazy. One of the girls on the afternoon shift called in sick at the last minute, and the supervisor asked if anyone would like to stay a bit longer—until she could find someone else to come in. Emily volunteered. She figured she could forego the gym today and use the extra money to put toward her wedding and honeymoon.

The shift ended up extending her workday another four hours; by the time Emily got home she was utterly exhausted. She turned her computer on and then picked up the phone to call Chris and tell him she was just going to have a nice bubble bath, grab a quick bite, and head off to bed. Not to worry about her because she was also going to unplug her phone so as not to be bothered with the evening calls by telephone solicitors. After hanging up, Emily went into the bathroom and turned the water on in the tub.

While waiting for the tub to fill she decided to check her email. What she found sent a shock wave through her bones—'ARE YOU LISTENING TO ME', was in the subject line... *"Dear Emily: you are still being very, very naughty. I told you what happens to very naughty people. Did you think about it? Did you ridicule someone today ... ignore someone just because ... blame someone wrongfully? Were you nice to someone ... really nice? Did you help*

*someone today, just because ... really help? I doubt you
even gave my message a second thought. Oh, believe it—
you are so pathetically naughty that I can't stand it! You
might still be able to turn this around and do something
about it. I am being generous giving you another warning
... but it is still up to you to seek reconciliation. If you don't,
retribution will come your way ... and don't forget all those
selfish, naughty friends of yours who are just like you. Pass
this on to them so they can get help too ... for every friend
you try to save the retribution on yourself might be
lessened ... you know the drill ... six to ten, maybe you
won't die ... one to five, you will ... signed: 666."*

"This is one sick bastard," Emily said as she was
about to hit the delete button. "Actually, I think I'll flush you
in the garbage can, you piece of crap, so you'll never be
able to bother me again!" Emily moved the email to her
'blocked sender' list, shut her computer down, and then
headed to the bathroom for her bath.

~

Camden was disappointed Emily hadn't shown up to the
gym. When he got home from work, he checked his emails
to see if she had opened the last one he had sent. Nothing.
He headed downstairs and told Emma he was going for a
walk before supper.

"But dinner is ready, Cam."

"I need to go for a walk," he shouted. "I've been
cooped up all day in that building ... I just need some fresh
air. Eat without me if you can't wait."

"Would you like me to come with you?"

"No! I want to be alone!" his voice was almost a
high-pitched scream as he slammed the door on his way
out.

Duke growled and went and stood protectively by
Emma's side. She patted his head. "It's okay, boy; Cam
probably just had a bad day at work." She sat down and ate
her supper, worried about her brother and concerned about
the feeling she was getting that they may be pulling up

stakes soon. She didn't like this. Things had never moved this quickly before.

Thursday, June 11, 2009

E mily didn't make it to the gym until Thursday. She and Chris had decided on having dinner out on Wednesday night, so she had gone home straight from work to get dressed for their date. There was no one at the front desk when she swiped in, but Camden caught sight of her as she was going into the ladies' change room. He had been coming in the back door from having taken out the garbage. He smiled and patted his pocket. The powder had been freshly ground last night. It was time.

When Emily finished her workout, she headed for the drink counter. To her surprise, Camden had her cherry smoothie waiting for her. "How nice of you," she said as she took a sip. "And you remembered my favourite flavour."

Camden grinned. "It's my job to know what our customers like and to service them accordingly."

"Well, thank you; you are sweet." Emily handed Camden the money for her drink and then headed out.

"She didn't even say goodbye," Camden mumbled.

Emily put the drink in her cup holder and drove home. She was thinking about the wedding plans she and Chris had discussed Wednesday night. When Emily pulled into her parking lot, she gathered her belongings from the car, including the smoothie, and headed up to her apartment. She looked at the large smoothie and decided that if she drank it now, she would not eat her supper, so she put it in the refrigerator for later. Emily had only drunk about a quarter of it: she had been taught well—waste not, want not.

Later that evening as she was watching television, her stomach started cramping and she felt feverish. She looked over at a calendar to see if it was close to her time of the month. About a week off. "Maybe it's going to be early this month," she reasoned as she got up to go into the kitchen and make herself a cup of peppermint tea.

Friday, June 12, 2009

Emily had had a restless sleep. Her stomach had bothered her all night, and she had gotten up twice with diarrhea. But she had to go to work, they were short-staffed. She only had to work a half a day, anyway. She opened her fridge and noticed the smoothie, but decided that probably all her stomach could handle at the moment was a piece of toast and a peppermint tea. The tea seemed to make her feel better, so she headed out to work. Emily threw her gym bag in the car, in case she felt well enough after her shift to go for a workout. She probably wouldn't make it to the gym on Saturday since she and Candice would be shopping for her wedding dress. Emily did not want to get out of shape, especially now.

By the time her shift finished Emily felt pretty good, so she headed for the gym. Camden was at the front desk, and she wondered why he looked surprised to see her. Emily thought he was a bit weird anyway, so didn't think anything more of it as she swiped her card and walked through to the ladies' change room. Had she turned around, she would have noticed the dark look on his face.

Camden swallowed hard and wondered what had gone wrong. Then he rationalized that maybe she hadn't drunk the beverage. He had noticed she'd only taken a few sips before leaving the gym. Camden patted his pocket, good thing he still had some powder. Despite the fact that she hadn't bothered to acknowledge him when she came in, he would have her drink ready for her again today.

Emily felt slightly embarrassed when she noticed the cup sitting on the counter as she walked up to the drink counter. *Two days in a row*, she said to herself; and then out loud: "I hope you aren't hitting on me, Camden." She furrowed her eyebrows.

Unfortunately, her serious look made Camden think she was angry with him and that she didn't appreciate his effort to be nice. He had no doubt he was doing the right thing—ridding the world of another self-absorbed, selfish person. "No, Emily, I don't hit on the customers. I'm just trying to be nice. Just to show you how nice, the drink is on-the-house tonight."

Emily felt really embarrassed now. "Oh, you don't have to do that. I didn't mean anything bad." She held out her left hand. "My boyfriend, Chris, asked me to marry him the other night. We set a date for September."

"How nice." Camden turned around. His head was starting to hurt. *"Too bad Chris is going to be a widower before he's a groom."*

Emily took Camden's turning around as her cue to exit. She picked up her drink and headed out. She decided to grab a few groceries before going home so she and Candice could devote the entire day on Saturday to dress shopping. She wanted to get Candice's dress picked out, as well. Emily was hungry. She hadn't eaten much all day, trying to let her stomach settle, so she finished off the smoothie.

Friday was Chris's night out with the boys and Emily usually did something with Candice, but since they would be together all day Saturday, they decided to forego their Friday night movie and get a good rest. Emily picked up a novel she had been reading and curled up in bed. She turned her clock-radio on and found her favourite station. "This is the life," she said as she snuggled down under the blankets and began to read.

About eleven o'clock Emily's stomach started to churn. A wave of nausea swept over her: she raced to the bathroom and threw up in the toilet. Her heart was beating faster than normal and she broke into a sweat. Emily splashed water on her face and looked in the mirror. Wow, was she ever pale! What the heck was going on? "Must be a bug," she mumbled as she crawled back under the covers. During the next hour, Emily threw up twice more and then diarrhea started. At twelve-thirty she called Chris to see if he could take her to the hospital.

"What's wrong, babe?" Chris asked as he came into the apartment. He stopped short when he saw how Emily looked. He grabbed a sweater from her closet and wrapped it around her, and then led her out to his car. She could barely walk.

Chris raced in to get a nurse and a wheelchair when they arrived at the hospital. Karen, the same nurse that had looked after Tyler, was just finishing her shift so she told the girls on the new shift that she would help the young fellow bring his girlfriend in. "What's wrong?" Karen inquired of Chris as they assisted Emily into the wheelchair.

Chris explained Emily's symptoms, and as if to confirm he was getting it right, Emily threw up. Karen rushed to the nurses' station and asked for immediate help. Once they had Emily cleaned up and lying in a hospital bed, Karen looked at her watch. She had to get home. Her sitter would be livid. This would be the third time this week that she was late.

Emily was hooked to an intravenous to replenish her fluids. The Emergency doctor ordered a sedative to be added so Emily could get some rest. She settled down and soon drifted off to sleep. By three o'clock the intravenous was finished, and she seemed to be improving. It was Friday night—well, early Saturday morning—and the Emergency department was overloaded with Friday night revellers, so the doctor signed Emily out. He told Chris to make sure Emily went straight to bed and if the symptoms returned, just to bring her back. The doctor stated that he thought it was probably just a touch of a bad flu, or maybe something Emily had eaten or drank.

Chris thanked the doctor and took Emily home. "I'm going to stay with you tonight," he informed her as he tucked her into bed. Emily didn't argue.

At four o'clock Emily bolted up in her bed as the pain riveted through her body again. "Oh, my God!" she screamed as she headed to the bathroom. Not knowing which to do first—sit on the toilet, or throw up in the sink, she opted for the toilet. The floor in front of her was covered with vomit when Chris reached her.

Chris helped Emily get changed and then insisted he take her back to the hospital. She didn't argue. "You need to call Candice for me," she mentioned. "I don't think I'll be able to go dress shopping today."

By the time they reached the hospital, Emily could barely move. Chris didn't wait to get a wheelchair; he scooped his fiancée up in his arms and rushed through the Emergency doors. "I need a doctor!" he shouted.

One of the nurses recognized Chris and Emily from earlier. She hurried over and led them to an empty bed. "Put her here. What happened? I thought she was improving."

"Obviously not," Chris said, a hint of sarcasm creeping into his words. "She started throwing up again, and when I flushed the toilet, I noticed blood. She looks like she's dying! Where's the doctor?"

The nurse told Chris the doctor was on his way. She brought her equipment over and took Emily's blood pressure. It was seventy over forty. She took it again: sixty-eight over thirty-nine. She raced out and was back in a few minutes with the doctor. He was different than the earlier one.

"Hello, son, I'm Doctor Campbell. Could you excuse us for a minute; I would like to examine your girlfriend."

Chris stepped outside the curtains. His heart was pounding. He began to pace. He couldn't believe this was happening. Emily was always so healthy. Being a nurse, she knew how to take care of herself. He could hear her throwing up behind the curtain. The nurse came running out and grabbed some towels. She barked an order to an orderly to bring a bucket and mop, said something to one of the other nurses, and then returned to Emily.

A nurse came up to Chris and took him by the arm. "Why don't you sit in the waiting room? I'll come and get you as soon as Doctor Campbell is finished. Your girlfriend is in good hands with him."

"I need to stay here," Chris insisted.

"You need to be out of the way for now so we can do our job," the nurse returned as she led him out to the waiting room.

Chris couldn't sit; he continued his pacing. He noticed a couple of nurses racing into Emergency with a cart. "Code Red" sounded out over the PA system. He began to panic. A couple of minutes passed, and finally, he couldn't take it anymore. He pushed through the doors and raced to where Emily was. The doctor and the nurses were standing around her bed. The doctor held two paddles in his hands; he nodded to one of the nurses, then placed the paddles on Emily's chest. Her body convulsed upwards.

"Again!" Doctor Campbell shouted.

Emily convulsed upwards again. And then she lay still. Chris crumbled to the floor and began to weep.

Monday, June 15, 2009

Jack turned on the early morning local news. Toby perked up when he heard there had been another mysterious death, which appeared to be caused by flu-like symptoms. The newscaster reported it was the third such death within the past couple of weeks.

The doorbell rang. *Oh no, hope it isn't Camden!* Toby jumped off the couch and landed in one of the easy-chairs. He watched Jack as he opened the door. "Hey buddy, haven't seen you for a while. What have you been up to? Coming in for coffee?"

"Sure, Jack. I was just on my way over to the gym and realized you lived here and might be up for a quick visit. I don't have to be to work until one today." A young man in his late twenties stepped through the door.

Toby sighed. Someone he liked. Andrew Fairfax. Andrew was a paramedic, and he and Jack had become good friends after the previous case Toby had solved. Andrew had been the first on the scene when the little girls had been brought out of the abandoned building.

"Did you hear the news this morning?" Andrew asked.

"You mean about the third person who just died from the flu?"

"Yeah. I was at the hospital last night when the boyfriend brought the girl in." Andrew paused and shook his head. "You know, Jack, I'm no doctor, but it sure didn't look to me like that girl had the flu. She was extremely ill. I talked to one of the nurses—Karen—she said she helped the boyfriend bring the deceased in the first time they came to the hospital. She said the girl had all the same symptoms of the young fellow who passed away the week before. She was shocked when she came back on shift Saturday and found out the girl had died." Andrew went through to the kitchen, poured himself a coffee, and called to Jack to see if he wanted another one.

"No thanks, I'm okay … still have some." Jack waited for Andrew to return to the living room. "So you think this is more than just a bad flu?"

"Like I said, I'm no doctor, but I was there dropping off another patient just before they went for the crash cart. That girl was convulsing terribly. And she was still throwing up. It wasn't like any flu I've ever had or seen!"

Jack stroked his hands over his whiskers. "What about the third person? Were they ever at the hospital—that you know of?"

"Not that I heard. I think that one died at home. But it might not be a bad idea to talk to some of her family members to see exactly what kind of symptoms she had before she passed."

Jack agreed. "Maybe I'll go and pay a visit to my buddy at the station and see if they can send someone over to investigate. I don't want to get too involved here, being retired and all."

Andrew broke the tension with a chuckle. "You shouldn't be retired, Jack; look at that waist of yours. I'll bet the captain would take you back in a second…"

"Too old, Andrew. Too many years in the force. I'll just talk to Bryce and let him take it from there. I'll keep you posted."

The two men exchanged a few stories before Andrew stood and said he had to go. "Thanks for the coffee, Jack. If I don't get to the gym, I'll miss my workout."

"Drop in any time," Jack suggested as he walked Andrew to the door.

"Will do."

As Andrew left Jack's house, Camden was coming down the sidewalk, headed for work. Toby returned to the back of his couch by the window. He noticed Camden stop and look at Andrew, and saw a disconcerting shadow pass across Camden's face. *Hmm, wonder what he's upset about now?* Little did Toby know, Andrew was on Camden's list.

Camden followed Andrew into the gym. Not a word passed between them. Camden had pegged Andrew to be next but thought that maybe it would be wiser to leave him till last since he appeared to be Jack's friend. The next victim should be the final girl anyway; he didn't want to make it look as though he had a pattern of any sort.

It was another bad day at work. Camden was happy he had made the decision to target the last woman he had picked before finalizing with the men. The third girl who had rubbed him the wrong way was Lauren Dagnell. Right from the get-go she had been rude to him. When she had come for a tour, Camden was all set to show her around. She had whispered something to Isabella, and then Paige was taking Lauren around the gym. As they walked away, Lauren had leant over and said something to Paige. They had both glanced back at Camden and laughed.

Today was even worse. Camden saw Lauren talking to Isabella and pointing over to him. Isabella was frowning and shaking her head. What had he ever done to Lauren? Why was she trying to get him in trouble? Graham was standing close to them when the interaction had taken place, so Camden asked him later if he had heard what had been said. All Graham could remember hearing was Lauren telling Isabella that Camden gave her the creeps and, if possible, could he not come around the equipment she was working out on. "Isabella said she would talk to you," Graham finished his story.

Camden's head started to pound. *Why? Why couldn't these people just leave him alone? They had to be destroyed! They were so inconsiderate. They had no idea what he had gone through in his life! They didn't care!* Camden thanked Graham for the information and excused himself to the washroom. Isabella was waiting for him when he exited.

"Take a walk with me, Camden," she ordered. When they were out of earshot of everyone, she continued. "One of the members has asked that you not go around her machines when she is working on them." Isabella pointed to Lauren.

Camden drew in a deep breath. "What reason did she give? I only do my job when I'm out there, Isabella. Honestly. I don't bother anyone."

"She said you make her feel uncomfortable. I just talked to you the other day about loitering around the machines; I hope you are not still doing that."

"I don't loiter, Isabella; I do my job!" Camden's voice rose in anger. "That's what I do out there—my job!"

"It's okay, Camden." Isabella made a motion with her hand for Camden to lower his voice. She bent in closer to him. "I understand that some members can be over-particular. I am just making you aware of this, and, once again, I am asking you to be more cautious. Maybe I should have Graham empty the garbage cans for a few days and leave you at the drink counter, just until things settle down. How does that sound?"

Camden didn't have a problem with Isabella's suggestion. "Actually, Isabella, that sounds fantastic. I enjoy mixing the drinks for people. Shall I tell Graham to get started on the garbage? I was just about to do it."

Isabella put her hand on Camden's shoulder. "I'll do it; I see someone at the drink counter." Camden noted who it was—Jack's friend, Andrew. As Camden walked over, he was bubbling inside. Things had a way of working out in the long run. It would be easier to do what he had to do, now he was going to be behind the drink counter all the time.

~

Toby pondered all day about the look on Camden's face that morning. He came to the conclusion the guy needed serious watching. Toby was sure Camden was up to something and that something was absolutely no good. He kept vigil at the window, waiting for Camden to leave work. Shortly after five o'clock Toby saw him coming down the sidewalk. He hoped Camden didn't decide to pop in and say hello to Jack, although Jack wasn't home, anyway. Camden walked on by. Toby headed for his cat door.

Once outside, Toby followed at a discrete distance. The last thing he needed was for Camden to see him and give him a boot. Toby skulked down in the long grass by the fence surrounding Camden and Emma's backyard. Emma was in the three-season room. Toby watched Camden go in the front door, and a few minutes later he came out to where Emma was. Duke stood up and greeted him with a tail wag.

Toby watched and waited. Emma and Camden appeared to be having an ordinary conversation, but, Toby thought he detected a note of concern on Emma's face when she shook her head after Camden had talked for a few minutes. Finally, she shrugged her shoulders and headed into the house. Duke followed her. Toby was about to head home when he noticed Camden's attention on a particular group of plants in the corner of the room. Camden was also warily watching the door Emma had just gone through. He started to pick something off of the plant. Just then, Emma poked her head out the door. Camden quickly shoved whatever he had picked into his pocket. Toby saw Emma's lips move, but he couldn't hear what she was saying. Camden said something in return; she nodded and disappeared into the house. Camden followed.

Toby hung around, watching, and just as he was about to leave he noticed a light flick on, on the upper floor. He looked around for something to climb. Near the lit window was a large tree branch, attached to an even larger tree. *"Well, it's been a while since I climbed a tree, but if I'm going to find out what Camden's up to, I'm going to have to do this!"* Toby began to make his way up the trunk. By the time he got to the spot where the branch veered off to the window, he was out of breath. *"I really am too old for this!"*

Camden was in his closet. He reached up and took down a box. When he opened it he took out his coffee grinder. Toby's head bent to the side, curious about what Camden would be doing with a coffee grinder in his room. Toby heard the back door open and Duke came bounding out. He ran right to the base of the tree and started barking. Camden was heading for the window.

113

Toby moved as quickly as his old bones allowed, and hid amongst the leafy foliage. Duke was going crazy at the bottom of the tree. Camden opened the window and shouted down to the dog. When Duke still didn't stop, Camden shut the window and the next thing Toby knew Camden was outside. He grabbed hold of Duke's collar and dragged him into the house.

"You want us to get kicked out of the neighbourhood, dog?"

Toby didn't like the dog, but he felt Camden yanked too hard on Duke's collar. *"But I don't have time to ponder on the finer arts of dog handling; I have to get myself out of here!"* Toby managed to scratch his way down the tree and then headed for home. *"I sure wish I could've seen what he was going to do with the grinder, though. I wonder if it had anything to do with what he picked off the plant. Oh well, maybe I'll be able to catch him another time. Whatever it is, I don't think Emma would approve, or Camden wouldn't have tried to hide from her the fact that he was picking things off her plants."*

Toby pushed his way through the cat door. "Hey, old man, there you are. I was beginning to wonder what happened to you," Jack greeted him.

"You have no idea!" Toby headed to his dishes, first having a drink of water and then digging hungrily into his kibble.

~

Lauren headed home after her workout. She was relatively new to Brantford. She had her own place, thanks to the divorce settlement. It wasn't as big as what she had been used to, but at least now she didn't have to always be looking over her shoulder, wondering where the next blow was going to come from. She hated the fact that she had to speak to the gym manager about the worker, but he looked so much like her ex-husband she couldn't stand having him around. Lauren had even considered changing gyms, but she had already paid for a full year and didn't want to lose her money. She closed her door and secured the locks into place: three on each door, just in case.

After the divorce settlement, Lauren had returned to school and graduated with a legal secretary certificate from Mohawk College. She had been lucky when the lawyer's office where she had done her co-op placement had an opening come up. They had been pleased with her work and she was hired on the spot.

She hadn't heard from her ex in six months, a good sign. He probably had another woman. Lauren wished whoever it might be had better luck than she'd had. After the last beating, the police had charged her husband and he was put on probation. As far as she was concerned, he should have served jail time! But, life wasn't that bad now … she was moving forward … she was in counselling … she was healing. The workouts were helping, and she was determined to keep them up on a daily basis.

~

When Camden returned to his room, he started to think about the ruckus Duke had caused earlier. There had to have been something up that tree outside his window. He walked over and closed the curtains and then retrieved the coffee grinder again. He took the seeds from his pocket, placed them in the mill's dish, and pressed the on-button. Then he poured the powder into a zip-lock baggie, which still had residue from his last batch. There wasn't quite as much as he thought there would be so he would have to pick more seeds later and add them to the mix.

After putting the grinder back on the top shelf of his closet and placing the baggie under his pillow, Camden turned his computer on. He pulled up his special email, made the name change, typed in Lauren's email address, and pushed send. He reclined back in his chair and smiled. It was sad things had to be moving so fast, but, in truth, it wasn't his fault—people were just so mean!

Tuesday, June 16, 2009

Lauren got up in the morning and turned her computer on. She hadn't bothered to check her emails last night. Her friend, Betty, was supposed to be sending her a note about when she was coming for a visit. Lauren scrolled down through all the spam. Nothing from Betty. Then she noticed one whose subject line said: 'JUST FOR YOU.' She decided to click on it. *"Dear Lauren: you are receiving this email because you have been very, very naughty. Do you know what happens to very naughty people? Think about it! When was the last time you ridiculed someone ... ignored someone just because ... blamed someone wrongfully? When was the last time you were nice to someone ... really nice? When was the last time you helped someone ... really helped? You are so pathetically naughty that I can't stand it! Only you can turn this around and do something about it. I have given you the warning ... now it is up to you to seek reconciliation. If you don't, maybe retribution will come your way ... if you have any friends who are just like you, pass this on to them so they can get help too ... for every friend you try to save the retribution on yourself will be lessened ... you know the drill ... six to ten, maybe you won't die ... one to five, you will ... signed: 666."*

Lauren's blood began to boil. How dare this person invade her personal space! She didn't have time to digest it now because she had to get ready for work, so she left it in her inbox.

After work, Lauren headed for the gym. She swiped her card and made her way to the change room. Camden was just coming out of the men's change room and crossed her path. She shivered and threw him a dirty look, not really meaning to. In the change room, Lauren looked in the mirror and shook her head. She shouldn't have done that. She should probably apologize to the young man, but she knew she wouldn't.

Camden returned to the drink counter and mixed a couple of drinks for some members that were waiting patiently for his return. He was boiling inside because of Lauren's attitude. Well, she had hers coming!

Lauren finished her workout and headed straight out the door. She didn't bother to stop for a smoothie; she wasn't hungry, and they filled her up too much. Camden was not happy about that. He breathed in deeply and tried to relax, realizing he was going to have to wait. He would send her a second email later; it was apparent she hadn't paid any attention to the first one!

Friday, June 19, 2009

Lauren didn't show up to the gym on Wednesday, and Camden was off on Thursday. He knew Lauren had received the second email though, and he was anxious to finish the job.

Lauren's fist came down hard on her desk when she read the email on Wednesday morning. She saw the subject line: 'ARE YOU LISTENING TO ME.' She clicked on it… *"Dear Lauren: you are still being very, very naughty. I told you what happens to very naughty people. Did you think about it? Did you ridicule someone today … ignore someone just because … blame someone wrongfully? Were you nice to someone … really nice? Did you help someone today, just because … really help? I doubt you even gave my message a second thought. Oh, believe it … you are so pathetically naughty that I can't stand it! You might still be able to turn this around and do something about it. I am being generous giving you another warning … but it is still up to you to seek reconciliation. If you don't, retribution will come your way … and don't forget all those selfish, naughty friends of yours who are just like you. Pass this on to them so they can get help too … for every friend you try to save the retribution on yourself might be lessened … you know the drill … six to ten, maybe you won't die … one to five, you will … signed: 666."*

She decided to run a copy of both emails and take them to work and show them to her boss. She was nobody's doormat anymore—least of all some sicko that sent out emails like this to frighten people. There had to be a way to trace where it was coming from. Lauren packed her gym bag and headed out the door. She had missed two days at the gym and was feeling it. She was going for sure tonight.

When Lauren's boss, Mr. Delaware, read the emails, he sat back in his chair and bit thoughtfully on the end of his pen for a few seconds. "I think you should take these to the police," he suggested. "Whoever wrote them is an incredibly sick individual. The police will probably have someone on their staff who can trace the I.P. address." He paused. "What I am afraid of the most is the fact that this email is dispatched directly to you. How does this person know your name? Do you know anyone who would send you something like this?"

Lauren thought for a moment. There was only one person she could think of who might be sick enough—her ex-husband. But he would be crazy to even attempt something like this because he should know it would be grounds for throwing him in jail. "Well, maybe my ex..."

Mr. Delaware butt in. "I am sure the police will question him. Tell you what—I'll give you an extra half hour at lunch to run these down to the police station. Ask for Captain Bryce Wagner. Tell him I sent you."

Unfortunately there was an emergency, and Mr. Delaware needed Lauren over the lunch hour. He apologized and suggested she go after work. If Captain Wagner wasn't in, she could leave the copies and a message for him, and Mr. Delaware was sure the captain would get back to her on Monday.

Lauren decided since it was so late when she finished work, and since the gym was closer to her work than the police station, she would go to the gym first. She could drop the letters on her way home.

Camden was happy to see her walk in. He smiled at her. To his surprise, she half-smiled back. Camden was actually having a good day. Even Paige was nice for a change, hanging up her sarcasm for a friendlier tone. At lunchtime, she dumped her problems on his shoulders. Paige had been close to tears, but because they were at work, she held them in check. Camden was not surprised she was in trouble with the way she flirted. He had asked Paige if she was going to tell the father and her reply had been that she didn't really know for sure which one it was; she had slept with both of them. Camden told her that she could always get a paternity test after the baby was born.

To himself, he had thought, *Slut deserves it*! When Vincent and Nolan had come in to work, Camden had looked right through them. They were no better than Paige in his opinion.

Lauren cut her workout short because she was anxious to get the letters delivered. Camden saw her enter the change room and after waiting about five minutes, he mixed her drink for her. When she came out, Lauren headed straight for the door.

"Lauren," he called out to her; "I have your smoothie ready for you."

She paused a moment and then walked over to the drink counter. "Sorry, I'm going to pass tonight. Some sicko has been sending me some pretty crazy emails, and I'm headed to the police station to drop off copies." Lauren swallowed hard. It was hard to talk to Camden: she had to keep reminding herself he was not her ex.

Camden felt a shooting pain through his head. He had to think quickly. "That's terrible," he finally managed to say. "How awful that someone would do such a thing." He reached out his hand to touch her arm. She saw it coming and pulled away. He blushed.

Lauren felt sorry, but pulling away from any advance made by a man had become second nature to her. "I'll take a rain-check on the smoothie, though. Maybe tomorrow— you working tomorrow?" she tried to smooth things over.

He managed to calm himself enough to say yes. As Lauren walked out the door, Camden dumped the drink in the sink. "Hey, you shouldn't have dumped that; I could have drunk it," Paige said as she popped her head around the corner.

"Too late—maybe next time," Camden answered as he crushed the cup and put it in the garbage can. "I have to empty this; do you mind watching the counter for me."

"No problem."

It was six-thirty by the time Lauren arrived at the police station. She assumed the captain would have left for the day, but when she asked at the front desk, to her surprise, he was still there. The receptionist laughed and told Lauren an old policeman friend and his famous cat had dropped by for a visit and they were in the captain's office reminiscing.

"I'll check if the captain will see you for a minute," the receptionist said as she got up and headed for his office. When she returned, she said, "Follow me."

Lauren was surprised at the scene that greeted her in Captain Wagner's office. An elderly gentleman, not in uniform, was leaning back in a chair, his feet perched on the edge of the big wooden desk. On the other side of the desk was another elderly gentleman, a shade younger, also with his feet on the edge of the desk. In-between, sitting in the middle of the desk, was a huge, orange cat! Lauren hesitated in the doorway.

The younger of the two men jumped to his feet and extended his hand to her. "Captain Wagner." He pointed to Jack. "This is my friend, retired Officer Jack Nelson and this fur ball is his famous cat, Detective Toby. How might I help you, miss?"

Lauren did not take his offered hand. Instead, she began her story of the two emails. Part way through the captain motioned for her to have a seat. Jack took his feet down from the desk. Toby listened intently.

"So, having saved the first letter," Lauren continued, "When the second one came in I realized whoever this was they were pretty twisted, and I thought it might be best to show the letters to my boss, Mr. Delaware. He was the one who gave me your name and suggested I bring the letters here."

"So the letters are still saved on your computer?" the captain asked.

"Yes."

"Could you bring your computer in so our tech expert can take a look and see if he can trace the I.P. address?"

"Sure. When would you like me to do that?"

"As soon as possible," Captain Wagner replied. "If you want to bring it right now, I'll wait around until you return."

"That sounds like a good idea."

"Before you go, though, I have a couple questions. Is there anyone in your life who would be sending these to you as a practical joke?"

"None of my friends would do this to me. They all know I've been through enough in the past few years."

"How about enemies?" Jack spoke for the first time.

Lauren paused before answering. She didn't want to blame her ex-husband or cast an accusation toward him, but there was a significant possibility that he, of everyone she knew, could be capable of this. "Only my ex," she finally answered. "But I don't think he'd go this far."

"Why is that?" Jack asked.

"Well, he'd end up in jail, for one. Our lives together weren't … ah … the most pleasant and he's walking a thin line with the law where I'm concerned. He's not supposed to have any contact with me."

The Captain bent forward. "We need his name anyway. With something like this, someone like him is our prime suspect. Since there doesn't appear to be any other enemies or prankster friends in your life, we would talk to him first."

"Ethan Wolf. He lives in Hamilton. I don't know his address though, or his number. You can probably get hold of him through his lawyer, or maybe even the Central Hamilton police station … yeah, they'd probably be the quickest. Ethan was there enough times, and I think his probation officer has his office there, as well."

Toby stood up and stretched. *"Poor girl."* He walked across the desk and jumped onto Lauren's lap, startling her. Jack laughed.

"Toby likes you," he said. "Not often he jumps on someone's lap."

Lauren stroked Toby's back and scratched behind his ears. *"Oh, this is so lovely; this girl has fantastic fingers!"*

Lauren missed having a cat and had recently contemplated picking up a couple kittens from the S.P.C.A., but she wanted to make sure she was well settled first. Ethan had ordered her to get rid of her cats after they were

122

married. She scooped Toby up in her arms, stood, and then set him back on the desk. "I guess I better get going if I'm to get my computer back here at a decent hour."

Captain Wagner saw Lauren to the door. "Just bring the computer straight to me; I'll arrange to have it looked at first thing in the morning. Make sure to leave a number where I can reach you."

"Thanks." Lauren headed out to her car.

Bryce Wagner returned to his office. Jack returned his feet to the desk. Toby was lying down. "Where were we?"

"We were discussing the three young people who died from this mysterious flu," Jack answered. "Do you think there might be a connection somewhere? I have a paramedic friend who just happened to be at the hospital the night the last girl who died was brought in. He said, basically, if that was a flu she had, he'd never seen anything like it before." Jack paused. "You know, I was wondering if it would not be a good idea to send someone over to the hospital to talk to the doctors or nurses who were on duty those nights. We don't want to jump to any conclusions, but..."

"I'm pretty short-handed, Jack," Bryce grinned, and it wasn't until his next statement that Jack realized why his friend was smirking. "How would you like to do a little freelance work here? You could go up to the hospital and snoop around. I'll give you a badge to show you are with the police."

Toby sat up at attention at the mention of Jack doing some police work. *"Come on Jack, say yes! This could be fun—life is a bit dull at the moment."* Toby stared at Jack.

"Looks like Toby wants you to say yes," Bryce chuckled.

Jack looked thoughtful for a moment. He *was* getting bored with retirement; a change in pace would probably do him good. "Okay, I'll do it. I don't want to get too involved, but I guess I can stop by the hospital and see if there is anything more to these deaths. The autopsy from the young man who died should be almost complete by now, shouldn't it?"

"All depends on what else is on the coroner's plate that takes priority over it," Bryce answered. He opened one of his desk drawers and handed Jack a badge. Toby meowed his approval.

Jack took the badge and stood. "Come on Toby, time to head home." He picked Toby up from the desk and headed for the door. "See you later, Bryce." As he was leaving, Lauren walked in with her computer and set it on the captain's desk.

~

Toby and Jack arrived home at eight o'clock. Jack was tired. He grabbed a beer from the fridge and plunked down in his favourite chair. Toby jumped up onto the back of the couch and stared out the window. Jack turned the television on and halfway through his program, he was snoring.

Toby noticed a familiar figure walking past the house. He had no idea why, but something inside him told him to follow Camden home and see what he was up to in his bedroom. Toby was still curious about the grinder. He jumped down and headed out the cat door. He was cautious not to follow Camden too closely.

Toby sat at the bottom of the tree outside Camden's room until he saw a light in the window. He climbed up to his branch, but stayed a little closer to the main trunk than he had before. *"Bingo, I'm in luck!"*

Camden was retrieving the coffee grinder and was taking a baggie out from under his pillow. The bag looked like it had beans in it. These were put into the mill, and Toby watched as Camden mixed the beans into a powder and then poured the powder into the bag. Camden smiled through the entire procedure, but to Toby, it was not a happy smile: it was sinister.

When Camden was finished, he placed the baggie back under his pillow, turned his light off and left the room.

Toby clawed his way down the tree and headed home. *"What the heck is that powder Camden is mixing up? And why is he so secretive about it? He was pretty careful not to let Emma see he was picking those seeds from her plant. Maybe I'll come and see Emma and nose around the plant. Maybe she'll tell me about it, and then I'll have a better idea of what Camden's up to. Of course I'll have to figure out a way to inform Jack, and that won't be an easy task."*

Toby pushed his way through his cat door. The lights were out in the living room. Jack must have gone to bed. Toby stopped at his dishes for a snack and a drink and then headed to the bedroom to join Jack.

Monday, June 22, 2009

Lauren had had a great weekend. Her friend, Betty, had come down from Toronto on Saturday and had stayed overnight. Lauren told her about the emails, and then the two young women went out and enjoyed their time together: a nice dinner and a movie on Sunday afternoon before Betty headed home. Lauren hadn't expected to hear from the police over the weekend, sure they had other more pressing matters to look after. She hoped it didn't take them too long, though; she missed having her computer. Lauren figured if she didn't hear from them by Monday, she would call them Tuesday.

She was up early Monday morning, not being able to sleep well. She got out of bed, thinking to go to the gym before work so she could stop by the police station afterwards. Lauren quickly threw her gym clothes on, grabbed a pair of slacks and a blouse from her closet, folded them neatly in her gym bag, and headed out the door.

Camden was working first shift on Monday. He had not been happy when Lauren hadn't appeared over the weekend, and he was beginning to worry she wasn't going to return. He would have to find a replacement for her if that were the case. Camden had considered Paige, but she was too close to home, and she was pregnant; he didn't want to kill a baby. Camden felt a surge of delight when Lauren walk through the door early on Monday morning.

"Good morning, Lauren," he greeted her. "You're early today."

Lauren breathed in deep. "Be pleasant," she mumbled to herself. To Camden, she replied: "Yes, thought to get this over with early because I have to stop by the police station after work and see if they are finished with my computer."

Camden raised his eyebrows questioningly.

"Remember, I told you about the emails I received?" Lauren reminded Camden.

He nodded. "Oh yeah ... sorry, I forgot."

"Well, the police are going to have a tech expert try and trace the I.P. address to see if we can find out who sent them."

Camden's face paled. He knew he shouldn't worry. He had taken extensive precautions, but then again, one could never be sure. He pointed to the clock. "I guess you better get started on your workout so you won't be late for work. Would you like me to have a smoothie ready for you when you're done?"

Lauren actually smiled. "That would be very nice; I skipped breakfast this morning—banana/pineapple please."

"No problem." Camden smiled back. He had an extra big surprise for Lauren. With her having gone to the police, he needed to ensure she would be too ill to be able to follow up on those emails. And if she didn't follow up, the police would probably just sweep it under the carpet and forget the entire issue.

Camden had Lauren's drink ready when she came out of the dressing room. She gave him five dollars and told him to keep the change. He almost had second thoughts about her, but it was too late: she had half the smoothie drunk before she hit the front door.

Around two-thirty that afternoon, Lauren started to feel nauseous. She thought at first that it was because she had skipped lunch, so she opened her desk drawer and raided her backup supply of energy bars. But that didn't help. In fact, her nausea increased to the point where she decided she better get to the washroom or she was going to upchuck all over her desk.

When Lauren returned to her station, Mr. Delaware walked out of his office to give her something to type up. He noticed how pale she was. "Are you okay?" he asked.

"I just feel a bit nauseous. Must be coming down with something," Lauren replied.

127

"You don't look well at all. Why don't you head home; this typing can wait until morning."

"I'll be okay—rea..." a sharp pain drove through Lauren's stomach, and she bent forward to try and stop the force of it.

"Go home! Stop at a walk-in clinic on your way, or the hospital. I read about some other people who died from some bad flu; maybe that's what you have, and if you catch it in time the doctors can help you." Mr. Delaware made his final point before returning to his office.

Lauren shut down her computer, grabbed her purse from the desk drawer, and headed out the door. She just wanted to get home; she didn't feel like sitting for hours in some walk-in clinic, or at the hospital's Emergency Department where she would probably pick up something even worse.

Another sharp pain doubled Lauren over as she walked through her front door. She ran as fast as she could to the bathroom and sat on the toilet. Her stomach exploded, but when she was finished, she felt a bit better. Lauren headed to the kitchen and looked through her cupboards for something light to eat. Finding a package of Cup-of-Soup, she plugged in the kettle and waited for it to boil. She was feeling scorching hot, which gave her reason to assume she was coming down with the flu.

"Hopefully, it'll pass by morning," she mumbled as she poured the hot water into her mug, then headed into the living room. Lauren curled up on the couch and turned the television on.

Tuesday, June 23, 2009

However Lauren wasn't better by morning. She had a dreadfully rough night and was feeling much worse. She called the office. No one was in yet, so she left a message on the answering machine, saying she was still not well; she would call later to let Mr. Delaware know of her progress.

She tried everything: more soup, juice, tea, water—it all went right through her. She noticed blood a few times, and she could not stop sweating. "This is like no flu I've ever had before," she mumbled after staggering out of the bathroom mid-morning. "But if I can make it through five years of living with an asshole like Ethan Wolf, I can surely survive this," she laughed weakly.

By mid-afternoon, Lauren was curled up in bed, too weak to even move. She had absolutely no strength left. The phone rang. She glanced at her night-table, looking for her portable. "Damn," she cursed. "I must have left it downstairs." The phone stopped.

A few minutes later, it rang again. Lauren remembered about the emails and her computer. "Maybe it's the police calling me ... I better try and get to it." Lauren forced herself to her feet and stumbled out of her room. She was dizzy and not sure if she could navigate the stairs to get herself to the living room. Her foot reached for the first step ... then the second ... then, there were no more. Lauren tumbled to the bottom of the stairs and lay still.

Wednesday, June 24, 2009

Captain Bryce Wagner was worried about Lauren. He had tried calling her at her home on Tuesday after her work had said she was sick, but she hadn't answered her phone. He had tried again this morning, and she still didn't answer. When he called her work again, they said she had left a message on Tuesday that she was still not feeling well. Bryce asked to talk to Mr. Delaware.

"Delaware, here, how can I help you?"

"It's Bryce ... you sent a young woman over to see me on Monday—about a couple of harassing emails. I have been trying to get hold of her, but she's not answering her phone: do you know where she might be?"

Mr. Delaware could only think of one possible place. "Well, if she isn't at home, she is most likely at the hospital or a walk-in clinic. She was pretty sick when she left here on Monday."

"What was wrong with her?"

"Said she was throwing up. I told her it was probably a touch of the flu and sent her home. She called in yesterday to say she wouldn't be in. Come to think of it, this isn't like her not to keep in touch. Maybe I'll go over to her house and check up on her. I don't think she has many friends in the city yet." He paused. "By the way, did you make heads or tails out of those emails?"

"Not of the actual emails, but the girl brought her computer in for us to check out. Our tech expert was out of town for a couple of days, but he's back now. He's going to look at it this afternoon. I'll give you a call if we find anything."

After hanging up the phone, Mr. Delaware sat for a moment in his chair and then he got up and headed for the door. "I'll be back shortly," he told the receptionist. Driving up to Lauren's house he felt a wave of apprehension wash over him. He knew himself well enough that this only happened to him when there was something terribly wrong.

He got out of his car and walked up to the front door and rang the doorbell. No answer. He tried the door to see if it was locked. It opened easily. Mr. Delaware looked around. He didn't want any of the neighbours to think he was a burglar but his concern for Lauren far outweighed his concern for his reputation. He pushed the door open and stepped inside.

Lauren lay at the bottom of the stairs, her body twisted from her fall. Mr. Delaware bowed over and felt for a pulse. The body was cold. The pulse was absent. He stood up, took out his cell phone and called the police. He asked to speak to Captain Bryce Wagner.

"Wagner, here."

"Bryce … it's Greg. I found out why Lauren didn't answer her phone. She's dead."

"Where are you?"

"At her place. After we had talked, I got worried and decided I would check on her. Like I told you, it isn't like her not to call in. Looks like she took a tumble down the stairs."

"I'll send an officer over right away. Don't touch anything," Bryce warned.

"You don't have to tell me that; I'm a lawyer."

In less than twenty minutes a police cruiser and an ambulance pulled up in front of Lauren's house. A couple of nosy neighbours came out onto their front porches to see what was going on. Mr. Delaware was waiting at the front door to let the officers and paramedics in. A yellow tape was put up across the front yard. It wasn't long before another car drove up and two newspaper reporters got out and tried to get through the tape. One of the officers stopped them at the door.

"There is nothing here for you to see, boys," she said. "Just a young woman had an unfortunate accident in her home."

"Are you sure it was an accident, officer?" one of the reporters questioned.

"We aren't sure of anything until we finish investigating the scene."

"So it might not be an accident then?" the reporter pushed.

"No further comments … now if you don't mind, I have work to do here." The female officer shut the door.

~

Somehow, someone leaked more information to the press than was expected. The six o'clock news broadcast how a young woman, Lauren Dagnell, was found dead in her home that morning. Her boss, Mr. Delaware, a local lawyer, who had become suspicious when she hadn't called into work, found the body. He was unavailable for comments. Police sources do not suggest foul play at the moment, but an autopsy will be performed on the body to see if there is anything else that could have led to the woman's untimely death.

~

Emma was watching the six o'clock news. The story of the young woman, who had been found dead in her home, shook Emma up. She called Duke over to where she was sitting and gave him a hug. "You wouldn't let anything happen to me, would you, boy?" Duke licked her face.

When Camden arrived home from work at six-thirty, Emma told him about the woman. "Did you catch her name?" Camden asked.

At first Emma thought that was a strange reaction for her brother to have, but then she thought that maybe since he worked in a place where a lot of people came and went every day, he might know the victim. "I think it was something like … Laura … no, that's not it … Lauren … that was her name. She worked for a lawyer, and he was the one who found her body at the bottom of her stairway. Do you know anyone named Lauren?"

Camden hid the joy he was feeling inside and shook his head. "Not that I can think of. Well, that's a shame." Camden saw the look on Emma's face and realized the

132

news story had upset her. After all, she was alone in the house quite a bit while he was working. "You have nothing to be afraid of, Emma," he began, taking her hands in his; "it sounds like this woman just had an accident in her home. Besides, you have Duke here to protect you; no one is going to get past him! I'm going upstairs to clean up; I'll be down in a few minutes for supper."

As Camden climbed the stairs to his room his face lit up: he punched the air, a victory salute. He wouldn't have displayed such happiness had he known Emma was watching him, wondering what it was that her brother found so humorous about a young woman's death.

~

Jack and Toby didn't have to wait for the six o'clock news to hear about Lauren's untimely death. Bryce called and asked if they could come down to the station so he could fill them in on what he knew so far and also find out if Jack had discovered anything at the hospital.

"Come in and close the door," Bryce said. He didn't waste any time. "There are no leads yet on the computer. Whoever sent the email knows computers and knows how to block access to their I.P. address. Our guy is still working on it. He said there might be another way." He paused for breath. "Did you find out anything from the hospital?"

Jack shook his head. "Nothing substantial. Doctor Campbell, who saw the first girl, wasn't too cooperative. Can't blame him I guess, with that young fellow's mum all over the hospital in regards to her son. There was a nurse who talked to me. She was on duty the night the young fellow was brought in, and she was just going off when the boyfriend brought his girlfriend up there. She told me the symptoms of both parties were similar. She also said she didn't think it was food poisoning or a case of the flu."

"What was her name? We will probably need to talk to her again."

"Karen."

"Good work." Bryce tapped his pen on the desk. "Wasn't there another young woman who died the same weekend as the Tyler fellow?" he questioned.

"Come to think of it, yes there was—a school teacher."

"I don't know ... I have a gut feeling that somehow these deaths are all connected. Find out who her family is and ask them if she was sick before she died."

"Am I on the payroll now?" Jack asked with a grin.

"I got no one better to help me out on this, and if it gets any more mysterious, I think we have more here than just the flu. My old police gut tells me something stinks. I also want to know if any of these other people who died received any vicious emails."

Toby was excited—not that people had lost their lives, but that he and Jack would be working on a real case together. As Jack and Toby were leaving the station, a couple of officers hollered over. "Hey there, Jack, how's that oversized orange cat of yours? Solve any more crimes lately?" They were laughing.

Toby walked out in front of Jack. The officers stopped laughing.

"Oh, there he is. Hey, Toby!" They came over and knelt down to give Toby a backrub. Toby absorbed every finger of it.

Jack waited patiently for Toby's backrub to be over, smiled at the officers, then picked Toby up and exited the building. He wasn't sure he wanted to get involved in this case, but Bryce seemed to need him so he would humour his friend until some unretired officers could take over.

When Jack got home, he went through his old newspapers until he found the one with the obituaries for the first two young people who had died. He noted Tyler's and moved his finger down until he came to Brianna Gates. He glanced over the list of relatives and wrote down her sister's name, Caitlin Carter, husband, Mitch. That should be easy enough if they were in the phonebook. Jack pulled out his phonebook and scrolled down the Carters until he came to an M Carter. He wrote down the number and then picked up the phone and dialled.

"Hello," a young woman answered the phone. Jack could hear children in the background.

"Hi, is this Caitlin Carter?"

"Yes, who's this?"

"My name is Jack Nelson ... I'm working with the police department on a possible case..."

"What does that have to do with me?" Caitlin interrupted nervously.

"I was wondering if I could come over and ask you some questions about your sister, Brianna."

"Brianna died at the end of May."

"I know. There was another young man who died the same weekend. I'd rather ask you these questions in person if possible." Jack paused a minute and thought about what Caitlin might be worried about. "What time does your husband, Mitch, get home from work? I could come over then if that makes you feel more comfortable."

"It would. He gets home at five-thirty. I put the children to bed by seven-thirty. Why don't you come by at eight?"

"No problem. See you at eight."

Jack fixed himself a bite to eat and then wrote a few questions on a piece of paper so he wouldn't forget to ask Caitlin anything. It had been a while since he had done a police investigation. He turned to Toby. "I have to go out tonight, old boy. Police work. Can't take you with me on this one but I'll fill you in on the details when I get back.

Toby flattened his ears and walked away with his tail in the air.

~

Jack didn't have a hard time finding Caitlin's house. She lived in a townhouse complex at the north end of the city. He rang the doorbell and was greeted by a young man who looked to be around thirty. Jack flashed his badge.

135

"Come in, officer," Mitch opened the door wider. "Have a seat in the living room; Caitlin will be right with us. Would you like coffee or something?"

"No thanks, I just finished my supper." Jack looked around the room and noticed the pictures of three boys on the wall. "Real handful, I bet," he smiled, pointing to the photos.

"That, sir, is an understatement."

Jack pointed to a photo on the fireplace mantel. "Your wife, or Brianna?"

"Brianna."

"She was a beautiful young woman."

"Yep."

A woman, whom Jack assumed was Caitlin, walked into the room. He stood and offered her his hand. "I'm Jack Nelson, the officer you spoke to earlier this evening."

Caitlin sat down. She looked haggard. Jack didn't think it was just from the three little rascals who kept her busy throughout the day. "What do you want to know about my sister?" she asked, melancholy threading her words.

Jack pulled out his notebook and flipped to the page where he had written his questions. "First, let me give you my condolences for the loss of your sister."

Caitlin nodded.

"Did your sister know a Tyler Acton?"

"Not that she ever mentioned."

"Did your sister have any illnesses that could have led up to her death?"

"Her name is Brianna." Caitlin's tone was taut. "And no, my sister was healthy—very healthy. Which is why it's so strange she died when all she seemed to have that night was a touch of the flu."

Jack's ears perked up. "She had the flu?"

At this point, Mitch spoke up. "Yeah, Caitlin told me Brianna had started to feel queasy and had broken out into a sweat not too long after supper the night before she died. That would have been May 29th—a Friday night—my night out with the boys. The girls were going to watch a movie."

"Get to the point, Mitch," Caitlin said.

Jack intervened with another question. "What did you have for supper that night, Caitlin?"

"Macaroni casserole."

"Any chicken in it?"

"No. The boys and I all ate the same meal … we didn't get sick." Caitlin wrung her hands together.

"Okay, so your sister—Brianna," Jack corrected himself, "she went home after eating, stating she didn't feel well, right? Did she call you at all that night?"

"No, she didn't call until Saturday morning. She sounded absolutely terrible on the phone; I could barely hear her voice. Said she needed me to come and take her to the hospital. Brianna never asked for help with anything unless it was something severe."

"She didn't say what was wrong?"

"No. I had to call a sitter because Mitch was working. I ran into an accident en route to Brianna's house and got caught in the traffic. By the time I arrived, Brianna was dead. I found her on the bathroom floor."

"Did you notice anything strange in the apartment?"

Caitlin didn't answer right away, so Mitch spoke up again. "The apartment was a mess. Caitlin said Brianna had thrown up in a few places and the inside of the toilet wasn't too pretty either—a lot of blood."

"Brianna's clothing was sopping wet, too," Caitlin added. I cleaned everything up before the ambulance came to take Brianna away."

Jack was busy writing. From the sound of things, Brianna had similar symptoms to the others.

Mitch ventured another bit of information. "When I read in the paper about that mother wanting to get an autopsy for her son, I suggested to Caitlin we do the same for Brianna, but Caitlin wouldn't hear of it. She just wanted to get her sister buried so she could be at peace. Do they know what killed the young man yet?"

"I don't think the autopsy results are finalized. If the police do think there might be a connection here, once they have the results of Tyler's autopsy, they are probably going to do the same with two other women who have also died from similar symptoms. They might ask you if we can exhume Brianna's body." Jack noticed Caitlin stiffen. "Only if necessary," he added quickly, to allay her fears.

Jack stood. "I think I have what I need for now. I may need to call upon you again though. Once again, Caitlin, I am sorry for your loss."

Mitch stood. "I'll show you to the door."

Jack was exhausted by the time he got home. Toby heard him come in and sat up, expecting a full rendition of what had taken place. Instead, Jack patted him on the head and walked into the kitchen.

"*You aren't going to get away that easy.*" Toby followed Jack, running to the refrigerator and sitting in front of the door.

"Okay, Toby, I'll tell you what went on; just let me grab a beer first."

Toby stepped out of the way.

Jack filled Toby in on the fact that it looked like Brianna had died of the same symptoms as Tyler Acton, Emily Foster, and Lauren Dagnell. Brianna hadn't made it to the hospital, and only her sister had seen the aftermath of what happened. Unfortunately Caitlin cleaned the mess up before anyone else got there. Her husband had suggested an autopsy, but Caitlin said no. She and her sister were close." Jack stood and downed the rest of his beer. "I'm going to bed, Toby. It's been a long day, and I have a feeling the days aren't going to get any shorter for a while. It's beginning to look as though there's a lot more to these four deaths than meets the eyes. You comin', old man?"

Toby followed Jack to the bedroom, and the two settled in for the night. Before he fell off to sleep, Toby's mind rehashed the facts. "*I'll bet there's a connection between Camden and all these deaths, which only started happening when he moved to town. But how? What's the link? I need to find one. I'm going to have to do some more digging over there—figure out what those seeds are that Camden is grinding up. Emma will know, but how do I get her to tell me? I'll figure a way. How would Camden know all these people; he just moved here and he sticks pretty much to himself. This is pretty tough. Maybe I'm meowing up the wrong tree..."* Toby finally fell asleep.

~

Camden was tired. He was not looking forward to the next couple of weeks. Everything had moved way too fast here in Brantford, faster than in any other place he had lived. There was no way he'd to be able to convince Emma they had to move so soon. And she was getting more observant of his moods; he was going to have to be more vigilant.

And now there was the issue of the autopsy and the fact Lauren had taken the emails to the police. No one had ever done that before. And her computer was there too. What if there was a slim chance his I.P. address could be traced?

Camden stepped out of his bedroom and looked at Emma's closed door. Good, she was sleeping. He went quietly down the stairs and out to the three-season room. He walked over to the corner where the special plants were and gathered some more seeds. He figured if he picked a few at a time over the next couple of days, Emma wouldn't notice. She didn't like him tampering with her plants.

He returned to his room, put the seeds in a baggie and shoved it under his pillow. Then he stretched out on his bed. Sleep wouldn't come. He reached under his bed and pulled out an old photo album. Most of the pictures were of him and Emma when they were little, then not until they were sixteen. The gap of about six years was when they were in foster care, years Camden wanted no memory of, yet years that still haunted him.

Camden turned the page to a picture of him, Emma, and their parents. He always thought his parents were only having the picture taken because that was what was expected. They weren't even touching him and Emma, not like in other families' photos he had seen where the parents had their arms around their children. His mother and father were distant in the image, just like in real life. And then, one day, they just weren't there anymore, and he and Emma had been forced into foster care.

Camden slammed the book shut and put it back under the bed. He curled up under the covers in the fetal position, put his thumb in his mouth, and went to sleep.

Thursday, June 25, 2009

Jack was up early. "You want to come down to the station with me, Toby?" he asked as he filled Toby's food dish. Toby looked up at Jack and meowed. "*Of course I want to come; what a dumb question.*"

When they arrived at the station, they walked straight through to Bryce's office. "Hey there, you look like a man who has some valuable information for me," Bryce greeted them.

Jack sat down and Toby jumped up onto the desk. "Hello there, old man," Bryce scratched behind Toby's ears.

"*Even he's calling me an old man now—I'll old man these two—well, I guess I can tolerate it since he's scratching behind my ears.*" Toby arched up, absorbing every stroke.

"I went to see the sister and brother-in-law of Brianna Gates last night," Jack began. "Brianna was visiting her sister on the Friday night; shortly after supper she developed stomach cramps and felt feverish. The next morning she called her sister and asked her to come and take her to the hospital. By the time Caitlin arrived, Brianna was already dead.

"Now, here's the thing: Caitlin said the apartment was a mess. There were several areas where Brianna had thrown up, and the sister said the inside of the toilet wasn't too pretty either. Said her sister's clothing was sopping wet. Unfortunately, Caitlin cleaned everything up before the ambulance arrived. I guess she was embarrassed for her sister; she mentioned Brianna was very tidy. She also said her sister must have been exceedingly sick because she barely ever asked for help.

"Caitlin's husband, Mitch, mentioned he had suggested to his wife, after reading about Tyler in the paper, that maybe they should have Brianna's body autopsied. Caitlin wouldn't hear of it. I mentioned—if it was necessary—we might ask if we could exhume her body."

"Good work, Jack." Bryce reclined back in his chair and folded his hands behind his head. "With this information and with what the Emergency nurse told you, we are either dealing with a horrific flu or, worse yet—and this is between us at the moment—a possible serial killer. Too many coincidences. Lauren's autopsy should be finished in a couple of days, and I'm going to call the coroner and see what is happening with Tyler's.

"I hate to keep leaning on you, Jack, but I was wondering if you could contact the family of the third girl, Emily Foster. Explain what is going on and that we would like to autopsy her body." He paused. "Do you think Caitlin will agree to let us exhume her sister?"

"I'm not sure if she will, but I think her husband will convince her it's the right thing to do," Jack answered. "I'll give them a call later when I know he will be there."

Bryce stood and extended his hand to Jack. "I can't thank you enough for helping out here." They started to walk to the door.

Toby jumped down from the desk. *"Hey guys, don't forget me! Feed me the facts and I'll get you the perpetrator. This afternoon I'm going to follow up on a couple of my own leads. I have a hunch who it might be, just need to connect the dots!"*

"I'll call you as soon as I have something solid on the two autopsies, or if our tech guy finds something on Lauren's computer," Bryce said as he opened the door for Jack and Toby. "See you later, Toby," he reached down and patted Toby on the head.

"You bet. You work your leads; I'll work mine!" Toby trotted out through the desks and was enthralled by the number of, "hey Toby", and "how's it goin', Toby" that he got. *"Boy, it's great to be a celebrity!"*

Jack had some stuff to look after during the afternoon, so Toby was free to do as he wanted. He decided to pay Emma a visit. He had to figure out a way to get her to talk about the plant Camden was so interested in. Toby headed over to Emma's after Jack left. She was sitting in the backyard reading a book. Duke was lying beside her. As soon as Duke sensed Toby's presence he stood and started barking. Emma looked over and noticed Toby pacing along the fence.

"Toby, hang on," she called over. She got up from her chair and patted her leg. "Come on Duke, in the house." Duke followed her, and she locked him in the kitchen. Toby snuck through the fence and was sitting in the three-season room when Emma turned around. "My you are a quick kitty for your age," she giggled.

Toby could hear Duke whining through the closed door. He gazed admiringly at Emma. *"Good to see you so happy."* Toby walked around amongst the plants until he came to the one Camden had picked the seeds from. He jumped up on a nearby stool and stretched his head out toward the leaves. He was just about to take a bite of one of the seeds when Emma hollered.

"No, Toby! You mustn't eat that seed. It's poison!"

"So that's what it is! Poison. Why would Camden want poison and what was he doing with it? I wonder now, even more than before, if these mysterious deaths are tied to him. If so, how? What's the connection?" Toby sat back on the chair, meowed, and stared at Emma.

As though Emma understood that Toby wanted to know more about the plant, she went into an explanation. "This is a castor bean plant from which they make castor oil. The oil is found in the seeds and has a lot of good uses, like lubricants for machinery and auto engines, paints' inks, soaps' waxes, cosmetics, candles, and crayons, just to name a few. I read in one place that they found evidence of its use in the Egyptian tombs where it was used for medicinal purposes as a purgative/laxative.

"However, if one takes too much of the oil it can result in poisoning. A lot of medical professionals feel the oil was dangerously used in a lot of folk remedies. There are some extremely toxic components of the castor beans, one of these being ricin, which is found in abundance in the seed and in smaller amounts in the rest of the plant. If you were to have chewed on that seed, you would have died, Toby. You must be careful and not eat any plant if you don't know what it is." Emma stroked Toby's back, and he rounded up to absorb her love.

"Well now that I know it's poison, I just have to figure out what Camden is doing with it." Toby jumped down from the stool and went to the door.

"Leaving so soon, Toby?" Emma asked. "I guess maybe you need a rest after that scare; I'm sorry if I yelled at you. There you go, come again; I do enjoy your visits."

Toby laid out on his back step taking in a little sun. He was worried about Emma. What if Camden was trying to poison her? He seemed devoted to his sister, but maybe he was becoming tired of looking after her; maybe he wanted a life of his own and the only way to have that was to get rid of her.

"I have to find out what he's doing with that powder, so I'm going to have to find a way to watch him, not only at home, but at his workplace too!" Toby decided to take a jaunt to the gym and see what kind of windows they had on the building, ones accessible for an old cat like him.

~

Camden was having another rough day at work. His head was pounding, and one of the clients had been extremely ill-mannered to him that morning. It was not the first time this guy had been rude to him, and Camden already had him selected for his next victim. Camden had been emptying one of the garbage cans Graham had forgotten the night before; he accidently dropped the bag, and the papers spilled on the floor.

As he was picking them up, he heard a voice say: "What a klutz! How could the gym hire someone like that?" The guy laughed. He was working out beside another fellow, who just shrugged his shoulders and kept pumping iron.

Camden looked up and saw Owen Bains. A couple of days before, Owen had been laughing with Vincent while they pointed at him. When he'd asked Vincent later what it had been about, Vincent had just grinned and asked

Camden what it mattered, it was no big deal. Owen was a fair-sized guy; Camden thought he would probably need a larger quantity of powder in Owen's drink. Life was closing in and it was time to try and get things wrapped up. Tonight, he would send out the first email to Owen.

~

Bryce had given Jack the phone number for Emily Foster's boyfriend, Chris. Jack gave him a call, hoping Chris would be available to talk. The phone answered on the second ring.

"Hey."

"Is this Chris Carmichael?"

"Yeah."

Jack identified who he was and asked Chris if there was a time they could get together and discuss what had happened to Emily. Chris wasn't too receptive.

"I don't want to talk about Emily right now," he answered.

Jack could hear the sadness in the young man's voice. He knew he would need to tread carefully. "We are concerned there may be more going on here than just the flu; there have been three other young adults who have passed away with similar symptoms to Emily's. I really would like to talk to you."

"Well, where are you right now?"

"I'm on the Gretzky Parkway, headed toward the mall; where are you?"

"I actually live close to the mall; how say we meet in the food court? No, wait, why don't we meet at Montana's––quieter this time of day and I'm not up to being around a lot of people just yet."

"I'll be there in five minutes; I'll be the old man waiting at the door for you." Jack thought to try and cheer the young fellow up.

"I'll be the young man who will look like he hasn't slept in two weeks." The phone disconnected.

Jack felt sick when he saw Chris coming toward the door of the restaurant. The young man had not been kidding; he looked like death warmed over—twice. The loss of his fiancée must have been an enormous blow to him. Hopefully this conversation wouldn't upset him too much more than he already was. As Chris walked through the door, Jack pointed at a booth in the corner.

"Would you like a drink, Chris?" Jack asked as they sat down.

"Just water will be fine."

Jack waved to the waitress. "Could we have a coffee and an ice water please?"

There was a moment of awkward silence before Chris opened the conversation. "So what would you like to know, Officer Nelson?"

"Call me Jack, please. What I need to know is exactly what Emily's symptoms were?"

Chris filled Jack in on what happened. "She called me around twelve-thirty. She was already really unwell; she was so weak she could barely walk. I drove her to the hospital, and the nurse who helped us was really nice—I think her name was Karen. Anyway, she got us some help right away, and Emily was hooked up to an intravenous. The intravenous finished in the middle of the night and she seemed to be slightly improved. The doctor said it just looked like a touch of the flu, possibly aggravated by something Emily might have eaten, so he told me to take her home. If she got worse, I was to bring her back.

"I decided to stay with her, just in case. It was a good thing I did, even though it didn't make any difference in the end. At least she didn't die alone. When we returned to the hospital, one of the nurses recognized us and put us through immediately. A Doctor Campbell was in attendance. Emily was so sick, officer. They shooed me out of the room and then I heard Code Red blasting out, and there was a cart being raced to where my Emily was. I tried to get to her! They had these paddles … and they were putting them on her chest … and she was convulsing and

... and..." Chris put his head down on the table and his shoulders started to shake.

Jack gave him a few minutes to settle down before he asked his next question. "Did Emily say anything to you about receiving a nasty email?"

Chris glanced up, a puzzled look on his face. "No, I don't think so. Not that I remember. I'd been away for a few days on business and had just gotten back. I gave her an engagement ring on Saturday; we were going to be married in September." He paused. "Is there anything else you need to know? I have to be somewhere."

Jack knew Chris didn't really have to be anywhere; he just needed to get out of there. "There is one thing ... who would we contact if we needed to have an autopsy done on Emily?"

Chris's face went white. "She's already buried," he choked.

"We would be asking permission to exhume her body. Three other people have died in the past month—all with similar symptoms."

"Are you saying someone might have killed Emily and these others?" Chris's eyes opened wide.

"We are not sure of anything just yet. We're hoping that maybe it is just a virus and if we are able to find out what it is, we can deal with it before it spreads. However, at this point, we are not ruling out foul play. One of the deceased received two very nasty emails."

"I see. I'll check Emily's email for you and give you a call if she did." Chris stood. "I gotta go." He pulled a piece of paper from his pocket and wrote a number on it. "This is my cell. If you need to talk to someone about exhuming her body, I guess that would be me. She hasn't seen her parents in years. I'm usually not home; you were lucky to catch me today." Chris handed the paper to Jack and left.

Jack sat quietly and finished his coffee. This was looking more and more like the work of a serial killer. But the question was: how were all the victims connected? There seemed to be no association at all. He paid the waitress for his coffee and left, heading for the police station to talk to Bryce. Jack hoped there would be some news on at least one of the two autopsies.

When Jack walked into Bryce's office, he knew right away there was an update. Bryce's face was creased with severe lines. "Close the door, Jack, and have a seat." He waited for Jack to sit down. "The autopsy report came back on Lauren, and it appears there was some kind of a poisonous substance in her system. The coroner does not think it is arsenic and he is going to be running further tests." He paused. "What did you find out?"

"I talked to Emily Foster's fiancé. He described symptoms exactly like the other three deceased. I've a bad feeling here, Bryce. I don't think we are dealing with the flu or food poisoning. I believe we have a serial killer out there—just a gut feeling. I asked the young man if Emily had received any nasty emails. He said she hadn't mentioned any, but he's going to check her computer and get back to me if she did. Anything from Lauren's yet?"

"No. The tech can't find anything. Whoever sent these emails is good." Bryce stood and walked over to his window. He stared out it for a few minutes. Jack let him be, knowing Bryce was thinking what the next best move would be. Finally he turned around. "We need to exhume the bodies of Emily and Brianna, and if we find the same traces of whatever poison this turns out to be, I am going to treat this as a murder case. I will probably call in an old friend of mine, Tessa Bannister, to help us out with profiling. We go back a long way, and I have used her before—she's good. I would like you to work with her. You have a nose for these kinds of things, too."

Jack scratched his head. He was being pulled in deeper than he wanted to be. "I don't know…"

"I need you, Jack." The tone of Bryce's voice was pleading for Jack not to say no.

"Okay … just let me know what you require."

Bryce asked Jack to talk to Chris and Caitlin about getting permission to exhume the bodies of their loved ones. He also asked if Jack would ask Caitlin about any strange emails her sister might have mentioned, and could he call Tyler's mum and ask if Tyler had revealed anything about the same. Jack left the office with several tasks to accomplish.

~

Camden couldn't wait to send his email to Owen. He raced up to his room when he arrived home, without saying hello to Emma. She was in the three-season room with Duke. He turned his computer on and pulled up the email, changed the name to Owen, and pushed send. Task finished, Camden headed downstairs, smiling.

~

Owen Bains left the gym in a hurry. He grabbed a banana smoothie for his supper because he had a house to show in half an hour and had forgotten his briefcase at the office. The guy at the drink counter—Camden—had looked at him weirdly so Owen hadn't bothered to leave him a tip. He seemed a bit of a creep lately; Owen had noticed Camden watching him several times, always with a disturbing look on his face.

Work had been lean for a few months. He guessed he had gotten into the real estate business at the wrong time—just as the economy had come crashing down. Thank goodness for his brother, Kevin, who had loaned him some money to keep him going until things picked up. Owen hoped tonight's showing would yield him a good sized commission. It was a big house with a substantial price tag. He pulled up to his office and ran in.

"Left my briefcase in my office," he explained to the receptionist.

She smiled. Owen was so forgetful, she didn't think he was actually going to make it in this business. Nevertheless, he was cute, and she wouldn't mind if he asked her out sometime. So far he hadn't taken her up on any of her clues. As he raced back out the door, she called out: "Good luck, Owen. See you soon—with a contract!"

"Sure thing, sweetheart."

Things didn't go quite as well as Owen hoped, but he was going to write up an offer. The couple lowballed the price and Owen knew the vendor would not accept it. That meant going back and forth, probably a few times before the deal closed—if it closed at all.

When he got back to the office to type up the offer, the receptionist smiled. "Any luck, Owen?"

"Probably not. The offer is extremely low, but it's our job to type them up and send them back and forth until we have a deal."

"Need help?"

"Nah, I have it."

When Owen was finished, he headed for home. He decided to take the offer to his client in the morning. He threw his keys on the coffee table and then went over and turned his computer on to check his emails, hoping there would be one there from Diana. It had been three months since she had spoken to him.

Owen glanced down the page and saw 'JUST FOR YOU' in the subject line. He didn't recognize the sender, but the title made him curious. He clicked on it. "What the frig!" he shouted as he read the email. *"Dear Owen: you are receiving this email because you have been very, very naughty. Do you know what happens to very naughty people? Think about it! When was the last time you ridiculed someone ... ignored someone just because ... blamed someone wrongfully? When was the last time you were nice to someone ... really nice? When was the last time you helped someone ... really helped? You are so pathetically naughty that I can't stand it! Only you can turn this around and do something about it. I have given you the warning ... now it is up to you to seek reconciliation. If you don't, maybe retribution will come your way ... if you have any friends who are just like you, pass this on to them so they can get help too ... for every friend you try to save the retribution on yourself will be lessened ... you know the drill ... six to ten, maybe you won't die ... one to five, you will ... signed: 666."*

Owen sent the email to his junk box, scanned to see if there was anything from Diana, and finding nothing, he shut the computer off and headed to bed. "Sick prick," he grumbled, "wasting valuable network space."

~

Camden checked his computer before heading off to bed. He stretched back in his chair and smiled when he saw Owen had opened his email. When he crawled under the covers, he spread out the full length of the bed before curling into the fetal position and going to sleep.

~

Toby was still thinking about what he had learned earlier that day. He was trying to figure out how he was going to tell Jack what he thought was going on. Jack had told him how the captain wanted him to help out on the case—that they both had the feeling there was a serial killer out there. Toby fully agreed, and he had a good idea who it was.

Friday, June 26, 2009

Jack received a phone call from Bryce early in the morning. The autopsy on Tyler had come in, and the coroner had found traces of the same type of poison in his body as he'd found in Lauren's.

"We need to move fast on this, Jack," Bryce said. "It's essential now to get the other families' permissions to exhume the bodies as soon as possible. Whoever is doing this is a sick person!"

"I'll get right on it," Jack stated.

Jack headed home, and when he got there, he retrieved the piece of paper Chris had given him and dialled his cell number. He got the call answer: "Hey, this is Chris ... leave me a message ... I might get back to you." Jack left his name and number and told Chris it was imperative he return his call as soon as possible.

Then Jack called Caitlin. He was hoping he would have been able to wait until Mitch was home. Caitlin answered on the sixth ring. It sounded like a child was crying nearby.

"Hello."

"Hi Caitlin, Detective Nelson here. Do you have a minute?"

"Sure ... Jimmy, come and get your brother for me! What would you like, detective?"

"We would like permission to exhume Brianna's body. We need to do an autopsy."

There was silence on the other end of the phone.

"It's important, Caitlin. We think someone is actually poisoning people. We may even be dealing with a serial killer!"

"My God," she breathed.

"I need to ask you another question ... did Brianna say anything about getting a nasty email or maybe even two of them?"

"No, she didn't mention anything like that. The only thing we talked about on the Friday night was that she had met some really nice guy at the gym. She didn't tell me his name, though."

"Do you have access to her computer?"

"Yes, it's still at her place. It might be password protected, though."

"Well, could you or Mitch check her emails for me? If she did have it password protected, I would like to pick up the computer and have one of our tech guys down at the station get into it. Would that be okay?

"I guess so."

"About the exhuming?" Jack asked again.

"Sure ... I guess. If she was murdered, I want to see the killer brought to justice. Do I have to sign any papers?"

"Yes, I'll bring them by this morning. What time's good for you?"

"Any time is as good as any." She hung up.

Jack let out a sigh. He looked at the phone almost willing it to ring. He needed to hear from Chris. He walked into the kitchen and poured another cup of coffee. Toby was sitting in his usual spot on the back of the couch. As Jack took his first sip, the phone rang. Toby's ears perked forward.

"Hello."

"Hi, this is Chris. How can I help you?"

"We need to do an autopsy on Emily's body; we need your permission."

"I don't know ... actually, I don't really think so. I don't want her body all cut up."

Jack was desperate. He hated having to tell all these people there might be a serial killer out there, but there was no other way. "We might have someone out there who is randomly targeting people. There was poison found in the bodies of two of the deceased. We need to see if the same traces are present in Emily. I already have the permission of the fourth person's relatives."

There was a clicking sound on the line. Chris was clicking a ballpoint pen. Finally, "Okay. Bring me the paperwork." Chris rambled off his address.

"One more thing, Chris—did you find anything on Emily's computer?"

"No, not that I could see, anyway."

"Would it be possible for me to pick up the computer and take it down to the station? I would like one of our techs to take a look at it."

"Yeah, I guess."

Jack called to Toby, "Want to come with me this morning, old man? I have to go to the station to pick up the forms for these guys to sign. Then I have to get them signed and back to Bryce so he can get the orders going for the exhuming."

Toby was ready and willing to go. The more he stayed involved in the investigation, the better off he would be when trying to figure out what was going on. In the meantime, he might find a way to get his suspicions across to Jack. He stopped by his dish on the way out, just for a snack. A first-class detective needed to keep up his strength.

~

Owen presented the offer to his clients at ten in the morning. As he suspected, they laughed at the price. He tried to explain to them that he had told the couple they were too low, but Owen could tell his clients were far from impressed. They wrote it back at full price, stating that would send a message to these people. Owen knew the couple would not be able to meet the price. He was aware that they badly wanted the house, but one could only have what one could afford. Owen, of all people, knew that.

He went back to the office and retyped the offer. The receptionist made eyes at him. Didn't she know he wasn't interested? He totally ignored her advances. He rushed past her and into his office. Later that morning, he managed to get hold of the couple who wanted the house.

They were devastated and said they couldn't afford any more than they'd offered and not to even bother with the papers. Owen called his clients and told them there was no counter-offer. Then he shredded the papers and drove to a local bar for a drink, and, maybe, a bite to eat.

~

Camden mentioned to Emma, before heading off to work, they might have to move again. It was not going as well at the gym as he had hoped. He had already started to look in the papers for another job. Isabella had been giving him a hard time and clients were picking on him and blaming him for things he wasn't doing. Camden told her that he hoped she wasn't too upset, but he could tell from the tears hidden in the corners of her eyes, she was.

"I thought you said it would be different here. I'm so tired of moving, Cam."

"I thought it would be different too, Em. I can't help it how people are."

"Other people don't seem to have the same problems we do," Emma stated matter-of-factly.

Camden's face clouded over. "What you meant to say is that other people don't have the same problems *I* do—isn't that right, Emma?"

Emma looked into her brother's eyes. She didn't like what she saw, and it scared her. She tried to adjust her position. "No, Cam, I meant us." She gazed down to the floor.

Camden's hand took hold of Emma's chin, and he lifted her face. His eyes were piercing. Insane. Emma was shaking. "Don't be afraid of me, Emma. I would never hurt you. I live for you. I live to protect you from the kind of people that I have to work with day after day. I do that because I am strong and you are not. You must understand that, Emma. You would never survive out there. People would eat you alive and then spit you out! You're my soul-mate, Emma—my twin. We would be nothing without each other." He paused, his eyes becoming more intense as

155

anger started to creep into his words. "I thought you appreciated everything I do for you!"

"I … I … do, Cam, I do." Emma backed away from her brother. "It's just that I am so tired of moving and, this time, it's happened so fast. If that Isabella person is giving you a hard time, why don't you talk to the man who hired you—Mr. Rawlings?"

"He won't listen to me, not if Isabella has anything to say about it. And she has all the others on her side. Paige hardly acknowledges me anymore, and the rest of the employees think I'm some sort of a creep. Only one who's half decent to me is Graham, and even he's been weird lately. You don't want me to endure that kind of treatment day after day, do you—just so you can stay living here?"

"No, I guess not." Emma felt weak. She walked over to the couch and sat down. "When will we have to move?"

"I only said that we might have to move," Camden reminded her. "I'm doing my best to make it work." Camden's face softened. "Right now, I better get to work, so I'm not late. That would just give Isabella more ammunition against me."

Emma finally allowed the tears to flow.

"Please don't cry, Em. I'll do whatever I can to stay here." With that statement, Camden headed out the door. He hated lying to his twin, but he had been doing it now for so long. His thoughts turned to Owen; Camden hoped he showed up today because he had a special surprise for him.

~

Jack drove to the station to pick up the forms he needed for Chris and Caitlin to sign. When he arrived at Chris', he noticed all the curtains were drawn. It was a beautiful, sunny day. Chris answered the door and reached for the paper. "Where do I sign?" he slurred.

Jack pointed to the spot. "Do you want to read it first?"

"I should be able to trust you, shouldn't I? You said this was just to give permission to dig up her body and discover the real reason she died, right?" Chris scribbled his signature and handed the paper back to Jack.

Jack thanked him and started to leave. "Oh, by the way," he said, turning around; "do you have Emily's computer?"

"Not here. I'll drop it by the police station later." Chris shut the door.

"Poor young fellow," Jack said to Toby when he got in the van. "He's been drowning his pain in a bottle."

From Chris' place, Jack drove over to Caitlin's. It was a different scene there, with three young boys terrorizing the living room, but the pain on Caitlin's face was the same as the pain on Chris'. She signed the paper for Jack, and, like Chris, she didn't bother to read it. Jack asked her about the computer.

"Mitch went over last night and checked her inbox. There was nothing."

"Would you be willing to let one of our tech guys look at it anyway?" Jack asked. "I know I said if you needed a password, but I really think it might be a good idea to have a deeper look."

"I'll get Mitch to drop it off." Caitlin turned as one of the boys started screaming. "Sorry, Officer Nelson, I need to attend to my children."

Jack drove to the station and went straight to Bryce's office. Toby followed close on his heels. A woman was sitting in front of Bryce's desk, looking over a pile of papers. Bryce looked up and smiled.

"Jack, I want you to meet Tessa Banister. She is the profiler I was telling you about. Tessa, this is Jack Nelson. I've brought him out of retirement to work on this case with us. He has been doing a little leg work for me already. And," Bryce pointed to Toby, who was sitting patiently beside Jack, "this is Toby. Toby is a decorated police investigator—helped us solve a crime a few months ago."

"What you should be saying, Bryce, is that if it weren't for me, you guys would not have solved the crime!"

Bryce continued, "With Tyler Acton's autopsy results showing traces of the same substance in him as what we found in Lauren, I didn't want to wait any longer to call in Tessa." Bryce saw the papers in Jack's hand. "Those the permission slips?"

"Yep," Jack replied as he handed them over. "Anything on Lauren's computer?"

"Nope; how about the others? Did they find any nasty emails?"

"No, but I asked for access to the computers anyway. They should both be dropping them off here at the station."

"Good. Sometimes people delete their junk mail or block the sender so it won't show up," Tessa mentioned. "There is a possibility these other people did not even open the emails if they didn't recognize the sender. Especially since none of them mentioned anything to anyone about a nasty email."

"I still have to talk to Tyler's mum," Jack mentioned.

"Good, get back to me as soon as you do," Bryce instructed.

Tessa knelt down and patted Toby on the head. "So, you're a celebrity, are you, Toby?"

Toby liked the feel of her hand. He gazed into her eyes. They were a nice, warm, brown. She had a pleasant smile too. "*I think I'm going to enjoy working with this lady. Might not be bad company for Jack either; he does spend a lot of time alone, except for me, of course. Maybe it's time I allowed him a bit of space.*" Toby purred loudly to let Tessa know how much he liked her.

Jack started to laugh. "Well, Tessa, you have passed the first test—Toby likes you." Bryce and Tessa joined in the laughter. "Come on, Toby, we have work to do. Let's go pay Mrs. Acton a visit." He paused in the doorway. "I'll see if I can get any other information out of her while I'm there."

~

Owen sat in the bar drinking for three hours. The only person left after the first couple of hours was an elderly gentleman; Owen latched onto him, telling him his life story.

"Mind if I sit with you?" Owen slurred. Not waiting for an answer, he pulled up a chair and sat down.

"Not at all, son."

"I've got big problems," Owen began. "Have you ever been through times when nothin' seems to go right?"

"A few times over my seventy-five years."

"Well, for the past six months—since Diana left me——nothin's gone right. I got no money, I got no home, I probably won't even have a job for long. To tell you the truth, it's probably only 'cause I work on commission that I'm still there. Sell a house—get paid. If I don't sell the house, some other agent will."

"You were married to this Diana?" the old man queried.

"Should've been. That way she wouldn't've been able to walk away so quickly."

"Why'd she leave?"

"Beats me."

"Has to be a reason. Women don't just up and leave a good man."

"Well," Owen took a gulp of his beer, followed by a sip of whiskey. "She claimed I was out too much—never home. I had to be; it was my job. Real estate's a dog-eat-dog business. When I lost my sales job—I used to sell industrial tools—I decided to take real estate courses. Oh, she was all for that, thinking we'd be rollin' in the dough.

"But then the market crashed and I couldn't sell anything. Girlfriend was workin' two jobs tryin' to make ends meet ... said I wasn't supportin' the household enough. I should've been cookin' and doin' the cleanin' ... I wasn't doin' anything else. She didn't understand ... I had to be out there tryin' to sell houses, even if I didn't sell one. If the broker thought I wasn't tryin', I could've been let go."

The old man looked at Owen. "So you must have tried really hard then ... worked 24-7 did you, son?"

Owen tilted his head.

"Don't get me wrong, son, I believe you probably did try hard to make your new career go well, but you must have been having a little fun on the side too. And the little lady got tired of paying for it, right?" The old man thrust his face closer to Owen.

Owen backed away. The old fellow had a point. That is what Diana had accused him of. But he had made up excuses, telling her he was trying to do customer relations and build a clientele. You never knew when someone you met would be selling their house, or just wanting to buy one. He emptied his beer glass and called the bartender for another.

"Don't you think you've had enough, son?" the old fellow mentioned carefully.

"Just one more."

Owen spent the next half an hour pouring out more of his problems and in the process polished off another beer and another shot of whiskey.

Finally the old man said he had to get going. His wife would be wondering where he was. "Take care, son, and don't be so hard on yourself. Things will work out if you work at them."

Owen watched the old man leave. "What's he know about hard times?" he grumbled as he downed the last few drops of beer. He looked at his watch and thought to go to the gym for a workout before heading home. He stumbled and almost fell as he left the bar.

~

There was a note on Mrs. Acton's front door directing visitors to use the side door. Jack knocked loudly; there was no doorbell. A lady, who looked to be in her early sixties, greeted him. Jack flashed his identification. "May I have a moment of your time?" he asked.

"Is this about my son?"

"Yes, ma'am, it is."

"Come in." She showed him into the small kitchen and directed him to one of the chairs at the table. "Would you like tea or coffee?"

"Coffee would be nice, thank you."

As Mrs. Acton was filling her kettle, she glanced out the window and noticed Toby sitting in the van. "Is that your cat in the van?"

"Yes, that's Toby."

"Well, bring him in. He doesn't look too happy sitting out there all alone."

"He's okay. Toby is used to waiting for me."

"Bring him in. I love cats. My Whiskers passed on to kitty-heaven about a month ago ... I haven't had the heart to replace him yet. I have some cat treats in the cupboard that I am sure your Toby might enjoy."

"I'm sure he would," Jack grinned as he got up to go and get Toby. There was no sense arguing with a woman who loved cats.

Toby was thrilled. Mrs. Acton put the treats in a little dish for him and poured him a saucer of milk. She poured Jack's coffee and then sat down at the table. "So, what can I do for you?"

"Did Tyler have a computer?"

"All young people have those things nowadays. He was always on it. That's why he didn't call me as much as he should have."

Jack smiled. "Did he tell you about receiving any unusual emails?"

"Not a word."

"Would it be possible to get into his computer and check it out? We would make sure you got it back."

"Oh, I gave it to his friend, Jason. It was just one of those laptop things." Mrs. Acton got up from the table. "Jason has been so good to me since Tyler died. He was with him that night at the pool hall, you know." She walked over to her phone and came back with a piece of paper. "Here's Jason's number if you want to call him."

"Thank you, Mrs. Acton." Jack took the piece of paper and put it in his shirt pocket. Toby was sitting beside

Mrs. Acton's chair. "You sure have made a friend there. Your treats must be more delicious than the ones I give him," Jack smiled.

"You don't give me treats—at least not tasty ones in special little packages!" Toby scowled at Jack.

Mrs. Acton sat down again. "The coroner called me earlier today. I have to go and see him this afternoon. He wants to tell me in person what he found out. I knew it wasn't just the flu or food poisoning. And now you're here asking questions; can't you tell me what's going on?"

Jack took a deep breath: "Three other young people have died of the same symptoms Tyler had. One of them, who was in touch with us because of a couple of nasty emails, and who had been found dead at the bottom of her stairs, was autopsied as well. The coroner found traces of poison in her, but as of yet, he hasn't figured out what kind, only that it is not arsenic. We have ordered autopsies on the other two bodies. I am investigating to see if any of the others, including your son, received the same kind of emails. So far we don't have a connection between any of the victims." Jack paused. "Would Tyler have mentioned any of these names to you: Brianna Gates, Emily Foster, or Lauren Dagnell?"

Mrs. Acton shook her head. "No, can't recollect. He went out with a Veronica a few months ago, but that didn't last long. My Tyler was a bit of a wild thing, especially after his dad died, but he was settling down. He was working at my brother-in-law's machine shop; George had just offered Tyler an apprenticeship, and I am sure he was going to take it."

"Okay," Jack stood. "Toby and I have to leave now. I'll be in touch. Thanks for Jason's number." Jack bent down and scooped up Toby.

Mrs. Acton went to her cupboard and returned with a packet of cat treats. "Here you go, Toby; you may as well have these."

Jack put them in his pocket and thanked her. Toby looked at Mrs. Acton adoringly and meowed a thank you.

Mrs. Acton stood at the kitchen window until the van was on the street.

"Lonely old woman," Jack commented.

"Yeah, but she sure knows how to buy treats for cats—not like someone I know!" Toby moved closer to the window and stared out at the passing houses.

Jack pulled over to the side of the road and took out his cellphone to call Jason. There was no answer. "Guess we may as well go home, old man, and maybe have a snooze. I'm not used to working so much."

Toby's tail swished, and he continued to stare out the window. He was deep in thought about what had transpired so far today.

~

Owen knew he shouldn't be driving, but he did anyway. Three hours of drinking without any food in his stomach was not the smartest thing to do, but he had done it before.

"Hey there, Paige, lovely lady of the jungle gym," he hollered out as he entered the facility.

Paige giggled until Owen came over and propped himself up on the counter. He reeked of alcohol. "What have you been up to, Owen? Had a few too many? It might be better if you didn't work out this afternoon. We wouldn't want you to get hurt now." Paige's tone turned serious.

Camden finished serving a customer at the drink counter and, hearing the commotion, came around to help Paige. "What's going on here?" he asked.

Owen looked at Camden. "None of your beeswax, bud! Butt out. This is between the lady here and me."

"You are drunk, sir. I think you should leave—now," Camden stated stiffly, emphasizing the word *now*.

"And if I don't?" Owen just about fell.

At that moment, Vincent and Nolan came up to the front. "Is there a problem here?" Vincent asked.

Their intervention seemed to settle Owen down. He backed up from the counter, put his hands up and

163

apologized. "I had a terrible day, guys. I'm so sorry. I'll leave."

"Maybe you should take a cab," Nolan suggested.

Owen waved his hand at them. "I'll be fine."

Camden was seething. Owen had treated him like a piece of crap. How dare he! He would find out soon enough! He wouldn't get away with treating people like that for much longer—his time was up. Camden went back to the drink counter.

Later that night, before going to bed, Camden sent Owen another email. He checked the baggie with the powder in it to make sure there was going to be enough to do the job quickly.

Monday, June 29, 2009

The weekend passed relatively quietly. Jack talked to Tyler's friend, Jason, and Jason gave him Tyler's laptop. However, there was a password on Tyler's email account so Jack couldn't access it. He would have to take it to the station Monday morning.

Jack learned from Jason that Tyler had been in a fantastic mood before he ate the chicken wings and downed a couple of beers—said Tyler had met a girl at the gym but hadn't told Jason her name. He had laughed and told Jack that Tyler hadn't even gotten the girl's phone number. When Jack asked him if he knew what gym Tyler was going to, he said Tyler hadn't told him.

When Jack came home from seeing Jason, he started going over some of his notes. Suddenly he sat forward in his chair. He had just thought of a possible connection. Caitlin had said Brianna had met some really nice guy at the gym. Jack made a note of this. He would tell Bryce and Tessa first thing Monday morning. They had both mentioned they were going to be out of town on the weekend.

~

Camden had Sunday off. He had been upset when Owen hadn't shown up on Saturday but figured he was probably hung over. Camden stopped by Jack's on Sunday for a couple of hours. Toby disappeared over to visit Emma. She looked sombre and nothing Toby did could cheer her up.

Monday looked like it was going to be a gloomy day. The rain clouds hung low in the sky. Emma was happy because she had told Camden on the weekend that the flowerbeds needed a good rain. They hadn't talked about the possible move on the weekend, but the cloud of it had hung over the house.

Camden packed his own lunch Monday morning; Emma was not up yet. He was worried she was falling back into a depression and it was his fault. But he would deal with it like he always did. She would come around like she always did.

~

Jack and Toby headed to the station early Monday morning. Jack had Tyler's computer, and he hoped the other two had been dropped off by now. "Morning, Bryce," he greeted as he walked into the office.

"Morning. Tessa will be right back." Bryce pulled a couple of papers from a pile on his desk. "I pulled some strings ... the other two autopsies were finished over the weekend. They found the same thing: traces of poison in their systems. The coroner is baffled and still running tests to discover what kind. Whatever it is, it sure works quickly. It seems that each one of the victims—I am calling them victims now—were healthy right up to within twenty-four hours of becoming ill." He paused. "Did you find out anything on the weekend?"

"Yeah. I talked to Tyler's mum. She gave Tyler's computer to his friend, Jason. I picked it up from him. Tyler had a password on his email, so we'll have to send it down to the I.T. department to crack it."

"Good work ... hi, Tessa," Bryce welcomed Tessa back, then added, "The other two computers were dropped off Saturday."

Jack continued: "Now Tessa is here, I did find out something that might be of interest to the case. Tyler's friend mentioned Tyler had been ecstatic that night—said he had met a girl at the gym. When I got home I went over my notes, and there it was, right in front of me: Caitlin had told me her sister had been excited about meeting a nice guy at the gym. I didn't think at the time to ask her what gym, but I'll give her a call later to see if she knows the name."

"That is excellent news, Jack," Tessa commented. "At least, we have something to go on now. Let's see if the others had any affiliation with a gym." Tessa sat down on the loveseat in the corner of Bryce's office—one of the perks of being a captain. Toby jumped up beside her and crawled onto her lap.

"*Jack, she's a looker ... invite her over for lunch ... you can go over the case with her ... come on, Jack ... just look at her!*"

"Toby, what are you doing? Get off Tessa's lap!" Jack looked embarrassed.

Tessa laughed and stroked Toby's back. He purred loudly and looked at Jack. "He's okay, Jack—really," she added to assure him.

They spent the next half hour discussing what they knew and some of their speculations. "Why don't we take the files and study them in one of the meeting rooms?" Bryce suggested. "That way we can spread out the papers and what pictures we have and try and make some sense of it all."

"Actually I have a few errands I must make this morning; would you mind going over these this afternoon?" Tessa asked, looking directly at Jack. She gathered the files and stuffed them in her briefcase.

Jack had no idea what came over him at that moment. A thought popped into his head and the words were exiting his mouth before he could stop them. "Unless you have a lunch date with someone, why don't we look at the files at my place when you're done your errands? I'll put together a bite to eat for us and then we can get to work. Maybe by then we'll have something more from the I.T. department on the emails from the other victims' computers." Jack ripped a piece of paper off his notepad and wrote his address on it. "Do you know where this is?" he asked, handing her the paper.

Tessa looked at the address. "Yes, I know exactly where you are. I don't have a luncheon date; it would be lovely if we had a bite to eat together." She reached over and gave Toby a scratch behind the ears.

Toby tilted his head. *"Oh, she has divine fingers! I could get used to them massaging me every night. How about it, Jack?"* Toby glanced up at Jack, purring loudly.

"See you guys later," Tessa said as she gave Toby a final pat.

~

Owen didn't have anything particular to do Monday morning. He'd had a rough weekend, sleeping most of Saturday, recuperating most of Sunday, and finally having his first decent meal in three days Monday morning. Owen decided to hit the gym before heading to the office; he needed to get back into a routine. Before leaving the apartment, he remembered he hadn't checked his emails over the weekend. Maybe Diana had a change of heart; he could only hope. He turned his computer on.

While it was firing up, he went into the bathroom and opened the drawer where he kept his pills. He popped one of the tranquillizers into his mouth: he'd been taking them since Diana left. When he returned to the living room, he clicked on his email. He had forgotten about the previous nasty one. He noticed one of the subject lines: 'ARE YOU LISTENING TO ME.' Owen clicked on it. *"Dear Owen: you are still being very, very naughty. I told you what happens to very naughty people. Did you think about it? Did you ridicule someone today ... ignore someone just because ... blame someone wrongfully? Were you nice to someone ... really nice? Did you help someone today, just because ... really help? I doubt you even gave my message a second thought. Oh, believe it ... you are so pathetically naughty that I can't stand it! You might still be able to turn this around and do something about it. I am being generous giving you another warning ... but it is still up to you to seek reconciliation. If you don't, retribution will come your way ... and don't forget all those selfish, naughty friends of yours who are just like you. Pass this on to them so they can get help too ... for every friend you try to save the retribution on yourself might be lessened ... you know the drill ... six to*

ten, maybe you won't die … one to five, you will … signed:
666."

Owen didn't have time for such nonsense. He sent
the email to the recycle bin and then emptied it. He
grabbed his bag and headed to the gym. Owen knew he
had to apologize to the employees there; he'd been a real
jerk the other day, especially to the guy who served the
drinks.

Camden was happy to see Owen come in shortly
after lunch. He greeted him with a nod of the head as he
passed by. Owen came up to the counter. "Hey man, sorry
about the other day; I'd had a terrible day. Hell, I've had a
bad few months. It wasn't right for me to take it out on you."

Camden was surprised at the apology. "That's okay,"
he replied. "I understand; we all have bad days once in a
while." He paused. "Would you like me to have a smoothie
ready for you when you finish your workout?" he asked.

Owen looked puzzled. "You'd do that for me?"

"Sure. I like to provide this service. I know how
thirsty you guys are after a vigorous workout."

"Well then, sure … let me think … make it a
strawberry/pineapple."

"No problem. Large?"

"Yeah, I didn't have lunch."

When Owen was finished his workout, Camden had
his smoothie waiting on the counter. Owen paid—no tip—
thanked him, and left. Camden smiled, not even bothered
by the fact that Owen hadn't tipped. He had only felt a
twinge of indecision when Owen had apologized so
sincerely, but the feeling had passed quickly.

Owen drove straight home. By the time he reached
his apartment the smoothie was finished. On his way in he
tossed the empty cup into the dumpster by the back door.

~

Tessa rang the doorbell at twelve-thirty. Toby raced to the
door, followed closely by Jack, who gave Toby a gentle

shove with his foot. "She can't get in, old man, if you don't move out of the way." Toby moved. Jack opened the door.

Tessa stepped inside and quickly scanned the living room. "How lovely," she commented. "Not exactly what I pictured."

Jack was puzzled. "What do you mean?"

"Well, it's pretty neat for a couple of old bachelors." They both laughed. Toby purred loudly.

"Let's have a bite to eat before we go over the files. Lunch is on the table." Jack pointed to the kitchen. "Lead the way, Toby."

They returned to the living room after lunch. Tessa pulled the files from her briefcase and laid them out on the coffee table. One by one she opened them. Jack came and sat down beside her; Toby jumped up and sat on the end of the coffee table. He wanted a cat's-eye view. The pictures of the four young people were heartbreaking to look at.

Tessa pointed to Tyler and Brianna first. "The only thing we know that these two have in common, other than the way they died, is they both belonged to a gym. She was a school teacher; he worked in a machine shop. She, according to her sister, was quite responsible; he, according to his mother, had a history of being irresponsible. She had her own house; he rented. I think we need to determine if the other two belonged to a gym, and then find out which ones. That's our strongest link, so far."

Jack mentioned that neither Tyler's mum nor Brianna's sister knew the name of the gym. He offered to call around and ask the different gyms in town if any of the victims were on their membership lists. "I actually know a young fellow who works for the one just down the street; I can start by asking him if he recognizes any of these names."

"Good." Tessa set her pencil down and pulled out her cellphone. "I'm going to call Bryce and see if they have been able to find out anything from the other computers." She stood and walked over to the window. "Looks like you have company, Jack." Tessa walked into the kitchen for privacy.

Jack opened the door before Camden could ring the bell. "I have a guest who saw you coming up the walkway," Jack explained when he saw the puzzled look on Camden's face.

"I was on my way home and thought to stop by. If you're busy, I could come another time."

"Oh, no; it's okay. I was actually just talking about you." Jack stepped aside and motioned for Camden to come in. "I was wondering if you would know any of these names as people who might attend your gym?" Jack said the names of the four victims as he and Camden made their way to the couch.

Camden furrowed his eyebrows as pain shot through his head. He shook his head slowly. "No, none of those names are familiar. I'll double-check tomorrow and give you a call." Camden was standing beside the coffee table. Toby stood, arched, and hissed at him.

"Whoa!" Camden jumped back. "What does your cat have against me, Jack?"

Jack shooed Toby off the coffee table. "Over to your couch, old man; you shouldn't be so rude to my guests." He turned to Camden. "Sorry about that; I don't know what gets into him sometimes."

"*I'll tell you what gets into me—people like him! Can't trust him—don't trust him, Jack. I know things. He's playing around with a poisonous plant. Don't believe him if he tells you these people aren't members of his gym; check the facts with someone else, Jack.*" Toby glared at Camden and then turned his back to him and stared out the window.

"You working on a case, Jack?" Camden pointed to the files. "These the people who've been in the news?"

Jack realized Camden shouldn't be looking at any of the information laid out on the coffee table. He quickly closed the files. "Sorry friend, you needn't see this stuff. And yes, we are working on that case."

Tessa walked into the room. Her eyes told Jack she had something important to tell him. Camden also noticed the look, and even though he would have loved to hear the information, he knew it wouldn't be divulged in front of him.

He headed over to the door. "Looks like you guys are busy; I'm going to go home." He saw himself out. Jack waited for the door to close and then turned and asked Tessa what she had found out.

"All of the other computers had the same emails on them, but like Lauren's, the I.P. address could not be traced. So we have another similarity connecting our victims." She reopened the files. "Was that your friend from the gym down the street?"

"Yeah ... said he didn't recognize any of the names but when he goes to work tomorrow, he'll double-check and give me a call."

"So we have two connections now, and the emails are definite confirmation we are dealing with a serial killer. But the victims are so random." She paused and pulled out her pencil. "Okay, let's see what else they have in common: they are all in their mid to late twenties. None of them was married, were they?" Tessa flipped through the papers.

"I believe Lauren was married but separated, and Emily had just gotten engaged," Jack informed.

Tessa continued. "Okay ... Emily was a nurse in a nursing home; she had little or no family around, but she did have a devoted fiancé. Lauren was a legal secretary, just went through a messy divorce, and was new in town." She tapped her pencil on the pad of paper. "Why three women and one guy? I could maybe squeeze out that all the women were in professional-type jobs, but Tyler doesn't fit in there with them."

Toby jumped down off the back of his couch and came over to Tessa. He sat looking up at her adoringly. *"How do I tell you there are going to be more victims? How do I show you guys what I know?"* Toby jumped up onto the arm of the chair she was sitting in. He rubbed his head on her shoulder and purred loudly. She reached over, absentmindedly, scratched behind his ears, and then returned to her profiling.

"Now we know all four victims received the same emails..." Tessa rustled through the papers in Lauren's file and pulled out copies of the ones sent to her ... "let's take a good look at this first one. The killer puts in bold letters in the subject line 'just for you'—and, he calls them by name."

"He?" Jack questioned.

"Yes, Jack—he!" Toby sat up at attention as Tessa continued.

"I am going to consider the killer male, for now, Jack. There are not many female serial killers out there. Now, where was I? Yes, he calls each victim by name, which tells us he knows them all somehow. Then he goes on to tell the victim they are naughty, and not just naughty, but very, very naughty. Then he asks them if they know what happens to naughty people."

"His explanation for what they are naughty about, though, is not really being naughty," Jack pointed out. "I don't think there is a person on earth who has not ridiculed or ignored or blamed someone for doing something they didn't do."

"Yes, to those of us who are normal, so to speak, those things would not be *very, very naughty*, but to our killer they are because he is the one who has been ridiculed, ignored, and wrongfully blamed. We are looking for someone with very low self-esteem and possibly someone who changes jobs quite often because they can't cope with even the most common aggravations of the workplace. At the workplace he is probably very much a loaner. Maybe, at first, he tries to fit in but always fails because when the least little thing goes wrong and he is to blame, he does not consider it his fault. It's always others doing it to him.

"He wants them to think about when they have been nice or have helped others because obviously they have not ever been nice or helped him. He calls them pathetically naughty because he, himself, feels pathetic."

Jack studied the letter. "But here he tells them they can do something about it, they can turn it around and save themselves and even their friends who are like them. He wants them to pass the email on to their friends?" He paused. "Yet, it seems he doesn't give them time between emails, which means something is escalating inside him."

"I agree. The perp doesn't give his victims time to repent. Look at the dates on these two emails Lauren ran off: they are only three days apart."

"But he says that for every friend they try to save their retribution will be lessened," Jack mentioned.

"No Jack, he says it *might* be; there is a big difference here between will and might. And he follows that up with *maybe* you won't die. The killer doesn't care what they do; he knows they are not going to forward these emails to anyone. He knows, in fact, his victims won't do anything about the emails and he is probably counting on the fact they are going to just delete them. He doesn't say what will happen to them if they send it to six to ten people because the killer does not care."

Tessa was silent for a few minutes as she studied the letter. "I don't understand his signature, though. 666?"

"That's the Mark of The Beast in Christianity, isn't it?" Jack offered.

"Yes, but why would the killer use that—I can't figure the significance. I'll have to think about it and come back to it later."

"There is a possibility this guy could work in a restaurant or a bar," Jack suggested. "Since the victims were all poisoned, the poison would have had to get into something they ate or drank."

"Good point, Jack. Wasn't Tyler at a bar when he got sick?"

"I believe so."

"But I think he was the only one, though."

"I keep coming back to the gym: both Tyler and Brianna belonged to a gym. They serve food at gyms, don't they?"

"Usually just drinks."

Toby's ears perked up at the mention of drinks. He wondered if the powder Camden was grinding up could dissolve in liquid and not leave a taste in someone's mouth so they wouldn't finish their entire drink.

"You know there is a possibility if we could get into the residences of the deceased we might be able to find a clue as to what gym they attended, and maybe some other clues as to a common denominator between them all," Jack threw out.

"You're right, Jack. Great idea. I'll call Bryce to get us clearance to go into the victims' homes. Now, let's look at this second email the killer sent Lauren. It starts off with 'are you listening to me,' once again in bold letters. He asks them what they are doing about the things he says they are naughty about. He doubts they even gave the first warning a second thought, but says they can still seek reconciliation. But he doesn't really care if they do or not because this is his last warning; there won't be anymore because their fate, in his mind, is already sealed. The second email is not really necessary; it's just a formality for him. His victims' fates were sealed the minute they were not nice to him or blamed him for something he may well have done but won't admit to.

"The killer cannot help himself once he sets things in motion. He is most likely very meticulous about his surroundings. I don't believe he is of a robust stature or he would not be killing in this manner. He is likely of slight build, and I am sure when he was a boy he was picked on at school and was forced to take the blame for many of the antics other kids did."

"If the killer is a male, and he is what you are saying he is, wouldn't he have targeted all males then?" Jack was puzzled by Tessa's reasoning.

"Not necessarily. He could also have been set up for big falls by the girls in his life—maybe even his mother. If he has a sibling, he was probably blamed for everything they did wrong, and, possibly, if the sibling is female, that would explain his desire to kill the women. If we take a look at all these women," Tessa laid the three photographs side by side, "they are all of a medium build and athletic."

Tessa looked at her watch. "I have to go, Jack. Can we continue this in the morning?"

"Sure, no problem."

"In the meantime, I would like you to follow up on the gyms in town; there are not that many in Brantford and your friend is going to get back to you in the morning from his gym. I'll give Bryce a call to get us keys for the victims' homes. How say we meet at the station at eight o'clock?"

Jack groaned. He wasn't used to getting up early every morning. "No problem, eight will be fine."

"Good, see you in the morning."

After Tessa left, Jack made a list of all the gyms in the Yellow Pages. He dialled the first one on his list and was told he would have to come in with his identification to prove he was a police officer. They had to protect their clients. He understood.

"Well, Toby, you feel like going for a ride?"

Toby lifted his head, looked at Jack, and then lowered his head back down and closed his eyes. "*I have other things I want to investigate, Jack—my own leads to follow up on.*"

"Okay, old fellow, I guess you deserve to rest. Hopefully I won't be long; maybe I'll get lucky and find a gym that they all go to on the first try." Jack wrote down the gym addresses, stuffed the paper in his pocket, and headed out.

When Toby was sure Jack was gone, he headed out himself. He sauntered over to the gym and walked the perimeter, looking for a window ledge where he could see from a good angle what was going on inside. "*I especially want to see what's going on where Camden works.*" The front of the building had a lot of glass, but it was thick and Toby couldn't see through it. Other than that, there were no windows on either side of the building.

As Toby walked around to the back, he noticed one window by the back door, but there was no ledge. He observed that the building had a flat roof and he thought maybe it might have one of those skylights like Jack had in his kitchen. *But how do I get up there?* Toby looked around and spied a couple of trees on one side of the building.

"*This is getting ridiculous. I'm too old for this; those are some big trees! Well, here goes.*"

Toby climbed as far as he needed to get to a branch that was close to the edge of the roof. He tread carefully along it and then jumped. He looked around and saw some dome shapes sticking up from the flatness.

"*Bingo! Skylights! Couldn't ask for anything better than those to be able to see what's going on in there.*"

Toby made his way to the first one. It was over the back of the gym. He padded up to the one closest to the front and peered down. It overlooked the reception area and the counter where people were served drinks. Toby didn't need to know any more for today. He would come back tomorrow when Camden was working. He turned and headed back to the tree.

~

Owen felt depressed as he looked around his empty apartment. It wasn't empty of things; it was empty of her— of Diana. The old man in the bar on Friday had been right on point when he had told him he had basically taken advantage of her. Owen had been a jerk. He turned the television on and started flipping channels. Nothing on but war and crime, and more war and more crime. Sad world … sad life he had. He fell asleep with the remote in his hand.

A couple of hours later, Owen awoke with sharp pains in his stomach. He looked at his watch. Four o'clock. Almost supper time. Maybe he was just hungry; after all, he hadn't eaten anything substantial since the early morning before going to the gym, and then he drank that smoothie after his workout. Owen opened the fridge to see if there were any leftovers. Nothing. He opened the freezer and noticed a frost-laden microwave dinner.

"This will have to do, I guess," he grumbled as he threw it in the microwave. A wave of nausea caught him off-guard. He shook his head and sat down at the kitchen table to wait for his supper to finish heating up. The dinger went off and Owen grabbed his meal and a fork and headed back to the living room. He flipped channels on the television until he came to a talk show that helped people deal with personal problems. He dug his fork into his food.

"Pathetic," he said as he watched a young couple discuss their problems on national television.

Owen was halfway through the supper when another sharp pain ripped through his abdomen. It was followed by a wave of nausea, and he broke out in a sweat. He felt as though he were going to pitch up his supper, so he headed for the bathroom. His legs felt wobbly. He no sooner reached the toilet and lifted the lid than his supper came up. He sat down on the floor and rested against the wall. He felt really sick now. He was dripping sweat, and his heart felt like it was beating a mile a minute.

"On top of everything else happening to me, now I'm getting sick!" he grumbled. He managed to stand, however, as he did, he vomited again. He noticed what he thought might be blood in the vomit. He lurched over to the sink and splashed water on his face and then rinsed his mouth. He looked in the mirror. "Pathetic." Owen opened the medicine cabinet and took out the bottle of tranquillizers. He rolled them around in his hands and then looked in the mirror again. Another wave of nausea swept over him ... he swayed over to the toilet and sat down on it, just in time.

When he was finished, Owen splashed water on his face again. Then he poured a glass of water, opened the pill bottle, and emptied it into his hand. He gazed once more into the mirror, lifted his glass in a salute, popped the pills into his mouth, and washed them down with the water. Somehow, he managed to make it back to his couch. He flicked the television off, picked up the phone and called the real estate office. The receptionist answered.

"I won't be in for a while—a long while," he slurred.

"Owen, is that you?"

"One and only."

"Are you sick? Do you need me to call someone for you?"

"Nope. Just tell the boss I'm off for a few days." Owen dropped the phone. "Shit!" he exclaimed as he reached for it and his stomach ripped with pain. Owen could hear the receptionist's voice calling his name. He pushed the off button on the phone and closed his eyes.

The receptionist was worried. Owen hadn't sounded well at all. She pulled his personnel file and flipped through it until she came to the sheet that had his emergency contact numbers on it. She picked up the phone and called Owen's brother, Frank.

When Frank arrived at his brother's apartment, he had to use his key to get in. He found Owen on the couch. There was vomit on the floor. Owen looked pale. Frank reached to his brother's neck and felt for a pulse. There was one, but it was weak. He picked up the phone and dialled 911. Then, knowing his brother better than he really wanted to, he walked into the bathroom and found the empty pill bottle. Frank returned to the living room with it, and sat down and waited for the ambulance.

Tuesday, June 30, 2009

A s Jack and Toby were about to leave the house on Tuesday morning, the phone rang. Jack looked at his watch. He was going to be late for his meeting with Tessa. The phone stopped and then as Jack was about to close the door the ringing started again. He decided whoever it was, they must have something important to tell him,

"Hello."

"Hey, Jack, glad I caught you. Andrew here."

"What's up, Andrew?"

"Me!" Andrew waited for a second for his joke to soak in. He heard Jack snicker and then he got on with his mission. "We got a call last night that I thought you might like to know about. It was for a young fellow by the name of Owen Bains. His brother called it in. When we got there, the brother handed me an empty bottle of tranquillizers and said he thought Owen had overdosed. He explained how distraught his brother was because his girlfriend had left him, and he was broke. Owen was barely alive. His pulse was down, his blood pressure was 60 over 35, and he was wringing wet.

"I was readily going to believe it was just an overdose until I noticed he had thrown up, and it appeared more than once, plus I saw traces of blood. When we lifted him onto the gurney, we noted he'd lost control of his bowels. I know you're working on a case of some young people who died from some of these same symptoms and I thought maybe you'd want to run down to the hospital and check out this fellow. He was still alive when I left. If you get up there right away, talk to a nurse named, Karen. She mentioned something to me: 'just like the others,' I believe it was that she stated."

Jack thanked Andrew for the information. He called Bryce and asked him to tell Tessa he was going to be a bit late; he had to check something out at the hospital—

possibly a fifth victim. Then he hurried out the door. Toby was waiting by the van door and Jack barely gave him time to jump up on the seat. Bryce had provided Jack with a portable siren; however, he hadn't used it until now. "Hang on, Toby, we're going for a ride," he warned as he reached his hand out the window and placed the siren on his van roof.

Jack pulled into Emergency parking and raced inside. "Is there a Karen here?" he asked at reception, flashing his badge.

"Just a minute." The receptionist got up and left. A few long minutes later she returned with a nurse.

"I'm Karen. How can I help you, officer?"

"You have a young man in here named Owen Bains?"

"We did."

"Did?"

"Yeah. We sent him down to the morgue about an hour ago." She paused and then motioned for Jack to follow her into one of the empty treatment rooms. She closed the door. "Owen had taken a lot of tranquillizers, so the doctor wrote his death up as an overdose..."

"What was the doctor's name?" Jack interrupted.

"Doctor Campbell," Karen replied. "But, personally, I don't think it was an overdose. One of the attendants who brought Owen in mentioned to me about the vomit in the apartment and he also said we would have to change the poor guy because he had messed his pants. If Owen had thrown up after taking the pills, in my opinion, the pills would have been up-chucked before they could do any real harm. Do you see where I am going here?"

Jack nodded. "So has an autopsy been ordered?"

"No, Doctor Campbell didn't think it was necessary."

"But you do?"

"Yes. I think Owen died from something else—I believe that it was the poison, just like those others." She paused, noticing the puzzled look on Jack's face. "I know about the poison because I'm friends with the coroner."

Jack nodded and then pulled out his cellphone and dialled Bryce's direct line. "I need you to call down here and get an autopsy ordered on an Owen Bains. The doctor has written him off as a drug overdose, but I'm having a conversation with a nurse who thinks otherwise."

"You got it, Jack."

Jack turned to Karen. "Thank you for the info. The captain is going to call over to the coroner to autopsy Owen. How can I reach you if I need to ask you any more questions?"

Karen wrote a couple of numbers on a piece of paper and handed it to Jack. "If I'm not at either of these numbers, you'll find me here," she said. "I have to get back to work now."

"Me too," Jack said as he followed her out the door.

By the time Jack and Toby arrived at the station, Tessa was going over some of the details with Bryce that she and Jack had discussed the day before. Tessa turned as Jack walked in. She didn't waste any time asking him how he had made out with the gyms.

"Dead end," he answered. "I had to go personally to each one; none of them had any of those names on their list."

"You didn't go personally to the gym beside our house!" Toby meowed for a moment of attention from Tessa. He rubbed around her legs and then jumped up on the captain's desk.

"Well, we know at least two of our victims belonged to a gym. We may have to look outside of Brantford, although I don't know why someone would travel out of town when there are so many fitness centres here. Are you sure you got them all?"

Jack hesitated at the accusatory tone in Tessa's words: he knew how to do his job. "I'm sure."

Toby looked at Jack. *"But you didn't get them all, buddy! You didn't go to the one where Camden works. But don't worry, I've got that one covered!"*

Tessa asked Bryce for the keys to the victim's residences. "Stop by the forensic department on your way out; they'll give you a kit in case you find anything of interest."

Tessa nodded and scooped up the big orange furball. "Let's go, boys," she ordered with a grin.

"Shall we take my van?" Jack suggested. "Toby enjoys being able to sit up front and look out the window," he added.

"Sure." She opened the back door of Jack's van and climbed in. "I think we should do the houses in order of the victim's deaths, starting with Brianna's." Tessa proposed.

"Sounds good."

Jack and Tessa walked into Brianna's house and were amazed that everything seemed to be in order and there was no dust anywhere. Someone—Jack knew who—had been keeping the place clean, almost like a shrine. He made a mental note to talk to Caitlin's husband, Mitch, about getting her some counselling. They wandered from room to room finding nothing that could help them.

Toby waited by the front door as he had been instructed. He knew the ropes—he was a detective. "*No contaminating the crime scene, but they can walk all over it!*"

Jack looked at the magnets on the refrigerator—a lot of gyms gave out magnets with their numbers. Tessa was flipping through a personal Rolodex sitting by the phone; she found no gym listing. Jack opened the refrigerator door; the fridge had been cleaned out.

Jack stood in the doorway of the bathroom where Brianna's body had been found. "What a waste!"

"What's that, Jack?" Tessa came up behind him.

"Nothing," he returned, sadly.

"Well, let's go to Tyler's; doesn't look like we are going to find anything here."

Tyler's apartment proved to have no more information available for them to consider than Brianna's had. It was evident Tyler's mum had tidied up, and some of her son's belongings were already in boxes. His fridge had also been cleaned out. Despite having been cleaned, Jack noted the stains on the carpet where Tyler had thrown up.

From Tyler's they moved on to Emily's apartment. When they walked in, they could tell no one had been there for a while. There was a pile of mail on the floor just inside the door, and the furniture was dusty. Jack walked into the bathroom and had to cover his nose from the stench. No one had even cleaned up after her. Tessa was in the kitchen checking out the refrigerator.

"Hey, Jack, I think we might have something here!" she came around the corner holding a plastic cup with a pink liquid in it. "Whew! What is that smell?"

"Death." Jack turned and closed the bathroom door and then steered Tessa to the living room. "What's that?" he pointed to the cup.

"Smells like some sort of a cherry drink. There is still a bit left in the cup. Maybe she started feeling ill before she could finish it."

Jack stroked his chin. "Or maybe it's the drink itself that made her sick. We need to bag it and send it over to forensics. It would be interesting if they found traces of poison in there. Too bad there's no logo on the cup because that would make our job a lot easier."

Tessa carefully bagged the drink. She and Jack took another look around and then headed to the van. Toby was waiting for them inside; he'd taken a pass on the third place, wanting to catch up on a few cat-zzzz!

Before heading to Lauren's place, they decided to drop the drink off at the station. "Whoever this killer is," Tessa commenced, "he is not leaving a whole lot of days between victims; we need to move as quickly as possible on any clues we find."

"I agree," Jack said.

"*Me too.*" Toby sat up and looked at the bag.

Tessa noticed. "Something we found in Emily's fridge, Toby."

Toby tilted his head to the side as he looked at the cup. Where had he seen a cup like that before? "*Come on, Toby, wrack that brain of yours!*" Suddenly, Toby remembered! He had seen Camden walking home a couple of days ago with such a cup! "*I'm right! I hate being right all the time, but I'm right. How do I tell Jack or Tessa before there's another victim? I gotta get home, check on Emma, and then get over to the roof of the gym and see what Camden is up to!"* Toby began to fidget.

"I think maybe Toby has had enough for today," Jack observed. "I suggest, before we go to Lauren's, I swing by my house and drop him off."

"Good man, Jack—read my mind."

"No problem," Tessa replied. "Why don't we grab a bite of lunch too? My treat."

Jack nodded. "Sounds good."

After dropping Toby at the house, Jack and Tessa grabbed a quick bite at a small restaurant downtown, then headed to Lauren's apartment. There was a semblance of tidiness to the place, however nothing of any importance was revealed that would warrant further investigation. Jack was studying her calendar and noted a date with a big red circle around it and the word 'freedom' written in the square. Tessa walked up behind him. "Looks like that was an important date for her," she commented.

"Yeah, probably her divorce. Now the guy can pretend to be the grieving widower," Jack sneered.

Tessa was thoughtful for a moment. "Did anyone ever check out her ex-husband?"

"I don't know for sure, but I would think Bryce would have had someone go and talk to him."

"We'll ask when we get back to the station." Tessa looked around one more time before suggesting they leave.

~

After Toby had been dropped off, he went into the kitchen to grab a bite to eat and a drink. He had no idea how long he would be gone so wanted to make sure he was well-nourished. Once the belly was satisfied, Toby headed over to Emma's; she was in her plant room. He meowed loudly. Emma looked up and motioned it was okay for him to come into the yard. She pointed to the house, indicating Duke was inside.

Toby went up to the door and Emma let him. She looked sad. Toby rubbed around her legs and began to purr. She knelt down and scratched along his spine. Tears started to drop onto his fur.

"Camden told me we have to move again. He informed me this morning I had to start packing. Cam said the owner has opened a new gym in Nova Scotia and he wants Cam to go down there and manage it. I asked my brother why him, and Cam said the guy who was lined up down there took sick and can't do it now. Cam said Mr. Rawlings was paying our moving expenses." Emma crumbled to the floor beside Toby and continued stroking him. "I don't want to leave, Toby. This has never happened so quickly before; I don't understand why we can't be like other people and just put down roots." Emma cleared her throat and sniffed. "It's almost like all the moving around we did when we were in foster care has affected him to the point where he just can't stay anywhere for too long. But this is ridiculous; we just got here. I'm sure Cam could have said no if he'd wanted to. I'm happy. I thought he was happy at work, too. He was for the first while, but then I noticed the signs: his moods when he came home, moods I'd seen before, moods that always got worse before our next move.

"There are times when I think to ask him to just let me stay somewhere; I could manage on my own. But then I remember how much he has done for me, especially after the rape," Emma was rambling on, providing Toby with a lot of information. "He was pretty angry when the guy got off on a technicality. We moved away and Cam started working at a gym. He's been working at gyms ever since. He's good at his job, I think. But now he tells me it hasn't been going so well here; people are blaming him for stuff he doesn't do … oh, Toby," Emma picked Toby up and buried her face in his fur. "I just don't know what to do anymore."

Toby stayed for another half hour before he decided it was time to leave. Emma continued to pour her heart out to him, and he learned more than he really wanted to. But without being able to talk, how was he going to get across his suspicions to Jack? He headed for the gym, climbed the tree, jumped on the roof, and sat down beside the skylight over the reception area. Camden was at the drink counter.

~

Andrew grabbed a few hours of sleep after his phone call to Jack. He planned on heading to the gym before his four o'clock shift. When Andrew walked into the facility at two o'clock, he was still thinking of the young man he had dropped off at the hospital. He had called the hospital before leaving home and was informed Owen hadn't made it through the night. Andrew swiped his card and headed for the change room, taking no note of who was at the reception desk. Toby saw him come in.

Camden was cleaning the counter and arranging the shelves. Toby noticed how he had turned, ever so slightly, to follow the direction Andrew had taken. Toby saw Andrew come out of the change room and head to the warm-up area, and Camden leave his work area and start to empty the garbage cans by the machines, starting in the warm-up area. Toby observed Camden talking to Andrew. Andrew just looked at Camden and Toby didn't see whether he answered or not because Andrew got up from his mat and walked away. Toby saw the look on Camden's face, though.

Toby spent the next half hour watching Camden watching Andrew. He got an eerie feeling that Andrew's life might be in danger, and Andrew was Jack's friend! Toby had to do something.

Andrew came out of the change room after finishing his workout and went up to the drink counter. Camden served him. Toby watched carefully. They appeared to be talking and Andrew wasn't happy after he took the first sip of his smoothie. Camden blushed, but Toby could tell by his body language he was angry. Andrew left the drink on the counter, bent down, picked up his gym bag, and headed for the door. Camden watched Andrew leave, his face contorted with anger. Toby had seen enough for now; he headed home.

He was crossing over the parking lot when he noticed Andrew getting into his car. He jumped up onto the front of the car, stared in at Andrew for a minute, and then jumped off. *"I got your back buddy; be careful."*

Inside the gym, Camden was still fuming. He had made the drink exactly as Andrew asked. He was sick of this guy being so arrogant and ignoring his friendliness. What could he have been thinking, trying to make friends with him anyway, especially when Andrew looked so much like the guy who had gotten away with raping Emma!

Jack and Tessa were in the living room going over the files when Toby arrived home. "Where you been, Toby? I thought you'd be sleeping all afternoon." Jack looked up as Toby entered the room.

"I've been doing your job, Jack—spying on the guy I think is murdering these people—keeping my eye on your friend—trying to figure out how to tell you." Toby jumped up to his perch by the window, lay down, closed his eyes and went to sleep. He needed a cat-nap.

The doorbell woke him up. Jack answered it and let Camden in. When Toby saw who it was, he sat up and hissed. His tail switched back and forth, and he hissed again. Camden glared at him. Tessa was watching closely.

"I checked the records, Jack," Camden began, "Those names are not on our membership list. I just thought I would drop in and tell you because when I called earlier you weren't home."

"Thanks, Camden, I appreciate you stopping by. I would offer you a drink, but Tessa and I have a lot of work to do here."

Camden gazed at the coffee table. He noticed there were five folders today. He couldn't help the smile that crossed briefly across his lips. Tessa looked at him strangely, wondering what he thought was so funny. "Another victim?" Camden pointed to the files.

"We think so," Jack answered.

"Any leads?"

Tessa intervened. "We are following up a few leads, but are being careful what we release to the press just yet." Tessa looked into Camden's eyes. She shuddered, not liking what she saw there. "We are closing in on the killer," she baited. Tessa saw the eyes darken.

Camden put his hands up to his temples. His head started to pound. He needed to get home. "I'll leave then and let you guys get back to work." Camden was getting bad vibes off Tessa; she could be dangerous. He had to get home and make sure Emma was packing, and he had to send out the final email. Andrew would only get one; there wouldn't be time for a second one before he and Emma would steal away in the night.

Tessa sat down on a chair after Camden left and she looked up at Jack. "There is something weird about that young man," she declared. "How long has he been your neighbour?"

"He and his sister moved here in May," Jack replied. "He's okay, loves his sister. Came here because of her health; she's seeing a doctor in Brantford, he said."

"What is wrong with her, Jack?"

Jack thought for a moment and then realized he didn't know. "Camden never really told me."

"Where did they live before?"

"Vancouver, I think he said."

Tessa made a mental note to check Vancouver for unsolved homicides that may have a similarity to what they were dealing with here in Brantford.

"Do the math, Jack. The murders started not too long after Camden arrived, and he's getting ready to run again! Emma said so! I'm even surer now … he's the killer!" Toby jumped down off the couch and joined Tessa on her chair.

"There is one thing I would like to do before calling it a day. I am going to head back to the station and take a look at the computer to see if there have been any other crimes like this anywhere in the country. I don't think this is the first time this killer has killed." Tessa put the files in her case.

"Neither do I!" Toby rubbed his head on Tessa's shoulder.

~

Camden stormed into the house. Emma was sitting on the couch. She looked like she had been crying. The boxes he had stored in the basement after their move and had brought up for her to start packing sat empty on the floor. He didn't have time to speak to her right now; he needed to send the email. He would deal with Emma when he was sure he had things in order. He rushed up the stairs to his room, turned on his computer, found his file, and sent Andrew his warning. Then he checked his baggie and saw he was going to have to grind some more beans. In his rush to get the email out, he didn't realize he'd sent the second one.

When Camden came downstairs, he found Emma had lain down on the couch and fallen asleep. How lucky could he get? He headed for the three-season room and was picking some of the beans when he felt Emma's presence. He turned and saw her standing in the doorway.

"What are you doing, Camden?" she asked.

He hesitated before speaking. What excuse could he give her? "I was just picking the seeds before we moved because we won't be able to take all the plants with us this time. I know how much you like the castor bean plant."

"It isn't me who likes that plant, Cam—it's you." Emma turned and walked back to the living room.

Wednesday, July 1, 2009

Andrew had the day off. Most places were closed for the holiday, however, not the gym. He figured a good workout would be the best way to start his day. "What do you think, Bear?" Andrew's dog, a Samoyed, smiled and wagged his tail. "You want to come along today? I'm going to stop by Jack's after my workout; you can play with Toby." Andrew walked over to his computer and turned it on. "Guess I'll check my emails before taking off."

It wasn't often Andrew checked his emails, and it took quite a while for them to download. The most recent one had a subject line, 'ARE YOU LISTENING TO ME.' Andrew was curious, so he clicked on it. *"Dear Andrew: you are still being very, very naughty. I told you what happens to very naughty people. Did you think about it? Did you ridicule someone today ... ignore someone just because ... blame someone wrongfully? Were you nice to someone ... really nice? Did you help someone today, just because ... really help? I doubt you even gave my message a second thought. Oh, believe it ... you are so pathetically naughty that I can't stand it! You might still be able to turn this around and do something about it. I am being generous giving you another warning ... but it is still up to you to seek reconciliation. If you don't, retribution will come your way ... and don't forget all those selfish, naughty friends of yours who are just like you. Pass this on to them so they can get help too ... for every friend you try to save the retribution on yourself might be lessened ... you know the drill ... six to ten, maybe you won't die ... one to five, you will ... signed: 666."*

Andrew turned his printer on and printed the email. He was sure Jack would want to see this. "We'll drop this by Jack's before my workout, okay, Bear?" Bear was just happy to be getting out for the day.

Unfortunately, when Andrew got to Jack's, his friend had already left. Andrew scribbled a note on the paper and

191

stuck it in Jack's door, then headed off to the gym. Camden was working the front desk: Paige had called in sick. *Of course,* Camden had thought. It was a holiday and yesterday he'd heard her making plans with Vincent.

~

Toby didn't accompany Jack Wednesday morning. He wanted to keep an eye on the home front. Soon after Jack left for the station, Toby headed out the door and took his position on the gym roof by the skylight. He watched Camden at the front desk. Being a holiday, there were not a lot of people coming and going, so Camden was looking after reception and the drink counter. Toby was just about to doze off when he saw Andrew walk in. He saw a peculiar smile creep over Camden's face.

Andrew stopped momentarily at the counter before heading to the change room. Toby watched as Camden mixed a smoothie and he saw him take a little bag from his pocket and pour some white powder into the drink. At first, Toby thought Camden was making the drink for himself, but then remembered seeing a little bag like that when he had been spying on Camden. Camden put the drink in the fridge.

Toby's heart beat faster when he saw Andrew come out of the change room and head toward the door. Camden took the drink out of the fridge and called to Andrew, offering him the smoothie.

Toby paced around the skylight, panic setting in. He knew what was in that baggie. Emma had told him how poisonous the seeds of that plant were. To his relief, Andrew was shaking his head. He raised his hand, gesturing 'no thank you,' and then turned and continued on his way. Toby breathed a sigh of relief. He watched Camden's face when Andrew refused the drink. At first, while Andrew was still within sight, Camden had been cordial, but once Andrew was out the door, Camden looked irritated. He took the drink and dumped it down the sink, rinsed the paper cup, and threw it in the wastebasket. Then

Camden took the garbage bag from the basket and proceeded to the back of the gym. Toby knew the evidence was headed for the trash. He would wait until Camden was back inside before leaving his post. Toby was confident he had the right guy and he was sure the next victim was Andrew!

Andrew was pleasantly surprised by Camden's offer of a smoothie, but he had other plans for lunch and didn't want to spoil his appetite. He had thought, on more than one occasion, Camden was a bit weird, but had rationalized that the young man was probably just trying to do his job. He looked like he had a lot on his mind most of the time. Andrew dropped Bear off at his house and then called his friend, Jody. They had dated a couple times, and since it was such a beautiful day, he asked her to go to Port Dover. They could stay, have supper, and then take a long walk on a quiet beach after the crowds left. Jody was happy he called and said she would love to go to Dover. Andrew said he would pick her up in half an hour.

~

By the time Jack arrived at the station, Tessa was already sitting at a computer with a smug look on her face. "I was right," she said as Jack entered the office. "He's killed before. I have pulled up two files: both unsolved crimes, both had six victims who died from poisoning, both were three females, three males killed in no particular order. And, just as the police were making significant progress, the killings stopped and the trails went cold." Tessa pulled up a file on the computer screen. It was dated September 2006 and was from the Winnipeg police department. She printed it off. Then Tessa pulled up another file dated June 2007, and then two more, March 2008 and the most recent one, May 2009. "The last one is from Vancouver," Tessa pointed out as she printed the reports off.

Tessa gathered the papers and laid them out on a table by the window. She motioned for Jack to come and take a look. She had a highlighter in her hand, and as she skimmed down each page, she highlighted all the similarities in the cases. The pink lines glared revealingly at the two detectives.

Jack sat back in his chair. "This means there will be one more victim—a male. But I've checked all the gyms in the area: not one of our victims are registered with them. Do you think the killer is changing his MO?"

"I don't think so; everything else is exactly the same—except for one thing. There was more time between the killings in these others. Since Vancouver, there was only about a month before they started again. The killer is escalating his kills, which means he is probably getting desperate about something. He will be packing to move again as soon as the sixth victim is finished; actually, my guess ... he probably is out of the area even before the sixth victim dies." Tessa put her highlighter down, stood, and walked over to the window.

"How well do you *really* know your new neighbour, Jack?" the question was asked pointedly.

Jack looked up, surprised. "Well," he began, "as well as anyone can get to know someone in a couple of months. He pretty much works and looks after his sister. Stops in at my place once in a while for a chat."

"What I'm getting at, Jack," Tessa continued, "is this ... he came here from Vancouver around mid-May, right?"

"Correct."

"He worked at a gym in Vancouver, right?"

"Correct."

"Did he mention to you where he worked before that?"

"I believe he has always worked at gyms..." Jack shook his head. "No, Tessa. I think you're barking up the wrong tree. Camden is a very gentle young man. He's devoted to his sick sister. He..."

"Is beginning to fit the profile, Jack. Face the facts." Tessa returned to the table and sat down beside Jack. She pointed to all the highlights. "Look ... all the victims of these other crimes were members of a gym ... the same gym in each city where the crime was done ... three males, three females, random; each time ... poison, which always threw the doctors off at first because it just looked like the victims had a severe flu or food poisoning of some sort. By the time they realized it wasn't the flu, the killer was almost finished and had moved on, leaving the trail cold. But here is the clincher: there were emails found. Not for all the victims, but I would bet my last dollar, if the police had investigated further, they would have discovered all the victims received the same emails.

"I have placed a call to a friend of mine at the Vancouver police department, asking him to forward me anything else he might have on this case. If I can get them to reopen their files and forward me a copy of the emails they found..." Tessa picked up the Vancouver file and scrolled down the paragraphs, "look ... see here, Jack ... three of the victims were noted to have received emails of a nasty sort.

"Camden is a loner. He is smart. He works in gyms. He moves around a lot. He was living in Vancouver before he came here. He claims it was because of his sister's health, but let me ask you, Jack, did his sister ever complain about her health? You had them both over for dinner one night, didn't you?"

Jack thought back to the evening of his dinner party. He remembered asking Emma about her health, and now he remembered her reaction. "Come to think of it, Tessa, she referred to her brother to answer when I asked about her health. She actually seemed surprised that was the reason they were here."

"When Camden was at your place the other day," Tessa pushed forward, "I noted some severe mood changes—not outwardly, but his eyes. Wasn't it he who told you none of the victims are registered at his gym?"

"Yes."

"And isn't that the only gym you personally did not go into and check out?"

Jack looked up and stared out the window. "Yes."

"I think it's time we paid Emma a little visit, Jack. I don't want to let Camden know we might be on to him because I don't want him to up and disappear. I think he is our killer. We just have to figure out why he is doing it—what's his trigger." Tessa gathered the papers and stuffed them into her briefcase. "Let's go see Emma. If Camden is home, we will wait until tomorrow."

"I think we should leave our visit to Emma until tomorrow anyway," Jack suggested. "It's already after lunch, and Camden left for work early this morning. He could be home anytime, and we wouldn't want him walking in while we are there."

"You make sense, Jack; we'll leave it until morning." Tessa hesitated. "It's a holiday—maybe we could do something relaxing, clear our minds and get a fresh start tomorrow."

Jack smiled. He had been thinking along the same line but hadn't known how to bring it up. "How about a nice drive to Port Dover, followed by a fish dinner and a walk on a moonlit beach after the crowds dissipate?"

"That sounds absolutely fantastic. Could we swing by my apartment so I can grab some swimming things?"

"No problem. I want to stop by my place and make sure the old kitty cat is well-fed. Toby will never forgive me if I don't have kibbles in his dish! Maybe I'll grab some swim trunks and a towel too."

When they arrived at Jack's house, he ran in through the back door, so he didn't see the letter Andrew had left in the front door. Toby was nowhere to be seen: Jack assumed he was visiting Emma. Jack filled Toby's dish, put his swimwear and a towel in a gym bag, then headed back to the van. On the way out of Brantford, they stopped by Tessa's place for her things.

"This is nice," she smiled at Jack. "Been a long time since I've done this."

"Me too," Jack returned. "Well, not since I have relaxed; I do a lot of that now I'm retired—too much actually. However, it's been a long time since I was in the company of such a beautiful woman."

"You flatter me, Jack."

"Be flattered then; I mean it."

Tessa looked out the side window. It had been a long time since she had enjoyed a man's company. Jack seemed to be the kind of man she could get used to having around.

~

Toby watched the van come and go. He was sitting by the fence at Emma's house, watching. Emma hadn't come out yet to tend her plants, and he was worried. "*I hope nothing has happened to her.*" He paced back and forth along the fence line. Even Duke was nowhere to be seen. Toby heard footsteps coming down the sidewalk—Camden. He crouched down in the long grass so he wouldn't be seen. He heard the front door slam when Camden went inside.

Before long, Camden appeared in the three-season room. He went straight to the castor bean plant. "*He needs more seeds to make more powder because what he used today got wasted.*" Toby still had no idea how he was going to reveal what he knew to Jack before it was too late for Andrew!

Emma joined her brother in the three-season room, but she took no note of what he was doing. She looked horrible. Her hair was unkempt, and her face was paler than Toby had ever seen it. There was no smile on her face and no light in her eyes. Her walk was nothing more than a staggering shuffle. Toby watched as Camden took his sister gently by the arm and directed her into the house.

~

Andrew and Jody were sitting in the restaurant when Jack and Tessa walked in. "What a surprise!" Andrew exclaimed standing and extending a hand to Jack. "Why don't you join us?" he pointed to the two empty chairs.

Jack looked at Tessa. She nodded approval. "What brings you to Dover?" Jack inquired.

"The beautiful weather, a day off, and a lovely girl!" Andrew grinned. "How about you?"

"The same." Jack blushed, and then everyone laughed.

"Would you guys like a drink?" Andrew asked as he waved down the waitress.

"I'll just have a ginger ale," Jack replied.

"I'll have ice water with lemon," Tessa added.

The couples ordered their meals and while they were waiting for the food to arrive Andrew thought to ask Jack about the letter he'd left at his front door. "Did you see what I left at your front door this morning, Jack?"

"I actually didn't use the front door since I left early; what did you leave me?"

"I received an interesting email—a threatening one. It was addressed 'you are you listening to me'..."

"Let me guess, the signature was '666,' " intervened Tessa.

"Yep."

Jack took a sip of his ginger ale. "The killer sends a second one out before he does anything. I want to know as soon as you receive it."

Tessa spoke up. "There is no guarantee there will be another email. This killer is escalating. We also don't know when the poison is administered to the victims as they seem to die pretty soon after the second email." She paused, thoughtfully. "Wait, you said the headline was 'are you listening to me'?

"Yeah," replied Andrew, a puzzled look on his face.

"That is the second email the killer sends; there might not be another one!"

Jack and Tessa filled Andrew in on some of the details of the case. They were careful not to mention specifics because matters were still under investigation. Andrew understood and said he would let Jack know if and when he received another email. Tessa reiterated it would be doubtful if he did. She didn't think the killer was going to waste any more time. Andrew promised to be careful.

When their meals arrived, they ate mostly in silence, with just the odd bit of general conversation about the demise of the world. They hadn't realized how late it was, so they forfeited their swim after the food. However, there was still time for a walk along the beach, which had almost cleared off, save for a few locals. The sunset was beautiful—bold and red—a sailor's delight, so goes the legend. About eight o'clock, Jack mentioned he would like to start heading back. Tessa agreed. Andrew and Jody were going to stay a tad longer; the night was still young for them.

~

Camden was worried. Emma hadn't looked like this for a long time, not since the rape. She was the last person in the world he wanted to hurt, but he had no choice now. He knew it would only be a matter of time before he was caught if he stayed in Brantford much longer. He couldn't understand why she didn't seem to believe his boss was sending him to Nova Scotia. She didn't understand why he just hadn't said no. Camden was also worried he wouldn't be able to finish what he had started. What if Andrew didn't come back to the gym tomorrow? He knew he had received the email.

On his way home from work Camden saw a piece of paper sticking out of Jack's front door. He walked up to the door and took the paper out, and when he saw it was his email, he stuffed it in his pocket. He was still agitated about the fact that his final victim was a friend of the only person who had been nice to him since he came to Brantford.

Camden decided, since he hadn't been able to finish the job today, he needed to send another email, still not realizing he was sending a duplicate of the second email. Emma hadn't packed any boxes so he spent the evening packing what they would be taking with them. She just sat on the couch and watched, tears in her eyes. Duke didn't leave her side.

After Camden sent the email to Andrew, he tilted back in his chair and muttered: "This is the last one, Emma—I swear—the last one." Then he shut off his light, crawled under his covers, curled into the fetal position, put his thumb in his mouth, and went to sleep.

Thursday, July 2, 2009

Emma was tired. She hadn't slept well since Camden told her they were definitely moving. She sat in the middle of the living room looking around at the boxes her brother had packed. She had half a mind to unpack them all to prolong the impending move. She stood and headed out to the three-season room. Duke followed close on her heels.

"You want to go outside, boy? You're getting tired of all these moves too, aren't you? We finally had a nice big yard for you." She opened the back door so Duke could take a run. The dog looked up at her and hesitated. "It's okay, boy. I'll be okay. I always am."

Duke started barking as two people came around the corner of the house. Emma recognized Jack, but not the woman with him. "Your gate was open," Jack pointed out; "so we thought you might be back here. How are you, Emma? You don't look well."

Emma grabbed hold of Duke's collar, pulling him back into the sunroom. "I'm fine, just a bit tired," she replied as she stepped out into the yard and closed the door on Duke. "To what do I owe your visit, Jack? Who is your friend?" Emma was puzzled as to why Jack had come over to the house, something he had never done before.

"Actually we are here on business. This is Officer Tessa Bannister. She and I are working on a case, and we want to ask you a few questions about Camden. Could we come in?" Jack pointed to the house.

"I'd rather you not. The house is quite a mess; I've been unwell for a few days, but I feel better today and am going to clean up later." Emma pointed to an old patio set. "We can sit here if you like."

Tessa was disappointed. She wanted to see the inside of the house. She got right to the point. "Has Camden always worked at a gym?"

Emma knew instantly she was going to have to be careful. Camden didn't like sharing too much information about their lives with strangers. "Not always," she replied, even though she couldn't remember a time when he hadn't.

"Oh, where else did he work?" Tessa pushed on.

"I think he worked in some group homes and even some retirement homes before he landed his first job at a gym."

"Where was that? The first one … at a gym?"

"I really can't remember. Why are you asking me these questions? Why don't you just ask Camden? He is better at remembering details than I am." Emma looked away nervously, knowing her brother was not going to be happy if he heard about this visit.

Tessa was not ready to give up. "You move around quite a bit, don't you?"

"Yes."

"Jack tells me that you and your brother moved to Brantford because of your health—to be able to see a specialist? Is that correct?"

"Also because he got a job here," Emma informed, ignoring the question about her health.

"Which was it Emma? A doctor for you, or a job for Camden? I need to know the main reason.

Emma stood. Tears encroached the corners of her eyes: she was confused as to why Jack was letting this woman ask her so many questions.

Jack noticed the turmoil on Emma's face, and he put his hand on Tessa's arm. "I think we should come another time, Tessa; maybe, as Emma mentioned, when Camden is home. We can ask him these questions." Jack winked at Tessa. "Emma is right—he's the one we should be talking to."

Tessa got the message and stood. She put a reassuring hand on Emma's shoulder. Emma flinched. "I'm sorry if I have upset you, honey, but we are investigating a series…"

Jack screamed out and slapped his arm. "Damn wasp! I think it bit me! Shall we go, Tessa?"

201

"I'll see you to the gate," Emma said. She stood for a few minutes watching the two police officers walk down the sidewalk to Jack's house, and then she closed and secured the gate lock. "I wonder who unfastened the gate anyway," Emma mumbled as she returned to the house. She opened the back door and Duke bounded out into the yard.

Toby, who had been hiding in the grass, headed home. He was upset with Tessa for making Emma cry. But then again, maybe that meant Tessa and Jack were suspecting Camden, which was a good thing. When Toby arrived home, Jack and Tessa were sitting at the kitchen table with a cup of coffee.

"She's covering for him, Jack. It was obvious." Tessa opened the conversation.

"She's fragile, Tessa, and not the one we are thinking is guilty here. He is her twin brother, and he's been looking after her for years. It's my understanding she went through some traumatic events in her life. Maybe the doctor she's supposed to be seeing here is a psychologist, and they just don't want people knowing such personal information. You were rough on her."

"I had to be. That's the only way to get the information I need sometimes. It's a tough world out there. I have the feeling her brother doesn't really make her life easy. I don't think she likes moving around, but she is dependent on him so has no choice. He is a controller. Most likely, because of their unique bond of twinship, she is the only person he has been able to control. Hell, I don't think he can even control himself most times." Tessa took a sip of her coffee. "This is good, Jack; what kind is it? Something really different is in it."

"Just the Nabob Morning Blend, with a touch of cardamom."

Toby meowed and looked accusingly at Jack, and then at his dish. Jack stood. "Sorry, old boy, been kind of busy lately."

"*You have no idea what 'busy' is! You should walk a day on my paws!*" Toby dug into his kibble, still keeping an ear on the conversation going on at the table. He was worried about Andrew, and Toby hoped he hadn't missed Andrew's trip to the gym today. He had been torn about whether to sit on the roof lookout or check on Emma when he saw Jack and Tessa headed her way that morning. Emma had won out. Toby had also been wracking his brain all night as to how to stop Andrew from drinking the poisonous smoothie that he knew Camden was going to try and get to him sooner or later. He hoped his decision to watch Emma hadn't made him too late to save Jack's friend.

~

Andrew was called into work early on Thursday morning. The phone rang at six o'clock: it was his supervisor. One of the guys had called in sick, and he couldn't get hold of anyone else.

"Yeah, they probably all know better than to answer their phones this early in the morning," Andrew grumbled into the receiver. His supervisor laughed.

Andrew packed his gym clothes and threw them in the car just in case he made it to the gym after work. He was enjoying his workouts and didn't want to get lazy like he had a few times before, especially after his conversation with Jody yesterday. He felt there was the real possibility of a long-term relationship blooming. Unfortunately he was asked to work overtime and didn't make it to the gym on Thursday night. He came home bushed, turned his computer on and checked his emails.

Bear pushed his head at Andrew's hand. "Okay, boy; I just need to check something out." Andrew scrolled through his inbox and noticed a subject that said: 'ARE YOU LISTENING TO ME' … he clicked on it … *"Dear Andrew: you are still being very, very naughty. I told you what happens to very naughty people. Did you think about it? Did you ridiculed someone today … ignore someone just because … blame someone wrongfully? Were you nice to someone … really nice? Did you help someone today, just because … really help? I doubt you even gave my message a second thought. Oh, believe it … you are so pathetically naughty that I can't stand it! You might still be able to turn this around and do something about it. I am being generous giving you another warning … but it is still up to you to seek reconciliation. If you don't, retribution will come your way … and don't forget all those selfish, naughty friends of yours who are just like you. Pass this on to them so they can get help too … for every friend you try to save the retribution on yourself might be lessened … you know the drill … six to ten, maybe you won't die … one to five, you will … signed: 666."*

Andrew pressed print and then picked up the phone and called Jack.

"Hello."

"Hey there, Jack … did you read the letter I left in your front door; I just…"

"Oh crap! I forgot to even look; hang on a sec Andrew; I'm sure it'll still be there." Jack set the phone down and went to the front door. He looked around and couldn't see a letter anywhere. He returned to the phone. "Nothing there, Andrew."

"Hmm, that's strange, I thought I stuck it good in the screen door. Oh well, I've run another copy will bring it over to you. It's the same as the first one! Would you like it tonight?"

Jack looked at his watch. "No need to bring it tonight, tomorrow morning is good."

"No problem then, see you in the morning." Andrew was relieved he didn't have to go out, he hadn't really wanted to. "Well Bear, how say we curl up and watch a movie?" Bear jumped up on the couch and wagged his tail.

~

Camden sat at the supper table and listened as Emma related the events of the visit from Jack and Tessa. Things were falling apart faster than he had imagined they would, and to top it all off, Andrew had not shown up at the gym today either.

"What is going on, Cam? Why were they asking so many questions about you and your work and where we lived, and the reason for us moving here?"

Camden wondered to himself how much he should tell his sister. He decided that a little knowledge would be better than none at all. Possibly it would quench some of Emma's questions.

"I think they are investigating a series of murders and they found some other similar cases where people who went to gyms were dying. For some reason, they are checking out employees of local gyms, as well." Camden paused. "Paige said they were in the other day when I was off, asking everyone all sorts of questions," Camden lied.

"So, we really are leaving because Mr. Rawlings offered you a job in Nova Scotia?"

After Camden had told Emma they might have to move again, he'd come up with the idea of Mr. Rawlings transferring him to another location. "I wouldn't lie to you, Em. I'm sorry this has happened, but it has. Mr. Rawlings was good to me by giving me this job; I don't want to disappoint him when he is caught with such a problem. And, he's paying our way there," Camden lied again. Emma didn't have to know he'd been putting money away for emergencies. He'd figure something out once they got there and she found out there was no job. "I need you to get the packing finished because we have to leave this weekend—Saturday, hopefully."

Camden reached over and pulled Emma into his arms and gave her a warm hug. "You did well today, Em, not letting them into the house."

Emma pulled out of her brother's arms. They didn't feel as comforting as they once had. "I'd like to go and lie down for a while. When I get up, I can help with some more of the boxes." Emma started up the stairs to her room.

Camden was relieved because he had been trying to figure out how he was going to get more beans. He hoped there were enough because he had used quite a few in his last harvest.

~

Toby decided to take a little jaunt over to Emma's. He stopped behind a bush just outside the fence when he saw Camden by the castor bean plant. Toby watched as Camden picked the beans and slipped them into his pocket. Emma was nowhere to be seen. Toby hoped she was okay.

Camden looked around nervously and then went back into the house. Toby moved so he would have a better view of the upper floor. He sat down and waited for Camden's bedroom light to turn on. When it did, Toby headed up the tree outside Camden's window. He slunk along the branch as far as he needed to get a good look inside. Camden had taken out his grinder and was dumping the seeds into it. Then he poured the powder into his baggie. Just as he was zipping the baggie shut, Emma appeared in the doorway.

Toby held his breath. Would she be in danger if she realized what her brother was doing? *"I'm not moving until I'm sure Emma is safe!"* Toby's tail switched nervously.

Camden shoved the baggie into his pocket and turned to face his sister. Toby couldn't hear what he was saying, but he saw the look of dismay cross Emma's face. She turned and left. Toby waited a few more minutes before he climbed down the tree and headed home.

Toby knew he needed to keep a particularly close eye on the gym tomorrow. He had no idea when Andrew would be working out, but he could not afford to miss him, especially if Camden was working. When Toby arrived home, Jack was relaxing in front of the television.

"Hey there, Toby, old man; want to watch some telly with me?" Jack called out when he heard Toby in the kitchen. "Your favourite show, *Law and Order,* is on," he added.

Toby came through into the living room and jumped up on Jack's lap. "Well isn't this something, old man— what's up?" Jack stroked Toby's back.

"*If only I could tell you, Jack, but I just haven't figured out how yet. So until I do, I'm going to have to do this one solo.*" Toby curled up on Jack's lap and went to sleep.

Friday, July 3, 2009

Tessa had been called out of town on Thursday for another profiling case, but Friday morning saw her up early and on her way to the Brantford station. She called Jack, but he said he had to wait for Andrew to drop off the email and then he would be over. When Tessa got to the station, she went straight to the computer Bryce had said she could use for the case and checked to see if she had any more information on the open cases out west.

She was in luck. There was an email from her friend in Vancouver. He had not only sent her his files, but he had also called Calgary and gotten hold of theirs, as well. His note was cheery...

Hi, Tessa: thought you might be interested in both of these files. I have also included pics of the victims from here and Calgary. To tell the truth, it is kind of eerie how much the victims from each city look alike. I've also included copies of the emails received by some of our victims. If I find anything else, I will forward it to you. Til later, Cole Palmer

Tessa pulled her files out of her briefcase and spread them out on the table while the printer was printing off the documents Cole had sent her. She gathered the papers from the printer and set them out beside the Brantford files and then stepped back. She turned and headed to Bryce's office.

"Bryce, I want you to see something; do you have a minute?"

When Bryce saw the pictures, he immediately caught sight of what Tessa had noticed. The photos also confirmed what Cole had mentioned in his email. There was an eerie amount of similarity in the individuals from place to place. Tessa pointed to the sixth victim from Calgary and Vancouver.

"Look at these two guys, Bryce; they could pass for brothers. They look familiar to me, but I can't put my finger on who I know with a similar appearance." She paused. "This guy is getting ready to kill again, and then he will disappear: we aren't any closer to finding out who he is than we were a couple of days ago. I have my suspicions but no concrete proof."

"Does Jack agree with your suspicions?" Bryce inquired.

"Not exactly." Tessa went on to explain about Camden, Jack's neighbour.

Bryce nodded. When she was finished, he walked to the door. "I'll wait until Jack gets here and then you two can go and have a talk with this fellow. Leave his sister out of it. By the sounds of what you said happened yesterday, she won't say anything to incriminate her brother. She probably doesn't even know what he has done—if it is him, of course—and if she does, she is too afraid to open her mouth." Bryce returned to his office.

~

After Andrew dropped the email off to Jack, he headed to the gym. He needed a good workout and knew there was plenty of time before he had to be on the job. Paige was at the front desk when he arrived.

"Good morning, Andrew, you're here early today."

"Missed yesterday," he answered. "Have to keep this body in good shape for the girls."

Paige laughed. "Have a good workout, Andrew."

"You bet."

~

Jack turned to Toby as he was getting ready to head down to the station. "Want to come, old man? You haven't been getting out much with me lately."

Toby looked up and then put his head back down on the couch and pretended to be asleep.

"Okay then, you rest … you're going to put on weight if you don't start getting out and about," Jack chuckled.

"Won't be putting on weight, buddy. I got things to look after, so get on your way so I can get on mine!" Toby opened his eyes to keep his lookout on the sidewalk. He knew Andrew was at the gym, but he hadn't seen Camden walk to work yet.

On the way to the station, Jack thought to stop in at the gym and double-check with reception about the names. Tessa's statement that this was the only gym he hadn't personally checked was nagging at him.

"Hi, how can I help you, sir," Paige greeted Jack.

Jack flashed his badge. "I need you to check your files to see if any of these names are on your membership list." Jack produced a piece of paper with the five victims' names.

"I can tell you right off that one of them is … actually, two," Paige pointed to Tyler and Owen. "Give me a minute, and I'll look up the ladies. If they don't come in too often, I don't always remember them. I remember the men because Tyler made a pass at me and Owen came in drunk the other day … I had to tell him he couldn't work out." She returned to the counter a few minutes later with the piece of paper. She had checked off all the ladies' names. "Looks like they're all members. Have they done something wrong?"

Jack wondered what planet this girl lived on and if she ever watched the news or read the paper. Probably not, he told himself as he looked at her chewing her bubble gum. "No, they haven't done anything wrong." Jack thought not to tell her they were dead—not yet anyway. He thanked Paige for the information and headed out.

As he was driving, Jack pondered about why Camden told him none of the victims were gym members. He was beginning to have second thoughts about his neighbour. A few blocks before the station, the van began to sputter. Jack looked at his gas gauge; it was below the red line. "Damn!" he yelled and hit the steering wheel. He managed to get the van pulled over to the sidewalk, got out, locked it, and began walking. He was not in the best of moods when he stepped through the door of Tessa's temporary office.

"Who ate your breakfast?" she smiled.

"Ran out of gas."

Tessa laughed. Then she got down to business. "Got the email?"

"Yep. And I got something else, too. I stopped by the gym down the street from me on my way here. All five victims belonged to that gym. Camden was lying to me, or maybe he just didn't have the proper access needed to see the entire membership list. I don't think he works front desk much." Jack was still trying not to believe Camden was involved in such a horrendous crime.

"Oh, I think Camden was lying to you, Jack," Tessa wasn't holding back any punches with her words. "By the way, what does the young man do at the gym?" she added.

"I think he mentioned doing a lot of the cleaning," Jack's face went pale, "and he works the drink counter, making and serving the members drinks."

Tessa pointed to the pictures on the table. "These are the sixth victims in Calgary and Vancouver, both men, which we know the next victim here is going to be. Look at them Jack; look at how much they look alike. They remind me of someone, but I can't put my finger on a name."

If Jack's face could have gone any paler, it would have. His hands began to shake as he picked up the two pictures. "Andrew!" he breathed.

"Oh, my God! Yes … Andrew! And he's the one who's received the email, isn't he? Do you know where he is at the moment?"

"At the gym. He was going there after he dropped off the email."

"We'll take my car," Tessa said as she headed out the door. "I hope we're not too late."

~

About five minutes after Jack left the house, Camden walked by. He looked into the window as he passed and gave Toby the finger. *Damn cat.*

Toby didn't waste any time. As soon as Camden was out of sight, he raced to the kitchen, pushed through the cat door, and headed for the gym. He climbed up his tree and took his post at the skylight over the drink counter. Toby had peeked in one of the other skylights on his way to the front of the building and saw that Andrew was still working out.

Camden was having a conversation with Paige, and he didn't look happy about what she was telling him. His face was sullen as he prepared his area to serve the customers. A couple of women walked up, and he made them smoothies. Andrew was still working out. Toby repositioned himself so he could see the change room—so he would know when Andrew was getting ready to leave. He still had no idea how he was going to stop this, but Toby knew he'd do what he had to so Jack's friend wouldn't die!

Finally, Toby noticed Andrew headed to the change room. Camden was watching Andrew, as well. He waited a few minutes and then began to mix another smoothie, even though there was no one at the counter. Toby watched as Camden poured the white powder from his baggie into the drink. He began to pace nervously around the window. Andrew was walking toward Camden, smiling.

"Damn, he's taking the drink. What to do? What to do?" Toby saw Andrew take a sip of the drink and then he nodded and put some money on the counter. He picked up his gym bag and headed out the door to the parking lot.

"There's only one thing for me to do!" Toby ran to the edge of the building, which breached the parking lot. Andrew was just passing by. Toby crouched on the ledge and then leapt off. He missed Andrew's back but knocked the hand holding the drink. The cup went flying into the air and landed on the asphalt.

Andrew cursed. "What the hell! ... Toby?"

Toby was lying on the asphalt. He wasn't moving. He could feel the pain in his front legs and his shoulders.

212

"At least Andrew can't drink the smoothie now!" His tail flapped weakly on the ground.

Andrew was kneeling down beside Toby when Tessa and Jack came roaring into the parking lot. Jack jumped out of the car and raced to his friend. When he saw Toby lying still on the ground, he fell to his knees beside his furry friend. "What happened here, Andrew?" Jack asked as Tessa came up beside him.

"Your cat just jumped from out of nowhere and hit me, Jack—spilled my drink all over the place. What has gotten into Toby? I thought he liked me."

Jack looked at the empty cup on the ground. He looked at the liquid surrounding it. "Who made the drink for you, Andrew?"

"The young fellow at the beverage counter; Camden is his name, I think."

"How much did you drink?"

"I just had a couple of small sips before Toby knocked it out of my hand."

"I think Toby just saved your life," Jack notified Andrew. "Tessa, we need to bag this cup and some of the liquid and get it sent to the lab for testing."

Tessa reached into her car and grabbed a plastic bag. She also put on a pair of gloves before she picked up the cup. "We'll need to have this dusted for prints," she pointed out.

Jack turned to Tessa. "I hate to request this of you, but I need to ask you to get Andrew to the hospital and then take Toby to the vet." He took out a piece of paper and scribbled down an address. "I have someone we need to talk to."

"I didn't really have that much, Jack. I should be okay," Andrew stated.

"Get checked anyway," Jack ordered. "This poison that is being used is pretty lethal, and if my guess is right, there was probably an extra-large dose in your drink. You will start to get cramps, and you will get the sweats, and then vomiting and diarrhea. Don't take any chances." Jack knelt down beside Toby and stroked his fur. "It's okay, old man, you're going to be okay. Tessa is going to get you to the doctor. You're a tough old detective…" A tear dropped down onto Toby's side. Jack wiped his cheek.

Jack gathered Toby up and handed him to Tessa. She'd already pulled a blanket from her trunk and had laid it on her backseat. Jack didn't wait for Tessa and Andrew to leave; he was already walking toward the gym entrance. Not seeing Camden, Jack approached Paige and asked her where he was. She pointed to the back door.

"He took the garbage out about five minutes ago. He hasn't returned yet. He might be in the washroom. I didn't see him come back in the building because I was serving a customer. What do you want him for?"

"I just need to talk to him," Jack replied.

~

Camden was taking the garbage out when he noticed the commotion in the parking lot. His head began to pound. It was all over. He knew it would be one day. Maybe now he could get some help—maybe. Or, maybe they didn't really have enough evidence and he would walk free. He had Emma to think of. He couldn't leave her. If he could buy some time, they could just throw a few things in the van and leave. Camden waited behind the dumpster until Jack walked into the front of the building and until Tessa drove out of the parking lot before he took off for his house.

He burst through the front door. "Get your things, Emma! We're going for a ride. Bring Duke."

"What do you mean, my things, Cam—what things?"

Cam was pacing in the foyer. "Think … think," he mumbled, hitting his head with the palm of his hand. "Don't panic her." He turned to Emma: "Just your purse. I want to take you out. You have been too cooped up here. Thought you could join me to pick up a few items for our trip."

"Why does Duke have to come with us; wouldn't it be easier to leave him home?"

"No, just get your purse and get in the van; I'll get Duke!" Camden yelled.

214

Emma was climbing into the van when Jack walked up. "Emma, where is your brother?"

"Inside. We are going shopping. He's just getting Duke. Why, Jack?" Emma's eyes grew round with fear. "You're scaring me, Jack; what's going on?" She started crying.

Camden saw Jack at the van. His head was screaming with pain. Duke was barking, and then he started running from the front to the back of the house. Camden decided he had to leave. He headed for the back door. As he went through the three-season room, he stopped for a moment and picked whatever seeds were left on the castor bean plant and popped them in his mouth. His teeth came down on the seeds, and he crunched them as quickly as he could, and then opened the door to flee. Emma would be better off without him. Maybe Jack would look after her.

Jack had caught a glimpse of Camden in the three-season room and noticed him putting something in his mouth. Jack hurried through the house and into the backyard as fast as he could to get to Camden before he swallowed whatever it was he'd taken. But Camden was running now, and Duke was also in the backyard.

"Emma!" Jack hollered. "Back here! Help me, Emma … call your dog off!"

Emma didn't know where she got the strength, but she managed to get out of the van and made her way to the backyard. She called to Duke, who had Jack backed into a corner. Duke was barking and growling. Emma raced to her dog, took hold of his collar and pulled him away, freeing Jack to go after Cameron.

"It's okay, Duke—it's okay, boy."

As Jack ran after Camden, Camden tripped and fell over a pile of weeds Emma hadn't cleared away yet. "We need to get Camden to the hospital," Jack hollered to Emma. "I saw him put something in his mouth. He picked it off that plant in the corner of the room." Jack turned to Emma as he placed a set of handcuffs on Camden. "What is that plant, Emma?"

Emma's face turned pale when she realized the plant Jack was pointing to. "That's the castor bean plant," she whispered.

"Castor bean … don't they make castor oil from that?" Jack questioned.

"Yes, but the seeds and the rest of the plant are poisonous." Emma turned to Camden. "Did you eat some of the seeds, Cam? What are you doing?" Then she shook her head. "What have you done?"

Camden hung his head and looked away. His stomach was already beginning to cramp.

"I need your van," Jack said to Emma.

She nodded.

On the way to the hospital, Jack called first to Bryce to tell him what was going on and ask him to send a couple officers to the hospital. Then he called the hospital, identified himself and the situation, and requested to speak to the attending physician.

"I have an individual here that has just consumed the seeds from a castor bean plant. I understand from his sister they're highly poisonous. I'm bringing him in right now. He will have to be under watch from the police because he is also our prime suspect in a murder case."

"Castor bean seeds, you say," the doctor said. "That means your fellow has ricin poisoning; you better get here as fast as you can. We will have to pump his stomach and then put him on an I.V. drip of saline and glucose. How far away are you?"

"Five minutes."

"We'll be ready." The doctor hung up.

Jack turned to Camden who was sitting in the back of the van. He was staring out the window and rocking back and forth as much as the seatbelt would allow. He had a peculiar smile on his face, and his eyes appeared vacant. "Why'd you do it, son?"

Camden didn't answer. He just kept rocking and staring.

Jack pulled up by the emergency door and got out of the van. He had to drag Camden out of the backseat because he had gone limp. Once Jack got him out, he literally picked Camden up and carried him into the hospital. A nurse came running up; Jack recognized her as Karen, the one he had talked to previously. She also recognized him.

"This way, Officer Nelson, we have set up for you in a private room. We thought it would be better that way."

Jack followed Karen into a room and laid Camden on the bed. She asked him to take the handcuffs off so they could get the stomach pump going and hook Camden to an I.V. "You can handcuff one hand to the bed if you like," she suggested when she noted the look on Jack's face.

Jack did so and then left the room. Tessa was waiting for him in the waiting area. "Do you think he'll make it?"

"Hard to tell; depends on how many he took. I didn't see any signs of cramping or such starting yet, but he was looking really weird. The doctors didn't know what they were looking for before, but the doctor I talked to on the phone, as soon as I said castor bean, he knew exactly what to do, so the possibility our perp will pull through is good."

"Great, then we can find out why he has done this." Tessa shook her head.

"How's Andrew?" Jack asked.

"He hadn't ingested too much of the drink, but they hooked him up to a saline and glucose drip just to make sure," Tessa replied. "The doctor said he'll be fine."

"Thanks for dropping Toby at the vet," Jack turned his attention to the hero of the hour. "What did they say? Or did you..." Jack was choking up and couldn't finish his question.

Tessa laid a hand on Jack's arm. "I dropped Andrew here and then took Toby straight to the vet. The old fellow is pretty broken up, Jack. Both his front legs are broken, and there is damage in the shoulders and back legs. The vet won't know until they operate how much. She is also going to do an ultrasound to see if there's internal bleeding. He's in surgery now; she'll call you when he's out."

Jack was doing his best to hold back his tears. "He's a tough old cat," he whispered huskily.

"He is, Jack … if any cat can pull through, it will be Toby. Andrew said he owes his life to the old furball and said when he gets better, he's going to buy Toby the biggest catnip mouse he has ever seen!"

"I have to go and check on Emma. She's probably a wreck by now. Thanks again, Tessa."

~

Emma was sitting on the floor in the middle of the living room when Jack showed up. She was rocking back and forth. Her eyes were red and swollen. Duke lay protectively by her side, his head on her leg. As Jack came through the door, Duke looked up and growled. Emma put her hand on his head and calmed him down. "It's okay, boy, Jack's a friend."

Jack was touched by her words. He sat down on a nearby chair and leant toward her. "How are you doing?" he asked, even though he knew it was a dumb question.

Emma looked up at him. "Not good." She paused. "I could never figure out why we had to move so much and always so suddenly. Camden was good at explanations, and I never questioned a great deal—until this time. Everything happened quickly here, but I don't want to move. I had made a friend—Toby. And you," she added.

Jack's heart skipped a beat when Emma said Toby's name. He wondered if he should tell her or if the shock of finding out what Toby was going through would damage her more. He decided to wait. "Once your brother comes out of the hospital, we will have to take him to a holding cell at the station. We will be questioning him. I need to see his room, if I could have your permission to do that."

"No problem."

"Did Camden ever see a doctor—a therapist of any sort?" Jack queried.

"When we were in Vancouver he was seeing a lady doctor. Her name was Lucy; I met her a couple of times. He told me he just needed to talk a few things out with her—about our childhood and stuff like that." Emma hesitated. "Camden has not had it easy, you know, but he's always been there for me. I don't understand … I just don't get it." Emma began to cry.

Jack saw a tissue box and retrieved one for Emma. "Here," he said as he handed it to her. "You wouldn't happen to have Doctor Lucy's number, would you?"

Emma shook her head. "No, I never knew it. Camden said I didn't need to."

Jack took out a pad of paper and wrote a note to get Tessa to call her friend in Vancouver. He should be able to find the doctor. Hopefully she can shine some light on what makes this guy tick.

"Would you like to stay at my place tonight?" Jack reached over and laid his hand gently on Emma's shoulder.

"Will Toby be there?"

Jack's heart fell. His face was sad as he began to tell Emma what had happened to Toby. "Toby must have known what your brother was up to, Emma. He was watching through the skylights at the gym, and when he saw Andrew exiting the gym with a drink Camden had just served him, Toby jumped from the roof right onto Andrew. He managed to knock the cup to the ground, but he landed hard on the pavement. Toby is at the vet's right now having surgery. He's a tough old cat; he'll be okay."

Emma began to cry again. "Oh no, oh no," she moaned through her tears. Jack reached over and gathered the young woman into his arms. She buried her face in his shirt and let the tears flow freely.

~

Tessa waited until the police officers who were going to guard Camden arrived before heading out to Jack's place. When she walked in, Jack was just laying a blanket over a sleeping Emma. He raised a finger to his lips. "She's exhausted, poor thing."

219

Tessa nodded and walked to the kitchen. "Where's her dog?" she inquired when Jack joined her.

"I made sure he had food and water and left him over there. I'll check on him later."

"Have you heard from the vet yet?" Tessa's voice was full of concern. She knew how much the cat meant to Jack.

"No, I was about to call," Jack answered. "Oh, before I forget, Emma mentioned something about Camden seeing a Doctor Lucy when he was in Vancouver. I believe she was probably some sort of psychologist because Emma said her brother went there to talk about things that had happened in the past. She didn't know the last name. Maybe you could call your friend out west, and he could do some investigating for us."

Jack called the vet's office and was informed Toby was still in surgery; they would call as soon as he was out … Jack was not to worry. They added that everything was going well, and, despite Toby's age, he was very healthy. They would be keeping him at the animal hospital for a few days for observation.

Tessa placed a call to Cole and explained what had happened. She mentioned that, if it were possible, she would appreciate it if he could try and find a Doctor Lucy who would have been seeing Camden Gale, probably up until May. Cole said he would see what he could do. He also mentioned that if Camden pulled through, he would like to come to Brantford on behalf of the Vancouver police department and sit in on the interrogation. Cole was assuming Camden was the one who had left a trail of death behind him in the west, and he was anxious to close some of their open cases.

When they finished their phone calls, Jack asked Tessa if she would like a drink. "A nice peppermint tea would be great if you have it," she replied.

"Sorry, no fancy stuff in this old bachelor's cupboards." He smiled and rummaged through his tea boxes. "Here's some Earl Grey; will that do?"

"Sure."

"I think I'll just have a beer," Jack said as he plugged in the kettle.

The two police officers—profiler and retired cop—sat looking at each other. Silence filled the room; it had been a gruelling time, and there was no rhyme or reason to any of it. They were both exhausted. They looked into each other's eyes, noticing each other's loneliness.

"Would you like to stay the night?" Jack asked. "I have a guest room."

Tessa looked up and smiled. "That'd be great." She wasn't quite at the point where she could say what she was thinking—that the guest room wouldn't be necessary.

Saturday, July 4, 2009

By the time Jack woke up in the morning, Emma was gone. He assumed she went home to check on Duke but decided it would be best to double-check. He slipped into some clothes and headed to her house. Just as he thought, Emma was in the backyard with Duke. She looked up and smiled as he entered.

"Did you sleep well?" Jack inquired.

"Well enough, I guess." Emma threw a ball for Duke to chase.

"Would you like to come back over for some breakfast?"

Emma shook her head. "I'm not really hungry." She noticed the look of concern on Jack's face and added: "I'll be okay; I'll eat later—honestly."

Jack hesitated. "Well if you need anything you know where I am."

"There is one thing I'd like," Emma said as Jack started to leave. "I'd like to go and see Toby."

Jack thought it strange that it wouldn't be her brother she wanted to see first. "I'll be going later this morning; you are welcome to join me. And, if you like, on the way back I can take you to see your brother," Jack offered.

Emma looked at Jack and he noticed the blankness in her eyes. "That won't be necessary just yet. Maybe tomorrow." She turned and threw the ball again. Duke bounded after it. Jack left and headed back to his place.

As Jack approached his back door, he smelled fresh coffee. Tessa must be up. "Good morning, Jack," she greeted him. "I hope you like your coffee strong in the mornings ... I do." She had two cups waiting by the coffeemaker.

"Would you like something to eat?" Jack asked as he opened the refrigerator and took out a dozen eggs.

"Actually, just a piece of toast with some jam, if you have it, would be enough for me. I'm not much of a breakfast person." Tessa poured the coffee and set the cups on the table.

"You don't mind if I keep my cholesterol up and have a couple of eggs with my toast, do you?" Jack chuckled.

"You go right ahead, sir," Tessa joined in his chuckle.

After breakfast they called the hospital to inquire about Camden and Andrew and were lucky to talk to Karen.

"Andrew is just fine. He didn't ingest enough poison to make him sick. We gave him the saline and glucose anyway and then sent him home." Karen confirmed what Tessa had already told Jack. She paused a moment. "As for Camden, he's still critical, but I think he'll pull through. It will take a few days. He has been talking in his sleep quite a bit."

"Any idea what he's saying?" Jack enquired.

"Most of what he says is incomprehensible, except when he says Emma's name."

"Well, we will be up shortly. I have to go and check on my cat, Toby."

"Yeah, Andrew told me how your cat saved his life—amazing."

"Yep, Toby is pretty incredible," Jack confirmed before he said goodbye and hung up the phone. He turned to Tessa. "If I could impose on you to drive me to a gas station, I can get some gas in the old beast I left on the side of the road. Hopefully, it hasn't been towed."

"No problem, Jack. I think I'll go home and change and then meet you up at the vet's, if that's okay with you."

Jack nodded. It was just fine with him. "We need to pick up Emma; she wants to see Toby."

"Not her brother?"

"Not yet."

"Hmm … strange."

"I thought so too … want me to swing by your place after I get gas and pick you up? That way we don't have to take two vehicles."

"Sounds like a plan."

~

Jack, Tessa, and Emma were asked to sit in the waiting room while the vet was retrieved. "Hello there, Jack," the vet said as she came into the room. "Your Toby is a pretty lucky kitty. I think this jump he did probably used up a few of those nine lives. I still have him heavily sedated, but you can look in on him if you like. Follow me."

Toby was sleeping on a blanket in a cage. Jack noticed how laboured Toby's breathing was. He had a cast on both front legs, extending up into the shoulder area. One of his back legs was in a splint.

"There was not as much damage to Toby's hind end because his front legs took the majority of the jolt when he landed. The ultrasound came back clear, showing no internal bleeding," the vet informed. "You can talk to him if you like; he may not respond, but he'll know you are here."

Emma was the first one to approach the cage. She opened the door and reached her hand in and gently stroked Toby between the ears. "Get better, Toby ... please," she whispered. "I want you to come home. You are so brave," her voice choked with emotion. She moved her fingers down to his side and then turned to Jack as she felt a small vibration from within Toby's stomach. "He's purring," she smiled. "He's going to be okay—he's purring."

Jack stepped forward and peeked in at Toby. "Come on, old man, there's work to be done at the house; can't have you slackin' off now, can we?"

Tessa stood back and watched the two people at Toby's cage. The sight made her feel warm all over.

~

On the way to the hospital, Jack asked Emma, again, if she would like to see her brother. Again, she said she would rather wait; she wasn't ready to see him. Emma said she would wait in the van—no need to go out of their way to take her home.

Jack and Tessa were only about twenty minutes in the hospital. Camden was still on the I.V. drip, but he was coming around. If he kept improving, they could probably move him to the police station by Monday or Tuesday. There was still a police officer posted outside his room; they weren't taking any chances on an early recovery and possible escape. Things like that had happened before, even when prisoners were handcuffed to a bed.

On the way out of the hospital, Jack looked at his watch. "How say we stop for a bite to eat? I doubt Emma has eaten today."

"Sounds good. If you wouldn't mind dropping me at home afterwards, I have some tasks I need to catch up on this afternoon. I don't expect to hear from Cole before Monday, but you never know."

Emma tried to protest when Jack mentioned lunch, but he and Tessa insisted she needed to eat. Finally she relented. Jack drove to Swiss Chalet, which was close to where Tessa lived. Emma only ordered soup and a bun, but at least she ate. After lunch Jack dropped Tessa at her place, and then he and Emma headed home.

Emma was extraordinarily quiet. Out of the blue, she began to speak. "I always wondered if there was something wrong with my brother—us being twins and all—but he has always been so good to me. Maybe I turned a blind eye to what might be happening."

"You had no way of knowing, Emma. Camden hid his secrets from you, probably because he does love you and wants to protect you from who he really is."

"But how is it that I didn't see what was going on? How many times did we just have to up and move with little or no notice? I should have insisted on knowing why ... all those people..."

"How many times was it, Emma?" Jack asked.

"Too many in the past six years."

Jack thought for a moment before he asked the next question. Emma saying the word six had triggered a thought in his mind. "Do you have any idea what significance 666 might have to your brother?"

225

Emma pondered for a moment. "I don't really know. Isn't that some sort of religious thing to do with the end of time? One of the foster parents we had was really into religion, and she was always talking about 666 being the mark of the devil. Why do you ask?"

"Your brother sent emails to his victims before he poisoned them and the signature he used was 666."

Emma shook her head. "No, I have no idea." Abruptly, she clammed up and looked out the window. When Jack stopped in front of her house, she got out and thanked him for taking her to see Toby. "If you're going tomorrow, I'd like to come along," she mentioned as she shut the van door.

Jack spent the rest of the afternoon tidying up his place. At five o'clock he thought to call Tessa and invite her over for supper. He was getting used to her company. There was no answer.

Tessa heard the phone ring, but when she saw it was Jack, she decided not to answer it. She had been thinking about what might happen if she let him into her life any further, and she was scared. Relationships scared her more than profiling and dealing with criminals, and Jack was someone Tessa knew she could get real comfortable with. She wasn't sure if she was ready to cross that line and was glad she hadn't suggested anything romantic the other night when her emotional guard had been down.

She'd call him later, but she didn't.

Sunday, July 5, 2009

Andrew stopped in at Jack's house with a couple of coffees on Sunday morning. "Boss gave me two days off. Just thought to drop in and see if you and Tessa would like to join Jody and me for brunch."

Jack looked at the clock. "I'll give Tessa another hour and then call her."

"How's the sister holding up?" Andrew asked.

"Better than I thought. In some ways, Emma looks almost relieved. I have no idea what their financial state is or how she's going to support herself when her brother is in jail, but I do know she wants to stay in the house and I intend to help her out in any way I can."

"Crazy how she didn't know all these years."

"Camden was good at hiding what he was doing. And, in all fairness to him, he loves Emma, and I don't think he would ever intentionally hurt her. He's done what he's done for some deep-seated reason that I am hoping will be exposed sooner rather than later."

"How's my hero, Toby, doing?"

"He's going to take a while to recover, but he'll be okay. He purred yesterday when Emma stroked him."

"I'm glad to hear that; he's an amazingly brave cat."

"That's what everyone is saying."

The two friends talked on about other things. Andrew touched on his hopes about Jody; Jack was glad to hear Andrew might have found someone to share his life with. At ten o'clock Jack called Tessa. Still no answer.

"Maybe she's gone out of town; they do call her in for other cases sometimes. You and Jody go along and have a nice lunch. I think I'll just hang around here and keep an eye on Emma. She wanted to go see Toby, too."

Andrew finally left: Jack walked over to see if Emma was ready to go to visit Toby. She was in her living room unpacking boxes. She looked up when Jack came in. "I don't know how I'm going to be able to stay here," she said, tears brimming in her eyes. "But I want to."

"If there is anything I can do to help, I will."

"Thank you, Jack, you are a good friend … first one I think I have ever had … that I remember, anyway."

Jack and Emma ended up going for a drive after visiting Toby. He was still heavily sedated, but his purr seemed a bit louder when Emma stroked him. Jack took her down to the Wilkes Dam and then they drove along the river road to Cambridge. On the way back to Brantford, Jack called Tessa again. Still no answer.

"How about I rustle us up some grub?" Jack suggested to Emma as they turned onto their street. "A couple of burgers and a salad?"

"That sounds lovely; I just have to go and check on Duke."

"Why don't you bring him over; I'll throw an extra burger on for him." Jack smiled.

Emma returned the smile.

After supper Jack put a movie into the DVD player—he didn't have cable—and the two companions spent a quiet evening together. Duke sprawled across the carpet and went off to sleep. At ten o'clock Jack walked Emma home and saw her safely inside.

"Your brother may be getting out of the hospital tomorrow."

Before Jack could elaborate further, Emma said "Give him my regards." Her tone was cold. "Thank you for the lovely evening, Jack. Goodnight." And the door closed.

Jack went home and called Tessa. Finally, on the sixth ring, she picked up. "You okay?" he asked.

"I just needed some time to unwind," she answered.

"See you in the morning?"

"I'll meet you at the station at nine o'clock. I have an email from Cole; he found Doctor Lucy. They are flying into the Hamilton airport tomorrow at noon. Would you like to go with me to pick them up?"

"Sounds like a plan. See you in the morning." Jack hung up the phone, went around and turned his lights off, and then headed off to bed. It was a lonely house without Toby.

Monday, July 6, 2009

Jack checked on Emma before he headed to the station. She assured him she was doing fine; she was busy cleaning the house. Jack asked her not to touch anything in Camden's room and also not to do anything with the castor bean plant. She guaranteed she wouldn't.

Tessa was already sitting in Bryce's office when Jack arrived. They motioned for Jack to come in and have a seat. "Camden is being released into our custody today. He is still weak, but he's out of danger. The hospital doesn't want the responsibility of looking after him any longer. I think we'll have to keep a twenty-four-hour guard on him," Bryce specified.

"Good idea," Tessa confirmed. "The fact he tried to kill himself by ingesting the beans shows he is emotionally unstable." She turned to Jack. "How's Emma doing?"

"Surprisingly well under the circumstances. She's unpacking the boxes her brother packed. She wants to stay … doesn't know how yet, but I said I would help her in any way I could."

"You are a good man, Jack Nelson," Tessa stated. She turned to Bryce. "What time is Camden supposed to be here?"

"Any time now. I just sent another officer up to the hospital to help escort him."

"I think we should wait on questioning him until we talk with this Doctor Lucy. She may know something that could help focus our interrogations in the right direction."

"Whatever you think, Tessa." Bryce stood and walked to his window. "You know, in all my years on the force, I have never been able to figure out why some people do the things they do. When do they break down and cross that line of being a human and decide to play God with other people's lives?" Bryce returned to his chair and shuffled through some papers.

Jack and Tessa got the message and took their leave. They waited long enough to see Camden brought in and put into a holding cell. Tessa left instructions for him to be watched every minute and that anything he might be able to use to take his life should be removed from his person and from his cell. She mentioned that she and Jack would be returning shortly after lunch with a doctor who would hopefully be able to enlighten them on Camden's past.

"Want a coffee?" Jack asked on the way out the door.

"Why don't we head to the airport and just have a coffee there, save us from stopping twice," Tessa suggested.

Jack nodded. "Your car or my beast?"

Tessa was still tired. "Your beast," she chuckled.

By the time they arrived at the airport, they only had about an hour's wait until the plane landed. Cole and Tessa embraced, and then introductions were made all around. On the way back to the station, Doctor Lucy was briefly filled in on what had taken place. "I'd like to talk with Camden alone if possible," she expressed.

Tessa nodded affirmation. "That won't be a problem, but we will be watching and listening through the two-way mirror, if you don't mind?"

"Not at all."

Doctor Lucy was escorted to the interrogation room as soon as they arrived at the station. Tessa had called ahead and asked for Camden to be moved in there before they arrived. Once again, she emphasized that he not be left alone.

Doctor Lucy sat down. Camden was sitting with his head buried in his arms on the table. "Hello, Camden."

He didn't look up.

"How's Emma?" Lucy knew Camden had a soft spot for his sister.

Still, he did not look up.

"I hear you have been busy since you came to Brantford," Lucy tried another avenue.

231

Camden finally looked up and smiled, but his eyes were like lost tombs buried in a dark abyss. "Who told you that?" his voice was scratchy.

"I heard it through the grapevine. I also heard you were busy in other places."

The same smile presented itself.

"So, how is Emma?" Lucy asked again.

This time Camden answered. "I don't know; they won't let me see her."

On the other side of the wall, Tessa turned to Jack: "I thought Emma didn't want to see her brother."

"She doesn't."

"Why then..."

"Because it's our fault he is not seeing her, not hers. Camden wouldn't blame her," Jack explained. They returned their attention to the interrogation.

"Why is that?" Lucy asked, continuing her questioning.

"Because they're evil."

"Who is evil?"

"Them ... the police ... evil ... evil ... evil!" He hit his head with his hands, an action that was becoming a habit.

"In what way?"

"Like all the rest were evil."

"Who are all the rest? The victims?"

"There were no victims," Camden snorted. "These people weren't victims—they victimized!"

"Who did they victimize, Camden?"

"Everyone around them ... I want to see my sister." Camden put his head back down on the table.

"I don't think that is possible right now, but I will see what I can do later—after you have answered a few more questions."

"I'm not saying anything more until I see my sister," Camden mumbled into his arm.

"Okay, I'll go out and ask the officers if they will allow it," Lucy said and walked out of the room. She approached Tessa and Jack. "Any chance Emma will come in and talk to him?"

Jack shook his head. "I can try, but she seemed pretty set on not seeing him just yet. I think she is afraid, but I don't know of what."

"So he doesn't know it's his sister who doesn't want to see him?"

"No, he doesn't know," Jack replied.

Doctor Lucy returned to the room and sat down. "They said no," she stated. "But I will keep working on them for you if you answer a few more of my questions."

Camden looked up. "Why should I believe you?"

"Have I ever lied to you, Camden? I thought we had a good relationship during our sessions."

"That's right ... everyone *thinks*. How would I even know how much you lied to me? The only person I can trust is Emma."

"How do you know that?"

"She's my twin ... she can't betray me."

"Who betrayed you, Camden?" This was territory that hadn't even been touched on when he had come to her in Vancouver. There had never been talk of betrayals.

"Everyone."

"Name names."

"Can't remember them all ... there were too many." Camden returned his head to the table.

"Would you like something to drink, Camden?"

He didn't answer.

She stood. "Well, I'm going to grab a juice ... sure you don't want me to get you something?"

Silence.

Doctor Lucy left the room again. "He is really closed up, more so than when I was seeing him. Makes me think he was hiding a lot then, especially since I know now what he has been up to here. I have also been in touch with a couple of doctors who treated him in other cities. They both mentioned that Camden can appear quite normal most times, but they always felt there were some very gloomy underlying issues going on in his head. One of the doctors felt there was a possibility that Camden was paranoid delusional, which would explain a lot."

Lucy looked through the window. Camden was still sitting with his head on the table. "I should have read the signs, but he left before I could get into deeper issues with him. I thought I was making progress, but I guess I was just scratching the surface—only what he wanted me to know. He's smart." She paused. "I am the only doctor he went to who was allowed to meet Emma—so he told me."

"Would you like me to get you something to drink?" Jack asked.

"An orange juice would be nice, thank you."

Jack come back with the juice and Lucy returned to the interrogation room. She sat opposite Camden, sipping on her drink. Finally, he looked up. "Shall we continue?" Lucy suggested.

Camden sighed.

"Why don't we start from the beginning? Who was the first person to betrayed you?"

"There were two."

"Who were they? Can you remember their names?"

"Mommy and Daddy."

Lucy didn't flinch. "How did they betray you?"

"By not caring."

"How did they not care?"

"They only cared for themselves. Our parents didn't care about Emma and me. That's why I had to look after her. She was always frail—because they didn't care enough to love us, to make sure there was enough food in the house … to pay the bills so we could be warm. They were selfish, mean people." Camden hit his head a few more times, then rested it back on the table again. "I want to go back to my cell. I won't say another word until I see Emma. I have to know she's okay."

"Okay, Camden. I think you have had enough for today. I will see what I can do to get Emma here tomorrow. You are going to have to talk to me, though, you know. The district attorney is laying some pretty hefty charges on you——and those are just here in Brantford. You are going to have to face criminal charges elsewhere, as well." Lucy paused. "There is a police officer here who flew in from

Vancouver with me; he has an entire file devoted to you. Six victims … just like here…"

Camden looked up and smiled. He'd thought Andrew had expired. He hadn't seen him in the hospital.

Lucy continued: "Well, not quite like here. There were only five victims here. Apparently, a cat saved the intended sixth one." She stood and walked out, having dropped her bomb. "You can take him back to his cell," she nodded to the officer waiting outside the door. "We are finished for today." Lucy turned to Jack. "What are the chances of getting Emma here tomorrow?"

"I'll try. Maybe she'd come if you asked her. It seemed as though she liked you when she spoke of you," Jack suggested.

"Well, it's worth a try. Lead the way."

Jack dropped Tessa and Cole off at his place, suggesting it would be better if just he and Lucy went to see Emma. Tessa agreed. "We can make ourselves at home," she stated.

"We won't be long," Lucy said as she and Jack went out the door.

Emma didn't answer the front door, so Jack and Lucy went around back. She was in her three-season room, watering her plants. Emma had put a sheet over the castor bean plants. Her face brightened when she saw Lucy. "Doctor Lucy! Come in, please. Forgive the mess," Emma said as she led her visitors into the kitchen. "I'm just getting things put away again. Have a seat." She pointed to the chairs around the table.

Lucy looked around. "You have a lovely little place here, Emma; are you comfortable?"

"I am now."

"I don't understand."

"Now I don't have to move again."

"Yes, I think one of the times I met you, you mentioned moving around so much bothered you, and you hoped you would be able to stay in Vancouver." Lucy paused. There was no easy way to say what had to be said. "Camden is very sick, Emma."

Emma looked away. "I think I know that. In fact, I think I have suspected it for a while now; I just didn't know what to do."

"But he really needs to see you, Emma."

"I don't know if I can … yet."

"He says he is the stronger of the two of you, but I don't think so. What do you think, Emma?"

Emma looked out the window. "I believe he is wrong. I think … maybe … he kept me weak. I've been reading a lot. I saw some programs on television and I looked up stuff on the computer Camden gave me for my room. He never allowed me to use his personal laptop. I began to realize it would have been better for me to get counselling after the rape—especially after the guy got off. But Camden said no; he said it was just another example of how the system failed us. So we moved. And moved and moved." She turned back to Jack and Lucy. "If you think it will help I'll see him, but not until tomorrow."

"That will be good enough; we will pick you up in the morning around nine. Is that too early?" Lucy asked.

"That's fine. I don't sleep much anyway." Emma turned to Jack. "How's Toby doing?"

"The vet said I could probably bring him home by the weekend."

Emma's face brightened, despite the moisture in her eyes. It was good to see her so relaxed. Jack and Lucy took their leave. On the way to Jack's, Lucy said she was sure Emma was going to be okay now that she was free of her brother.

Tuesday, July 7, 2009

Emma stood outside the interrogation room and gazed in at her brother. A tear slipped down her cheek. She turned to Lucy: "He looks so lost."

"He is lost, Emma," Lucy stated quietly. She laid a hand on Emma's shoulder. "He needs you now. Are you ready?"

Emma nodded and followed Lucy through the door. Camden stood when he saw his sister. Emma didn't approach him. She sat in a chair beside Lucy. "How are you Camden?" she asked in a firm, quiet voice.

There was a puzzled look on Camden's face as he sat down. This wasn't the fragile sister he had known. There was something different about her. "I'm okay," he finally answered.

"What have you done, Camden?" Emma looked her brother straight in the eyes. "No one ever hurt you so badly that you had to kill people."

Lucy was shocked at Emma's statement, but she thought to sit back and let her continue when she noticed the look on Camden's face—disbelief!

"You understand, don't you, Em? You were there when we were growing up ... you suffered too. I tried to protect you from them, but I didn't always do such a good job."

"Are you talking about our parents, Cam, because if you are, they couldn't help what happened to them. I heard Daddy telling Mommy that he had lost everything."

Camden butt in: "Do you know how, Emma? Do you know Daddy Dearest gambled away all his money—money that was supposed to feed and clothe and put a roof over his family's heads!"

"But that was him, Camden. That was Daddy, not all these innocent people the police are saying you killed."

"Same thing, Emma ... look what happened to us! We ended up in foster homes!"

"They weren't all bad," Emma insisted. "Just a couple of them," she added with a grimace, remembering the tragic homes they'd had to endure.

"Your memory isn't as good as mine, then," Camden spit sarcastically. "Besides, I shielded you from a lot of the bad stuff. Most of our foster parents were just in it for the money. And look at what happened at the last home we were in—the bastard husband raped you!"

Emma repeated her statement: "But that was him, Cam, not all these innocent people. You have done a terrible thing, and you are going to have to go away for a long time. That hurts me because I am going to miss you, but that's the way it is." Emma stood. "I won't abandon you, Cam, but I won't support what you've done either." She turned and walked out. When she got outside the room, she collapsed in Jack's arms.

Tessa had an idea. She wanted to show Emma the pictures of all the victims. This way they might be able to get a handle on why Camden had picked the ones he did. She would run it by Jack first, though. Tessa took Jack by the arm and pulled him aside. He agreed it was a good suggestion.

Emma was shocked when she saw the victims' pictures. When the sixth victim was laid out, she began to shake, and a fury of tears started flowing. Cole brought her a chair, and she sat down. Jack put a reassuring hand on her shoulder. Tessa waited. Finally, Emma got herself under control, cleared her throat, and pointed at the sixth victim. "He looks like the man who raped me." She paused. Then she pointed to some of the others and identified them as either foster parent look-a-likes or as persons who vastly resembled her parents.

Tessa looked at Cole and Jack. "I think we have some of our answers now as to what type of victim Camden was targeting—his alleged abusers and those whom he thought were abusing his sister."

After Emma had left the room, Camden went quiet. Lucy let him be for a time, wanting to give him the chance to recuperate from his sister's words. Finally, she opened the conversation. "Emma is right, you know, Camden. It isn't anyone else's fault that some people were not kind to you. I think you have a serious problem, but I also believe there is help for you."

"It doesn't matter now." Camden took a deep breath. "What's going to happen to Emma?"

"Emma will be okay. Jack is going to help her get situated. She wants to stay in the house you rented. She is happy there. In fact, she has unpacked all the boxes you packed."

"But she has never been on her own."

"She is now—thanks to you." Lucy pushed her chair away from the table. "I think we have done enough for today. The district attorney will be coming in to see you later. I believe it would be in your best interest to co-operate with him." Lucy peered into Camden's eyes. "For Emma's sake," she added before turning and walking out.

Camden stared after her. His shoulders sagged in defeat. He breathed in deeply and shuddered as he released his breath. All he could think about was that Emma was forsaking him. Without her, he had nothing to live for. A police officer came into the room and led Camden back to his cell. He lay down on his bed, curled into the fetal position, stuck his thumb in his mouth, and closed his eyes.

~

Lucy put her arm around Emma. "I have to return to Vancouver tomorrow," she informed. "I have patients there who are depending on me." She reached into her purse and pulled out a business card and wrote something on the back of it. "This is my personal email, Emma. I would like you to keep in touch and let me know how you are making out. Will you do that?"

Emma took the card and slipped it into her pocket. "Yes." She turned to Jack. "I'd like to go home now, please."

Tessa came over to Emma and took hold of one of her hands. "You are a brave young woman, Emma. We don't always know why some things happen to us in our lives, but it is not the happenings that always matter, it is how we handle them. Camden didn't handle his issues very well. Now, hopefully, he will get the assistance he needs to get better. Unfortunately, he will spend the rest of his life behind bars. I am going to make some calls for you and get you in to see a good counsellor. You will need some professional help to get you through this and through some of the incidents that happened to you in the past."

"I won't be able to afford it," Emma said. "I still have to figure out how I'm going to put food on my table and pay my rent."

"You let me worry about the counsellor's fees. I am sure Jack will look into the other for you."

Emma nodded and then followed Jack out to his van.

Wednesday, July 8, 2009

When the District Attorney, Brody Kaufman, walked up to Camden's cell on Wednesday morning, he was shocked at the sight of the young man lying on the bed. Camden was still curled up under his covers, his thumb in his mouth. There was almost a peaceful aura surrounding him.

Brody turned to the officer with him. "Too bad we couldn't send this young fellow back to where he seems to be at the moment and let him start over again, correcting all the wrongs he perceives have been done to him, and all the ones that were done to him."

"Not sure it would have made a difference, Mr. Kaufman; some people are just wired wrong—in my opinion, anyway." The officer scowled at Camden.

Brody Kaufman noticed the look on the police officer's face. He was saddened there was so much pain in the world and so little empathy toward the afflicted. He glanced in the cell again. Camden was beginning to stir. The officer banged on the bars.

"Get up, Gale, there's someone here to see you."

Camden's eyes opened. Brody flinched at the emptiness he saw there. A door opened at the end of the hallway and Tessa approached. Brody had worked on cases with Tessa numerous times.

"Good morning, Brody," she greeted. She looked in at Camden. "I guess it will be a bit before we get started." Tessa turned to the officer: "Sydney, could you get Mr. Gale cleaned up and then bring him into interrogation room three please?"

"Yes, ma'am." Tessa noticed a hint of contempt in Sydney's voice.

"Be gentle, Sydney; we want Mr. Gale in one piece––unblemished," she added with a stern look. Tessa had heard about how the odd prisoner sometimes had 'little accidents' while in Sydney Couzen's care. A couple of court cases had even been lost due to such incidents, and the department had been sued. Tessa had no idea why Couzen was still on the force, and she wished it wasn't him who was here this morning.

"Is Jack going to be joining us this morning?" Brody asked as they were leaving the cell area.

"I believe so. He was driving Doctor Lucy to the airport early, around seven, and then going to check on Toby..."

"Toby?" Brody raised his eyebrows.

"Jack's cat. Detective Toby."

Brody started to laugh: "Yes, I remember now. Toby solved a case a few months ago, the one where the officer kidnapped his own kids."

"That's him," Tessa grinned. "And he saved the life of the last victim in this case. Right now Toby is lying in the animal hospital, all broken up because of his heroic deed."

"What did he do?"

"He jumped off the gym roof and knocked the drink out of Andrew's hand. Unfortunately the jump ended up like more of a fall and both his front legs and shoulders were broken, and one of his back legs. Last I heard, though, Toby is doing fine and should be home by the weekend."

"Quite a cat!" Brody exclaimed with admiration.

"You got that right." Tessa opened the door to the interrogation room. "We may as well wait in here. I can show you the files we have, and Doctor Lucy left us copies of her files and the files she brought from other doctors."

Brody Kaufman sat back in his chair, a thoughtful look on his face. "What do you think, Tessa—what is this young man all about?"

"Doctor Lucy and one of her colleagues diagnosed Camden as paranoid delusional. Watching the interview and listening to him leads me to believe they are right on target. The emails Camden sent told the victims how bad they were to others." Tessa handed Brody a copy of both of the emails.

Brody scanned them and set them back on the table. "And you are telling me his sister was totally unaware of all that was happening? Tough to believe."

"Actually, there are a lot of times when I wouldn't consider such a scenario either; but I've met Emma. She was, and still is, in her own little world—a world created partly by the traumatic rape she lived through and partly by the brother who tried to protect her."

"He tried to protect her by killing innocent people?" Brody questioned, his eyes narrowing.

Tessa pulled the files closer and pointed to the pictures. "All of these people resemble individuals who were in Camden's and Emma's lives—people who, in Camden's opinion, treated him and his sister badly." Tessa pointed to two of the male victims. "These two men could pass for brothers, no?"

"Pretty damn close."

"They look just like her rapist."

"I see."

There was a knock on the door, and Jack entered. "Where's Camden?" he asked.

"Should be here any minute," Tessa replied. "Have a seat. You know District Attorney Brody Kaufman, don't you Jack."

Jack extended his hand: "Yes, we've had the pleasure many times before. Been a while, though—how are you, Brody?"

"Fine, Jack—you?"

"Not sure if I like being pulled out of retirement; I was getting real comfortable living a life of leisure," Jack smirked mischievously. Brody laughed.

There was another knock on the door and Sydney entered with Camden. He looked so small. The chains around his ankles were attached to the handcuffs, and Camden was stooped over. He walked with a shuffle. Sydney pushed Camden into a chair on the opposite side of the table. Tessa threw Sydney a dirty look.

"That will be all for now, Sydney," she informed him. "We'll call when we are finished." Tessa waited for Sydney to leave before turning to Camden. "Camden, this is District Attorney Brody Kaufman. He is here to talk with you about what you have done. I do need to inform you, though, if you wish a lawyer to be present on your behalf we will get you one. Do you want a lawyer?"

Camden looked from Tessa to Jack to Brody. His eyes were void of life. The dark circles around them emphasized the paleness of his face. His black hair was lifeless and unkempt. His fingers locked together and he twirled his thumbs. Then he looked directly at Jack

"Should I have a lawyer, Jack? You're my friend; you tell me."

"It is the right of everyone to have a legal representative present, but if you wish to talk to Mr. Kaufman…" Jack didn't get to finish.

Camden reclined as far back in his chair as he could. "I think I want a lawyer," he smirked.

Tessa stood and left the room. On her return, she told Camden a court-appointed lawyer would be arriving soon. "Is there anything you want to say to us before they get here?" She was hoping for something.

Once again Camden turned to Jack. "Should I say something, Jack? You're my friend; tell me."

Jack was puzzled as to what Camden was doing. The vacant look in his eyes had been replaced with a look Jack couldn't quite read, and it was not a pleasant one. "Only if you want to, Camden," he finally answered.

"Good. Then will you tell Tessa to stop suggesting I talk? I know she's out to get me. I know her kind. I've had to survive through many of them. She isn't like you, Jack. You're my friend."

Jack frowned. "I am *not* your friend, Camden, not after what you have done."

Camden smiled. "What have I done, Jack? Tell me."

"Why don't you tell me?" Jack turned the table. "Tell me what you have done, Camden."

"I don't have to say anything. I have rights."

"Like those people you killed had rights?" Tessa hit her fist on the table.

Camden smiled. "What people are you talking about?"

Tessa was frustrated. The scared young man she had witnessed yesterday, and again this morning in his cell, was gone. This Camden would be much harder to deal with. She watched as Camden lowered his head and then squeezed his hands to his temples. She was about to ask him if he was okay when the door opened: a young male lawyer walked in. He extended his hand to Brody and introduced himself.

"Mr. Kaufman … Travis Simons. I've been appointed to represent Mr. Gale. Could I have a few minutes alone with my client, please?"

Brody nodded to Tessa and Jack. "Let's go for coffee." He handed Travis the files on Camden. "You might want to take a look at these first."

Travis scanned through the files and then turned his attention to Camden. "These notes say you have been a busy boy on more than one front. What do you say?"

"I say a man is supposed to be innocent until proven guilty. The justice system is just like everyone else who abuses: it hangs the innocent. I did what I did to protect other people from getting hurt by the nasty, inconsiderate people around here!"

"So what you are telling me … your lawyer … is that you did commit these murders?"

Camden sneered. "Of course, I did. However, don't they have to prove it first?"

Travis sighed. *This guy is totally nuts*, he thought to himself. *Just my luck that my first pro-bono would be a nutcase!* "Yes, they do have to prove beyond a reasonable doubt that you committed these crimes," he finally answered.

"So what do they have on me? Did anyone see me put poison in these people's drinks? It could've been someone else at the gym. Did they check out Paige; she makes a lot of the drinks—Graham, too. No, they assumed it was me because I'd run home that afternoon … because

I had a headache. They barged into my home, without a warrant I might add, and arrested me in front of my sister."

"Well, if you weren't guilty why did you try to run? It says here you were running away and that you grabbed a bunch of castor bean seeds and stuffed them in your mouth. Those are poisonous, aren't they?" Travis pointed to the papers in front of him. "And then you spent a few days in the hospital being pumped full of saline and glucose so you wouldn't die. What do you say to all of this?"

"What am I supposed to say? They were out to get me. Don't you see—it would be easier to blame someone like me than to go after the real killer!"

"But you just told me that you killed these people." Travis's patience was wearing thin.

"Well, the way I see it is: you are my lawyer, and you are supposed to respect our confidentiality, right?"

"I am expected to represent you to the best of my ability; to the letter of the law," Travis answered.

"Then I'm going to plead not guilty and let them prove otherwise!" Camden put his hands to his temples. "I need a drink," he moaned. "I'm withdrawing my confession; I didn't do it," he added.

"I'll be right back." Travis left the room. Tessa, Jack, and Brody were waiting outside the door. "He needs some water."

"What do you think? Is he willing to talk?" Brody asked.

"He wants a trial," Travis replied. "He wants you to be able to prove, beyond a reasonable doubt, he committed these crimes."

"Is he insane?" Tessa shouted.

"I believe he is," Jack stated.

"Which is probably the direction I will have to take," Travis mumbled. "Now I need to get my client some water … excuse me."

Brody turned to Tessa and Jack. "I have to be in court in half an hour. Keep me posted. I want everything you have on this guy. Talk to a judge to get a search warrant for his house and confiscate everything in his room. Hopefully the sister hasn't already cleaned it up."

"We asked her not to," Jack said.

"Well, for her sake, I hope she didn't. Call me when you have everything. The problem here, as I see it, is we really don't have a witness that saw him put the poison in the drinks—other than your cat, Jack, and I doubt we can put Toby on the witness stand. Camden's lawyer can argue someone else put the poison in the smoothies."

"But he had the plants in his house!" Tessa protested.

"Sure he did; so could someone else have them in their house. Get his computer. Hopefully, it will have the emails still on it—the ones the killer sent." With those words, Brody turned and left.

"I'll get Bryce to make the call to the judge," Tessa said. "I also have to fill Cole in on what's going on. He thought this would be an open and shut case so he could get Camden expedited back to Vancouver to face those charges."

Jack headed for the front door. "I'm going to talk to Emma; maybe she can make her brother see the insanity of what he is doing."

"Don't bet on it. And, hopefully, she hasn't had a change of heart and removed any of Camden's personal possessions. If she has, our ass is on the line for having trusted she wouldn't!" Tessa called after Jack.

"And that would make her an accessory, wouldn't it?" Jack stated.

"Yep."

As Tessa headed to Bryce's office, she passed Travis. "Good luck, young man."

He smiled, but it wasn't what Tessa would have classified as a cheerful smile. "Thanks," he said and headed to the room where Camden was waiting. He set the bottle of water on the table and sat down. Travis tapped his pencil on the files in front of him.

"There is a lot of evidence against you, Camden. There is only one way I can plead you as not guilty and expect you to get off—you will need to plead insanity." He stopped, waiting for a reaction.

There was none. Camden sipped on his water and then set the bottle on the table. His eyes were once again empty pits of torment; his lips were sealed. Travis called for an officer to come and return Camden to his cell. "I'll look at this stuff and come by tomorrow."

Camden hung his head and shuffled out of the room.

~

Jack knocked on Emma's door. It took her a few minutes to answer. "Sorry, I was upstairs." She opened the door wide for Jack to enter.

Jack's heart skipped a beat. Hopefully, she wasn't tampering with evidence.

"I took an empty box up to Camden's room and left it on his bed. I figured you could put anything you need to take into it." Emma walked into the living room. "Would you like something to drink, Jack?"

Jack breathed a sigh of relief. "No thanks. Tessa should be here soon with a warrant to obtain Camden's belongings."

"I would have just let you take them, Jack. You know that, don't you?"

"Yes, but this way it's legal. Camden's lawyer won't be able to fight the technicality of an illegal search and seizure."

"He won't."

"Camden wants to plead not guilty, Emma."

The shock on Emma's face was genuine. "Excuse me? He wants to plead innocent?"

"Yep … that's what his lawyer told us."

"His lawyer?"

"Yep, he asked for a lawyer." Jack sat back in the chair and observed the confusion on Emma's face.

"Who is paying for this lawyer?"

"Court-appointed."

"He wants to plead not guilty?" Emma still could not believe what she was hearing. She had added up a lot of things that had happened over the years, and she knew, deep down, her brother had a problem—he was guilty.

"Yep." Jack gazed directly into Emma's eyes. "Is there any way you can talk to your brother and convince him this road he is thinking of taking is madness? Your brother is mentally sick, Emma; he needs help. He wouldn't survive a week in a maximum security prison. I know what he has done is horrible, and I would like to see him rot in jail for killing all those people, but I also see how sick he is. Can you help us help him? If anyone can get through to him, you can."

"Let me think about it. I'll give you my answer in the morning."

They heard a car pull up and stop in front of the house. Emma went to let Tessa in. Tessa handed her the search warrant and then nodded to Jack to follow her upstairs. "Show us Camden's room," she ordered Emma.

"First on your left," she replied without moving.

Jack and Tessa looked around Camden's room. Jack unhooked the laptop and put it in the box Emma had provided them. Tessa inspected the closet, finding the coffee grinder. "Look what we have here, Jack! Bingo! The appliance he used to grind the seeds … still some residue in the cup."

Jack was looking under the bed: he pulled out the well-worn photo album. He flipped through the pages, then placed it in the box.

Finding nothing else of value in the room, Jack and Tessa headed downstairs, thanked Emma for her co-operation, and headed out the door. Jack told Emma he would call her in the morning for her answer. She nodded and closed the door. Emma watched the car leave and then headed out to her three-season room to tend her plants. Duke was waiting at the back door. She opened it and let him in.

It didn't take long for the police's I.T. guy to find the emails on Camden's computer. He smiled as he told Tessa that that evidence alone would be enough to put Camden away for life. The coffee grinder also tested positive for castor bean residue. Tessa left the station with the knowledge that Brody Kaufman was going to be one jubilant district attorney.

Thursday, July 9, 2009

Emma called Jack's house at eight in the morning. "I'll talk to my brother," she said. "I'm ready whenever you want to come and get me."

On the way to the station, Jack thanked Emma for making this decision. She just looked out the van window and said nothing. When they arrived, Jack escorted her to Camden's cell.

"I'd rather talk to my brother in private—in his cell," she expressed. Jack motioned for the officer who was guarding the cell to let her in.

"Hello, Camden." Emma sat down beside her brother on the bed. He pushed himself up and backed up to the wall at the head of his bed.

"Emma, what are you doing here?" His voice was barely audible.

"I have come here to talk some sense into you, Cam. The police tell me you want to drag this whole thing through court. Do you really think that's wise? You'll end up in prison, and I won't be able to come and see you there. If you plead insanity, they'll be able to help you." Emma reached out for her brother's hand. "Please, Cam, for me. Don't make me go through a trial and all the publicity that comes with it. I'll never be able to show my face outside the house."

Camden hung his head. He raised his hands to his temples and rubbed hard. He was in so much pain. He just wanted everything to go away. He hit his forehead a couple of times, tears in his eyes.

"They have your computer, Cam, and they took a coffee grinder from your room. They seemed pretty happy about that. If you make a deal with the district attorney, this could be over before you know it. They'll put you in a maximum security mental hospital, so I'll be able to visit you all the time."

251

"You will?" Camden looked into his sister's eyes.

"I promise."

"I'll think about it then."

"Don't take too long, Cam; I need you to do this for me—for us. Remember what you always say to me ... together, forever ... you and me."

Camden nodded.

"I have to go home now," Emma rose and bent over and kissed her brother on the cheek. "Please do what is right," she whispered in his ear. And then she was gone.

Camden agonized over what his sister had just told him. He knew she was right. He couldn't be so selfish and expect her to visit him in a maximum security prison. Camden was not fool enough to believe he would get off. He curled up on his cot, put his thumb in his mouth, and stared into space.

When Camden's lawyer arrived later that morning, Camden told him he was ready to make a deal.

Travis breathed a sigh of relief.

EPILOGUE

Saturday, July 11, 2009

It was going to be a joyous day. Toby was coming home. He would still be laid up for quite some time, but the vet had promised that with a lot of tender loving care, Toby would be as good as new in no time. He had the heart of a lion.

Jack, with Andrew and Emma's help, had arranged a welcome home party. Several police officers, including Tessa and Bryce Wagner, would be present. Jack fired up the barbeque and threw on steaks; nothing but the best for his Toby.

Andrew and Emma watched over the goings-on when Jack went to pick up Toby. The guests hid in the backyard. Toby thought something might be up when he smelled the barbeque. *"Bit closer than the neighbours' ... wonder what Jack is cooking me tonight. He should know I can't chew very well yet."*

As Jack walked out to the back deck, with Toby in his arms, everyone jumped up and hollered surprise. Toby almost had a heart attack. *"These guys should be careful. I am very fragile right now; the old ticker has had just about enough for a while!"*

"We have to be careful with Toby," Jack mentioned, "he'll still have the casts on for a few weeks. I think he would enjoy company, but not for too long at a time because he'll need his sleep to recuperate faster." Everyone laughed when Jack mentioned sleep.

"I don't think cats have to be encouraged to get their sleep," one of the officers hollered out.

Bryce stepped forward with a big box. "Toby," he began, "once again, we don't know how to thank you. You have proven ... beyond any reasonable doubt ... you deserve to be awarded this plaque and this badge for your

253

great detective work. It is an honour for me to present it to you."

Everyone clapped.

Andrew stepped forward. "Toby, to thank you for saving my life, I have placed an order at the pet store for your treats to be delivered on a weekly basis—the best treats a cat could ever wish for."

Everyone clapped again.

Toby looked around for Emma. He saw her standing off to the side. Jack noticed the direction Toby was looking, and he motioned for Emma to come forward. As soon as she reached into his box and stroked his head, Toby began to purr.

~

Later that night, alone in her house with Duke, Emma smiled. It was good to be alive. It was good to finally be free. It was good to be able to stay in one spot now, for as long as she wanted. Camden was a good brother. He had always been willing to do anything for her, especially after the rape. He would never know. No one would ever know that she had known all along what he was up to. She had been very careful to play the part of the fragile victim and Camden had never suspected—not once. Neither had anyone else.

Emma had observed how angry Camden was after the guy who raped her walked away with a mere slap on the wrists. She had listened to his speeches about revenge against everyone who had wronged them, including their parents. She had remained passive and delicate, and he had stepped up to the plate to make life decent for her. In return, she had looked after him well, making sure his meals were always ready and the majority of the household duties were looked after.

The only problem was they'd had to move around too much. And then the moves had escalated, and Emma began to tire of moving. She decided she wanted stability. When they moved to Brantford, she had hoped she would have time to get him to stop; she would stop playing on her fragility and show him she was okay now. That is why she had mentioned that she see a counsellor; she wanted to move forward with her life.

But Camden had too quickly gone right over the edge: there was no stopping him. She saw how tortured he was. Emma would sometimes look in on him during the night when he was sleeping, and she saw how he curled like a baby and sucked his thumb. She even knew how to check his emails, and she was aware of his special one, which he sent to his victims. She knew what he was doing when she heard the grinder in his room.

Emma always made sure she looked after the plants, especially the castor bean plant, which she had suggested they buy. She remembered the day she had told Camden all about the castor bean plant and what it could do, and she could still see the look of amazement, and then excitement, on her brother's face. He was smart; he'd figure a way to work it out.

Emma thought back to her childhood: to her negligent parents who thought of no one but themselves; to the kids at school who teased her and Camden without mercy; to the day she and Camden entered foster care because their parents had been arrested for fraud; to the six foster homes they were subjected to, only two of them being warm and protective. She remembered the beatings she and Camden had to endure, and the beatings he would take for her. Those thrashings had made her tough— tougher than Camden.

However, her strength had been temporarily shaken on the day the last foster father they lived with had raped her. She had staggered from her room and had run from the house out to the barn. She had thrown herself into the hay, her only comfort at the time being a couple of big orange farm cats. That is where Camden found her when he returned from delivering something for their foster father. Her clothing was ripped, her face streaked with tears, her legs streaked with blood!

Camden had gone to the police, but it hadn't done any good. Their foster father was a respected man in the community and who were they—just a couple of kids who had already been through five other foster homes. One of the officers had even snickered and suggested Emma had asked for it. The officer had been unaware Camden had heard him, but he had, and he told Emma how disgusting the man was—as much as the man who'd raped her!

Later that night, Camden had told her to pack her bags, they were leaving. They would survive; he would look after her. He was fed up with everyone else ruining their lives. It was time to take charge. During the next few months, it had been difficult; Emma had had to listen to Camden rant and rave about everything and everybody. He went through several jobs, always losing them because someone had done something to him or blamed him for something he didn't do. She soon began to put behind her what had happened, but she was careful not to let Camden see that. She liked the new Camden, the one who wanted revenge.

Camden had gone to see a few doctors and had even been admitted to the mental health hospital at one time, but she had always kept her distance from the medical organizations. She wasn't willing to have them start probing into her mind. And Camden had been protective of her, even in this, when she explained to him how devastating it would be for her to have to remember the entire rape ordeal—and the other abuses inflicted on them.

Emma remembered the day she was looking at the newspaper with her brother and he was scanning the job listings. She had pointed to the ad for a gym. She had told him that lots of different people went there, and she had warned him there might be some not so nice ones, too, but he should just ignore them. She had known Camden wouldn't be able to do that. She had secretly talked to one of his doctors; she knew her brother was paranoid delusional and should be taking medication to help him control his urges. Camden did take medicine sometimes,

Are You Listening To Me?

but even then it wasn't the pills he was supposed to be taking. Emma had always switched them with a placebo.

It was after Camden got the first gym job that he truly changed. It was then he started to pick the seeds from the castor bean plant, always thinking he was hiding it from his sister. Emma ensured there were plenty of those plants available to him. He had started to take charge with an authority she had never seen before, and at first, it had been fun, but it had grown tiring.

When Camden met Doctor Lucy, he began to change. Emma couldn't have that; she wasn't ready to let go, so she suggested she pay Doctor Lucy a visit. She had told her brother she didn't have to go over events from the past; she just wanted to meet the woman who was making such a difference in her brother's life. After the visit, Emma told Camden she didn't think Doctor Lucy was right for him, which, again, was something no one else knew. It was shortly after that conversation that Emma had heard the grinder for the sixth time, and she knew they would be leaving very soon.

"Come along, Duke," she said as she got up and went out to the three-season room to water her plants. She gave an extra bit to the castor bean plants to ensure their hardiness. One never knew when they might be needed again.

"They were right, Duke—I am the strong one."

About the Author

Mary M. Cushnie-Mansour resides in Brantford, ON, Canada. She is the award-winning author of the popular "Night's Vampire" series. Mary has a freelance journalism certificate from Waterloo University, and in the past, she wrote a short story column and feature articles for the Brantford Expositor. She has also published five collections of poetry, two short-story anthologies, a youth novel, nine bilingual children's books, and a biography.

Mary has always believed in encouraging people's imaginations and spent several years running the "Just Imagine" program for the local school board. She has also been heavily involved in the local writing community, inspiring adults to follow their dreams.

You can contact Mary through her website
http://www.writerontherun.ca
or via email
mary@writerontherun.ca

CPSIA information can be obtained
at www.ICGtesting.com
Printed in the USA
LVHW052222221020
669596LV00016B/1650

9 781728 772684